I0655295

SHADOW SOUL

R. MICHAEL CARD

Gryphon's Gate Publishing

Shadow Soul

Copyright © 2018 R. Michael Card

Published by Gryphon's Gate Publishing

Cover Art by Darko Tomic

All rights reserved. No part of this book may be reproduced in any form or by any means without written consent, excepting brief quotes used in reviews.

This is a work of fiction. Names, places, characters, and events are entirely the product of the author's imagination or are used fictitiously, and any resemblance to persons, living or dead, actual locals, events, or organizations is coincidental.

Gryphon's Gate Publishing

550 King St. N.

PO Box 42088 Conestoga

Waterloo, ON

N2L 6K5

ebook ISBN978-1-988115-63-4

Print ISBN978-1-988115-62-7

I<small>T WAS A BEAUTIFUL SUMMER'S DAY, AND FOR JUST A MOMENT,</small> as she walked, Caerwyn closed her eyes and drank in the sensations of the afternoon. She tilted her head back to feel the sun's warmth full on her face. A pleasant, cooling breeze ruffled her clothes, tousling the stray hairs that had escaped her ponytail, in a refreshing counterpoint to the heat of the day.

Where she'd grown up—in the Afgenni lands far to the South—the wind wouldn't have been half as pleasant, hot and blasting. There was no respite from the heat of summer, even in shade. It sat on you, a physical thing, oppressive and heavy. In the rainy season, there was shade enough, but the heat was made worse by the moisture in the air, from which there was little relief. In the dry season, the air sucked moisture from a person, desperate and unyielding. It was a harsh life, but she'd loved it.

Here in the North, the summers were much milder and more pleasant, it seemed.

Other sensations came to her, clear and crisp, while her eyes were closed. The rough rope in her hand, the clop of hooves from the donkey behind her, the creak of the wheels of the wagon it pulled. Birds sang in the forest to her right which bordered close along the road they traveled. Their calls were light and cheery and made her heart feel lighter as well. Not that her heart was that heavy these days, just... uncertain.

She'd been traveling with Jais of Kilian's Hollow for nearly a month, moving north and east along various roads like this. They had grown closer in that time, and yet also more distant. They were friends now and firmly so. She trained him in various combat techniques when they stopped at night and before they began in the morning. He was getting good too, improving with every session, drinking it all in, and now bested her roughly one time in six. Yet still, his natural talent carried him more than his skill, but he was getting closer to a tipping point. Caerwyn hoped that soon he'd advance from his initiate's ways to become a steady warrior, less raw, more refined.

This made him a fine addition to the team, which had been just her and Barami—her stalwart companion from the South—for so long. As a friend and fighting companion, Jais had knit quite well into their little group. But as anything more...

Caerwyn had come north looking for a mate, someone with whom to have a child. She didn't know where her intense desire to bear offspring had come from, but after her exile from her home in the South it had come on strong and never let up. She didn't need or want a husband, no connections of that sort. She needed only the child, one of drahksani blood.

When she'd first met Jais, she'd thought him an ideal match for her, and so a good potential mate to give her that child. But now... she was certain, despite all their camaraderie, that Jais wasn't the man for that. He was young and unable to dissociate the intimate act from their friendship. He'd admitted as much. If he was going to have a child, he'd want to be a father *and* a husband—which didn't work for her.

She was better on her own and always would be. She'd had far too many close friends and family ripped away for one reason or another and remained wary of getting too close to anyone. She never wanted to feel that pain again.

Though, she did have Barami—as close a friend as any. He hadn't left her.

The big, dark-skinned warrior hadn't changed much this last month. He was still his old self, protecting her and pining for her in equal parts. He'd accepted Jais into their group after a little adjustment, though he still called him Brakka half the time, a reference to a large and stubborn beast of burden in the South. Jais didn't seem to mind the name.

Opening her eyes, she glanced around. Barami and Jais were both ahead of her, talking quietly. She took a moment to size them up, comparing the two, as they were quite opposite in appearance.

Barami was tall, taller than Caerwyn herself by a half a head. His skin was a deep brown, his head bald. He moved with the easy grace and readiness of a tested warrior. Strapped to his back was his shield and his large sword, Oken Adi—which meant "stalwart friend" in the Southern tongue. Pretty much the only attribute he shared with Jais was a well-muscled frame. He was old for a warrior, a few years past forty.

Jais was shorter and broader through the chest and across his shoulders. He was perhaps just a touch under average height for most men, but he made up for it in bulk. He was thick with muscle... everywhere and incredibly strong. This was a gift of his drahksani heritage. A heritage she shared with him and which provided her own build and strength. Jais looked younger than he was, perhaps five years less than his twenty-two years of age. His skin was well tanned, his light brown hair long and shaggy—awkwardly shorn by knife to keep it out of his eyes since he wore it loose. It blew about his head in the light wind. His gait as he walked was more the rolling stride of a farm boy than a warrior. That's what he'd been a month ago, when she'd met him; A hunter and woodsman leading a simple life. That had all changed the day she'd arrived, and they'd gone off to hunt krolls—massive misshapen beasts who knew only hunger and destruction. He hadn't held a sword before that day, and now two blades sat in scabbards across his broad back.

He'd been so innocent then, thinking he wanted adventure, pining for a good fight. In some ways, he remained innocent, but in others... He'd watched his family, and the girl he loved, die. He'd faced horrible creatures and come out of it changed.

She sighed.

She wouldn't wish that on anyone. Yet he represented so much for her... mostly hope. She'd found one drahksan and perhaps together they could find others.

And maybe somewhere down the line she'd find someone to give her the child she so desperately wished for.

An arrow hit the ground just behind the two men up ahead.

Perhaps it was Caerwyn's distracted thoughts which had made her careless. She hadn't heard the twang of a bowstring. She was shocked into alertness, but the damage had been done.

Barami's grunt of pain came a moment later as he crumpled to his knees. The arrow had gone completely through his abdomen toward the right side. He was alive... for now, but he wouldn't be participating in the fight to come.

The shot had come from the forest to their right; a high vantage point.

She dropped the rope leading the donkey and wagon and threw herself to one side, toward the forest, drawing her short sword as she rolled up behind a tree. A quick glance around showed Jais doing something similar, though he'd come up behind a jagged stump and had to stay in a crouch to remain hidden from their unknown assailant.

Her heart raced, ready for battle, but she calmed her mind. She couldn't think of Barami right now. End this fight quickly then hope to Suur he was still alive. Which meant she couldn't wait for the assailant to come to her. He could remain hidden and pick them off when they came out of hiding. She was fairly certain it was only one foe, or at least only one with a bow. Otherwise, there would have been more arrows at the same time. If this had been bandits, they'd have tried to eliminate as many as they could with ranged weapons first.

She spun out from behind the tree and darted to another one. As she did, she glanced in the direction she thought their attacker might be. She hoped to see if he had any companions or get a sense for his location. She got lucky. She saw a man dropping from a tree branch, bow in hand. Now the question became... was he the only one?

Yet even though she'd only gotten a passing glimpse of him—her breath caught. It might have been only a glimpse, but she knew this man. She would never forget him.

He was the same man who'd ruined her life... twice.

She called out to Jais, needing to warn him. "Jais, careful! It's a dragon hunter!"

Dragon hunters had come out of the great purge of drahksani, dozens of years ago. After the wars which had killed off so many of their kind, the remaining drahksani had gone into hiding. These men had been trained to find and kill drahksani.

This same man had killed Caerwyn's parents, her birth parents, nearly thirty years ago in the far western kingdom of Domara. Then he'd found her again just a little over a year ago in her adoptive home of the Afgenni Empire in the Far South. How he kept finding her, she had no clue, but today she'd end his quest against her once and for all.

She darted around her tree and charged toward the spot where the man had been. He was still there, arrow nocked and ready. She ducked, and dove into the underbrush, slamming against a tree, scraped and bruised for her effort, but she'd avoided the arrow.

"I'll kill you, Gosse!" Perhaps she should have kept quiet, but she couldn't help herself.

She'd learned his name last year when he'd gotten her exiled from the South after exposing her as drahksani, and it had been seared into her memory.

Laughter greeted her, but not for long. He didn't want to give away his position.

"Caer!" Jais' urgent call caught her attention. He was peaking around at her from behind the stump he used for cover. Her charge a moment ago had put her ahead of him. He showed her his bow, now strung and an arrow nocked. The message was clear: she needed to draw Gosse's attention so Jais could pop up and fire. The only question would be, did he have a clear shot?

She hoped so.

She let out a war-cry, a wordless sound of fury, and spun around from behind the tree—charging at where Gosse had been a moment before. He wasn't there now. Looking around frantically as she ran, she couldn't see him. When she reached where he'd been, she spun around.

Her keen ears heard the nearly simultaneous twang of two bowstrings.

She had to move to see what was happening. Through the trees, she caught sight of Jais running to the edge of the forest. Gosse sprinted away from her, he'd dropped his bow and had a sword out. Jais was half turned away from her, clutching his side, and drawing a sword.

She'd end this now.

"Dav—" She cut herself off. Her magical spear Davlas was no more. Summoning it was a habit she hadn't broken, apparently. She had bought a few regular spears... but they were not on her. They were in the wagon.

"Suur's Sweaty..." She gritted her teeth and instead drew out her sling from one pouch, and a stone from another. She loaded the leather cup, swung, and released.

Gosse dove out of the way at the last second, and the stone instead struck Jais in the shoulder.

"How...?" She felt a chill take her. She dare not fire again.

Putting away her sling, she ran toward the two. She pulled her shield from behind her, sliding it on her other arm, then drew her sword again.

But she couldn't seem to make her legs work fast enough. Jais was faltering, her wound to his shoulder hampering him as was the one on his side. He could only use one sword, in his off hand. His other hand held the gut wound, staunching it. He was retreating, moving farther from her.

It was clear Gosse was the better swordsman and would win this fight... if Caerwyn hadn't been there.

She yelled again. She didn't want to. She'd hoped to have surprise on her side when she came in behind Gosse, but she needed to distract the man, get him away from Jais.

It worked.

Gosse stepped back and away from Jais, to one side, though not before a quick flick of his sword send Jais' blade out of his hand. Jais was defenseless, but she was getting close and Gosse was focused on her now.

She lashed out with all the pent-up fury built up over the last thirty years. She couldn't help it. She knew somewhere in her head that she should be cold, calculating, that emotions only got in the way in a fight, but her heart wouldn't listen. This was the man who had killed her birthparents and taken her family from her twice! He would get no quarter.

But by all the gods, he was good!

It occurred to her only then, that she'd never actually seen the man fight. She'd been spared from seeing his encounter with her parents, and when he'd found her in the South, he hadn't need to fight, just let everyone know she was a drahksan. They'd turned on her and done the rest.

She could tell Gosse was clear of mind, eyes focused. His sword moved with swift precision to block her attacks. He fought with two weapons, but the other wasn't a full sword, just a long dagger. Even though he was old for a human—hair gray, skin worn and wrinkled around his eyes—he was still amazingly fast and agile. He was not a big man, but he did have more years of training than she, and it was clear he kept himself in prime form.

He ducked under a slash from her sword and danced away. Her sword wasn't as long as his, so she had to get in closer. It was to his advantage to be farther from her. She lunged in and swatted his sword aside with her shield. But that left her open as he threw that off-handed dagger. She ducked and tried to charge in close while he was defenseless on his off-hand side, but then a faint noise from behind her caught her ear.

A grunt of pain.

No.

She bashed him aside with her shield as she drew close then drew back herself, glancing toward the sound. Jais had his bow in hand, good... but Gosse's dagger was now stuck in his shoulder, the unwounded one.

Jais was still up and clear of eye, but pain was evident on his face. He wouldn't be able to use his bow. He took up his sword once again and drew close to the fight.

She couldn't decide if this was a good idea or not.

Jais was good, yes, but they hadn't practiced a lot of two on one fighting. One had to be very careful when fighting along side an ally against a single opponent, as it was easy to get in each other's way. She prayed to Suur that wouldn't happen.

Without his dagger, Gosse had turned side-on to her, his sword arm out in front—less of a target. Unless she was going to chop his arm off first, she would have even more trouble getting in close to use her shorter weapon.

She circled him, hoping to get Jais behind him, but he was too smart for that. He kept dancing back away to keep them both in his field of view. The best she could do was get around to one side, directly across from Jais, who'd moved in closer by now. Jais wasn't looking so good. He hadn't removed the dagger from his shoulder, and the wound was bleeding profusely. He was managing to keep the injured shoulder still at least, using that arm to press the wound on his abdomen on the same side. That meant he was wielding his father's sword in his off hand, using the shoulder she'd wounded earlier. He tried a few test lunges at Gosse, but the man would either move back or turn the blade away.

Caerwyn struck while Gosse was turned away, deflecting Jais' blade. But her blade wasn't long enough. She caught him, but only a shallow wound, barely slicing through the light armor on his side.

Gosse spun, and with his free hand, grabbed her sword hand. She'd been trying to get as much reach as she could out of her shorter blade, lunging in, which meant she was off balance. He pulled, and she stumbled forward as Gosse stepped out of the way. Jais was charging in, swinging. She ducked, falling forward. She felt Jais' blade score along her shoulder, but not deep. Her sword was tossed to one side as she landed on her hands. She rolled along the ground, trying to get away from the fight, yet expecting a killing blow to come. When it didn't she scrambled to her feet and looked around.

Gosse was disappearing into the woods, picking up his bow along the way.

"After him!" she shouted to Jais, but the young man only sat heavily in the middle of the road.

"I'm done," he said.

She ran to the edge of the forest. Gosse was gone into its depths. She shouted back at Jais. "Track him! I can't let him get away again!"

"I'm in no condition to go anywhere," he called back. "And..." His gaze turned to Barami and her heart froze.

Gods, Barami!

She needed to go after Gosse, but she wouldn't be able to track the man through the forest. Jais could, but he was injured, and he was their only healer, even if his healing skills were still uncertain. He needed to stay and tend to Barami. This left her with the horrible choice of letting her friend die or pursuing the man who had ruined her life... twice.

She let out a feral scream of frustration.

2

Jais' vision swam. His breathing was short, and he was trying to calm himself and breathe deeper to keep from passing out. It was the pain from his wounds, more than the exertion of the fight, which gave Jais pause.

After a moment, he got up, unsteady on his feet, staggering over to Barami, to fall next to the man. Jais' wounds would heal given time; he possessed exceptional healing. It was one of his drahksani abilities. But that didn't mean he wouldn't pass out. Barami needed to be healed before that happened. He felt at the man's neck, as his aunt—a practiced healer—had taught him, and thankfully found a pulse. With little finesse, he rolled Barami onto his back, lacking the energy to be nice. Jais put a hand directly over the wound in Barami's gut and focused on healing.

He hoped this would work.

Healing was a gift from his mother's side. Jais' experience with it was limited, having only healed a few times before, and that had been during the fight with the krolloc—the massive monstrosity that had been controlling the krolls attacking his village. Previously, he'd just sort of... done it, and he still didn't really know what he was doing. There had been no need to practice in the weeks since then.

He knew he needed to push energy into the wound to heal it, but he lacked skill. His aunt had never trained him. She'd hidden the fact that he was drahksani from him, trying to keep him safe. Then she'd died, leaving him with many unanswered questions. There had never been time for training. All he knew of healing was the little she'd mentioned in passing while working on others, and the little that his father's spirit had passed on to him, through the sword it now inhabited.

He'd hoped he'd have the time to learn more later.

But for now...

He let out a long grunt as he simply tried to infuse some of his life-force into Barami. It worked! He could feel the wound closing, the blood stopping, Barami's pulse growing stronger. He didn't even know how he was feeling these things, but he did.

Once Barami was out of danger, Jais stopped, not wanting to give too much of his energy while he was injured, and even then, he was exhausted from his effort.

Caer had joined him some time while he'd been concentrating on healing.

"Will he live?" she asked.

Jais nodded.

"And you?"

He grimaced. "I'll be fine. I'll heal. Nothing fatal." His breath was short though and his vision was narrowing. He was close to passing out. "Sword!" he said urgently tapping around, feeling the ground for where he'd dropped his father's sword.

She looked around, and a moment later pushed the grip into his palm. He moved his hand from the grip to the blade, touching the cold metal.

Father! Help me. I need some of your energy.

This was also something he hadn't done since that fight. His father's spirit had spoken to him in his time of need but had been silent since then.

I am here. Take this. Energy flooded into him, and he blinked as the fatigue and exhaustion was pushed to the side for a moment.

He released the sword and reached over to his shoulder. He tried to pull out the dagger still embedded there. However, between the pain from the wound Caerwyn had inflicted on his other arm and the fact that any movement of the blade caused searing agony down his arm and into his back, he couldn't pull it out.

"Oh for..." Caer said and, pushing his hand aside, pulled the dagger out.

Jais cried out as a wave of agony washed over him, but it was gone quickly.

"Thank you. I'll heal in time, but I don't know if I have the energy to do it myself now. If that man comes back..." He saw her expression at the mention of the man. She'd known him. That was clear enough. She'd even called him by name, Gosse... or something...

"Who was he?" Jais asked.

"The man who killed my parents," she said softly, though there was a certain intense menace in her voice.

That explained a lot.

"If I heal myself I'll probably knock myself out. Better I'm alert in case he returns."

She nodded. "Thank you." She took a moment to scan the

forest edge. "And knowing him, he'd attack when I least expect it. I would appreciate an extra set of eyes." She glanced at his other shoulder. "I'm... sorry..."

He grimaced and shook his head. "Don't worry about it. It's not that deep. I know you weren't trying to hit me." That didn't stop it from hurting like Holn, though. He didn't know how she could have missed, but she had. This Gosse was a slippery fellow.

She gave a quick smile, seeming relieved, then was up and moving, getting them back on the road.

She retrieved his bow and quiver then loaded the still unconscious Barami into the wagon. She took some of the cloth and blankets they used for their bedrolls and tents and made Jais a bit of a padded seat, which would face the forested side of the road. Then, binding his wounds as best she could, she helped him over and into the wagon as well. It wasn't comfortable, but it wasn't that bad either. Even as the wagon continued down the road, and the wooden wheels bumped along, he found it tolerable.

For her part, she kept the donkey between her and the forest, trying to shield herself from potential danger as she led it along.

Jais scanned the forest as they went but saw no threats.

"How much farther do we have to go?" he asked as they moved on. He didn't know where they were heading; they were off any maps he'd ever seen. He knew only the kingdom of Erestin and they'd long since crossed the eastern border of that small realm into lands unknown to him. The village of Thresh, where they'd bought this wagon, was the farthest village to the east he'd ever heard of. They'd left that behind weeks ago.

He didn't know where they were going, only that Caer

had a "sense." Her "sense" being the ability to feel other drahksani, something he couldn't do. That wasn't a surprise. All drahksani had different abilities, sometimes vastly different. His were focused on strength and combat, along with healing, traits passed from his father and mother, a warrior and healer respectively.

"We're close," she said. "Perhaps we'll get there by the end of the day?"

Given they were down a warrior and that he, himself, wouldn't be much good in a fight, Jais certainly hoped so.

SURE ENOUGH, SEVERAL HOURS LATER, AS THE SUN WAS SETTING in the west behind a row of mountains, they came to a town. It was sizable, much larger than Klaston's Green, or Thresh, which had been the largest settlement Jais had ever seen.

They crested a hill and found the town nestled in the valley below them, snug up against the curve of a river, which meandered south. The forest, which they'd skirted all day, continued down the hill and then fell away to the south. It probably provided much of the building materials and heat for the town. There were farms up the hills on both sides of the valley, and a bridge which spanned the river. At the center of town, there were large buildings, two or three stories tall with smaller buildings farther out. It looked well established and cozy at the same time.

One thing was for certain, they'd be sleeping in beds tonight and after the afternoon bouncing along in the wagon, Jais was thankful for that.

There was a wooden palisade around the town, about twelve feet high, with a wide gate where it met the road.

Caer stopped at the gate as dusk settled over them.

"Good timing," a man called out. He was pushing one side of the wooden gate shut. "We were just closing up for the night. "What brings you to Cold River?"

"We're looking for someone," Caer called out. "Most immediately we're looking for a healer if there's one in town. We were attacked by bandits on the road and have a couple injured men."

"Bandits? In these parts? I'll have to let the town council know. Haven't had bandits in years."

"What's the gate for?" Jais called out.

The man must not have seen him in the gathering gloom of twilight and peered up over the wagon for a moment. "Oh, hello there. The gate's mostly for wolves and the occasional bear. It keeps them from wandering into town when their hunting's not so good."

"A healer?" Caer asked, as she passed through the still open side of the gate.

"Yes, sorry. There's one in town, a good one too. You're lucky. Her name's Elria. You'll find her at The Boar this time of day. It's a tavern near the bridge. But I wouldn't recommend staying there unless you're well off. The Setting Sun is a better choice for most. It's just there, on the edge of town, along the main road. Can't miss the sign. It's bright yellow!" The man pointed.

"Thank you," Caer said and they were moving again.

Jais watched the man close the other side of the gate and felt a bit better. That wall wouldn't stop any determined man from getting into the town, but still. He let his guard down a little and tried a little self-healing on his stinging shoulder.

He was tired. Even just a little healing and he found himself slipping into sleep. He nodded off, coming awake when the wagon stopped in front of the Setting Sun Inn.

He remained awake enough to stagger inside to a room, but once in a bed, was out the instant he hit the mattress.

Yet his dreams were troubled, filled with swordsmen he couldn't beat and wounds that wouldn't heal.

3

CAERWYN'S DAY WAS NOT DONE. BY THE TIME SHE'D HAULED Jais and Barami to a room, it was full dark out. She left them to sleep while she went to find the healer, wanting to get her friends tended to as soon as possible. Both Barami and Jais looked to be doing well, but she wasn't going to take any chances. She wanted them both up and able sooner rather than later, what with Gosse still out there.

Oil lanterns lined the streets, illuminating them well. The buildings changed from low, smaller structures to taller, larger ones as she walked farther into town. Few were awake at this hour, and the windows were dark.

She was on edge and couldn't stop the feeling that she was being hunted, watched, stalked. She looked around as she walked, but there were only a few townspeople about on the streets, no concerns there.

It took her a moment to identify why she was feeling this way.

In all the commotion of getting to town, getting her friends settled, and going out for the healer, she'd forgotten why they'd come here.

A drahksan.

When the man at the gate had mentioned a talented healer, she'd thought that might be who they sought, but now, as she made her way to The Boar tavern, she didn't sense the drahksan ahead of her, but somewhere off to her right... and up?

She looked in that direction. The houses or buildings here were uniformly three stories tall and all built together in a long row. Was the drahksan in one of those buildings? Perhaps in an attic? They seemed higher even than that top floor.

She shook it off. She could find him or her later, after she found the healer.

She hurried onward to The Boar tavern. A boar's head, intricately carved from a chunk of wood, hung above the door marking the building. The windows glowed with light, creating pools in the dark street. Even out here, she could hear the din of many people within.

She opened the door and was met with the scent of ale and roasted meat, with an undertone of stale straw, sweat, and worse. The noise of people shouting and cheering greeted her. She stepped within and looked around.

The far wall was ablaze with three large hearths, all cooking something. The center one had a full boar roasting on it, the other two had pots bubbling away. There was a long table in front of the hearths where meat was being sawed off another already roasted boar and plates of various foods were being put together by a crew of men and women. Ale flowed freely from several large casks at the left side of the room. In the same place on the opposite side, a long stairway ran to a second floor. Everywhere else was a mass of people, sitting or standing, talking or shouting. Smaller round tables lined the edges of the room, with four much larger ones, long and square, dominating the centre of the room. One of the long tables seemed to have a great group around it, all turned inward at something, cheering or groaning in turns at whatever they were watching. There would be no way to yell out a name over the din of the crowd so finding the healer seemed unlikely without help.

Caerwyn pushed her way up to the long bar where food was being prepared and poked the large man carving the boar.

"Hello!" she called out over the noise. "I'm looking for a healer? Elria?"

"Eh?" the man said only seeming to have noticed her just then.

She tried shouting louder. "I'm looking for Elria, the healer!"

"Ah!" He nodded then pointed to the big group at the long table. "Red hair!" the man shouted. "Can't miss her."

Caerwyn surveyed the group. As far as she could tell, there were only a few women present, and none had red hair.

She drew closer. Better to be sure before she went back to ask again.

She began pushing her way through the tight crowd, not easy, given their boisterous nature and intentness on whatever they were watching, but she was a dragon-blooded warrior and she was stronger than she looked.

She pushed through the final row of onlookers and... there she was.

Caerwyn gaped for a moment.

Elria's hair was indeed hard to miss. Flame red, it stood out like a beacon, as did her clear green eyes. That wasn't what caused Caerwyn to gape though. The woman was downing a flagon of ale... in one go... and by the look of the many empty flagons in front of her, it wasn't her first.

Elria slammed down her mug, and the crowd went wild with a great cheer. There was a grin on the woman's lips, and a heady rose color to her cheeks, but she didn't seem that drunk. The same couldn't be said for the men drinking with her…

It looked like there had been three others. Two were now face down on the table. The last was swaying wildly as he lifted his own flagon. He tilted his head back to drink, but instead just kept falling backwards into the crowd, the mug slipping from limp fingers as ale spilled on him and the floor.

Another cheer as Elria rose sharply in victory.

Caerwyn's sense hadn't deceived her. This woman wasn't a drahksan, but she certainly could hold her liquor. She wasn't even swaying as she stood, raising a hand to acknowledge the roar of the crowd. Some money was exchanged, and a portion of it went to Elria herself. After that, the crowd began to disperse.

Caerwyn slipped around the table quickly and caught hold of the other woman's arm.

"Elria?" she asked. "The healer?"

The woman nodded. "I am she." There was a heavy accent to her voice, not from these parts, much harsher and a little sing-song. "Who are you?"

"My name is Caerwyn, and I just came to town. I have some injured friends if you wouldn't mind taking a look at them?"

"Now?"

"Now, yes."

Elria shrugged and brushed off her green dress, removing the remains of dinner and smearing a few splashes of ale. She was not as tall as Caerwyn, but she wasn't far off, which was odd. Most women were much shorter than she.

"Lead the way," Elria said and Caerwyn nodded, heading out of the tavern.

"What happened to your friends?" Elria asked once they were out in the quiet night, walking swiftly back to The Setting Sun Inn. She kept pace with Caerwyn's long strides. She was certainly a woman who would stand out, what with her hair and her height, perhaps even more than Caerwyn herself. "Sickness? Wolves?"

"Swords and arrows," Caerwyn said. She decided it would be best to stick with her story about bandits for now. "We were hit by bandits on the road today."

Elria didn't break stride, but her expression was just as the gate's man had been, shocked. "Bandits? Truly? That is odd."

"That's what I've heard, but it's true. You'll see the wounds for yourself."

Elria nodded and they continued quickly to the inn.

It was only as they neared their destination, that Caerwyn felt the call of the other drahksan again. She looked up to the roofs on her left and saw a man there, crouched low in the shadows of a chimney. He was looking at her. She knew from the pull within her, he was the man she was looking for. Meeting his gaze, she nodded. But she didn't have time to pursue that now. She needed to ensure Elria saw to her friends.

4

Volfard's heart nearly stopped.

She'd seen him.

She'd looked straight at him. Her gaze had locked with his for just a moment... and she'd nodded at him.

But how had she known? Unless she felt him the same way he felt her. He'd felt it for some time now. Not knowing what it was, it was simply a call to some deep part of him. Only that evening as he'd felt it draw incredibly close, had he ventured out and seen... her.

But he hadn't expected her to see him. The fact that she had, scared him more than anything had in a long time.

He scampered down the other side of the steeply slanted roof and threw himself off, flying over the alley behind the building to land on the roofs on the other side.

Then he ran.

He had no fear of those within these houses hearing him. He'd always been light on his feet. Even when running, he padded along like nothing more than a mouse. Yes, a mouse, that's what he was. As invisible and unassuming as any small rodent. Even though his name meant wolf's heart, he'd never felt like much of a predator. Though perhaps he was a mouse with the heart of a wolf? Even that didn't feel right. He might be cunning and fearless like a wolf, but wolves were also predators and aggressive, and he wasn't like that at all.

He scurried down the side of the row of houses into another dark alley then ran along the dark streets, keeping to the shadows, hidden from everyone until he reached his home. It wasn't much, but it was secret and safe, and that's what he prized most for his dwelling.

He'd spent his life sneaking into the homes of others. He would only take what he needed to survive, a little food, supplies, other such things. He didn't steal for pleasure or gain. It wasn't his fault that he could easily slip into their homes, through open windows or bypassing simple locks. It wasn't his fault if they kept their dwellings so easy to get into. He thought it much better to have a hidden place, a secret place, where the door didn't look like a door. That was how one kept to one's self and didn't get pilfered from.

But once he was settled into the one chair he had, he found he couldn't relax.

Who was this woman?

No one had ever seen him before; he'd made sure of that.

More than just her having spotted him, there was... everything else about her. She wasn't like any woman he'd ever seen. That healer she'd brought back to her inn came close to being as... odd. Both were foreign and tall and possessing of qualities which were not inherently womanly. But even more so than the healer, who still wore dresses and filled them out well enough, this new woman wore leathers and armor and carried a sword and shield. She was a warrior. That was altogether different than the hard-drinking healer with her strange accent.

He had to know who she was.

It ate at him, her difference, and how easily she seemed to have spotted him. He needed more information. Luckily, he had sources.

He slipped out of his tiny ramshackle home and slid like a shadow through the night. Out of the town proper, he went, and across the small field to the sentry wall around the town.

As he suspected, Aric the night gatesman, was sitting out on the road on a small stool, leaning against the gate, looking up at the stars.

"Aric," Volf whispered. The corresponding shudder of shock through the man was always fun to watch.

"By the gods, man! Stop doing that." Aric put a hand over his heart. "I'm not as young as I used to be. You'll scare the life right out of me one of these days."

Volf chuckled, just a little. "Sorry." He stepped out of the shadow in which he'd hidden himself, allowing himself to be seen. "I'm curious about some people that came into town today. A woman with two men in a wagon."

"Aye, yes, they came in just as the gates were closing for the night. Didn't seem that curious to me. Though the woman did look ready for anything. Can't say I seen too many women carrying a sword and shield, 'cept when those Northerners come down for supplies."

"I don't think she's a Northerner." Though Volf didn't want to say how he knew. He'd sensed her coming from the west, not the North. He hadn't been close enough to hear her talk, so he didn't know what her accent was like. "Did she sound like one?"

"No, didn't have that same lilt as the Northerners do. Though she was looking for that Northern healer that's in town. But I suspect she wasn't so much looking for a Northerner as she was just for a healer. Those two men with her looked pretty rough. Can't believe bandits are threatening the roads again."

Volf didn't much care about bandits. He'd spent his entire life in this town and didn't plan to go anywhere.

"What did she sound like? Western?"

Aric shrugged in the darkness. Volf's eyes were quite good at picking out details even in all but complete darkness. "Can't say as I know what westerners sound like. We get so few through these days. But she did sound a little odd. Don't know how to describe it. There was an accent, but I couldn't place it."

Volf nodded.

He was starting to form a picture of her: a foreign warrior woman, tall and sure.

He thanked Aric and slipped back into town.

He climbed to the roofs opposite the Setting Sun Inn, hoping to see her again, but curtains were drawn over the window of her room.

He didn't know if it was her in the room or not. There was a second call. He hadn't been able to discern that there were two until she'd gotten into town, but when she'd gone for the healer, he'd still felt something calling to him which remained at the Setting Sun as well. And now, he could sense one of them moving about the inn, while the other remained still in one of the rooms.

As night drew on and he saw no more of her, he eventually began his nocturnal routine of slipping in and out of people's houses to gather bits and pieces of food and supplies. Never enough to draw attention, only enough to meet his needs.

Then he retired to his small abode to ponder this new woman... and what she might mean for his life.

He had a feeling something was about to change.

But he liked his life, and the thought of change worried him deeply.

5

JAIS BLINKED A FEW TIMES AS HE WOKE.

Then he winced as someone dabbed the shoulder with the dagger-wound. It was a cooling, wet cloth, but it still stung against the injured flesh.

"Caer?" He rolled his head to one side and saw... a rather stunning woman sitting next to him.

"Aye, no. Elria am I, a healer." The woman nodded her head in greeting. Waves of red hair tumbled about her head, glinting like true fire from the light of the single candle in the room. If that wasn't strange enough, her eyes were the clearest, purest green Jais had ever seen. For a moment, he lost himself in that tender gaze. Any words he'd been about to speak flew from his mind as his mouth hung open. It was only after a long moment staring at her that he realized he was being rude and snapped his mouth shut.

He also became aware that his shirt was off, and he was half-naked in front of this woman.

"Ah... hello," he said then cleared his throat.

She laughed, and it was a light and free sound, like music.

"A tough one, you are," she said softly. "Most men of these

parts would be right blown down by such a wound as this."
Her accent was odd, light and lilting, but her turn of phrase
was even more odd. He'd never heard anyone speak like her
before.

"He is a special one, yes." That was Caer's voice. But being
on his back with the red headed woman so close—what had
she said her name was... Elria—he couldn't see much of
the room.

"Caer, are you there?"

"Yes," came the reply. She moved toward the foot of his
bed and came into view. She looked tired, though that could
have been the candlelight at an odd angle against the planes
of her face.

She nodded to the woman tending him. "I sought out the
healer in town to take a look at you and Barami. If we
encounter... bandits... any time soon I wanted to be sure you
were in fighting shape."

"I doubt you'll be finding many bandits in Cold River,"
Elria said offhandedly.

Jais knew what Caer was saying though. Caer still
mouthed the words 'dragon hunter' probably to be certain he
understood. He nodded. Bandits probably wouldn't be seen
inside the city, but a single man might easily sneak in. They
needed to be on guard.

"How is Barami?" Jais asked.

It was Elria who answered him. "Well enough. There be a
wound there, sure as day, but it be mostly healed. More of a
concern are you. I'll look in on your friend in a moment."

Caer nodded, her gaze moving off to something else in
the room and her face growing a little more drawn.

He could just imagine her thoughts. Blaming herself for
Barami's injuries, for bringing the dragon hunter down on
them. Though Jais had no idea how anyone could have

found them, in the middle of nowhere as they were. There had to be something else at work here. It couldn't be Caer's bad luck that had somehow summoned the dragon hunter. Yet she'd blame herself anyway. He might not have known her for much more than a month, but spending every moment with her had given him a fair view of her mindset. Somehow, she thought she could control the world around her by sheer force of will and when things went wrong, it always seemed to be her fault. She carried far too much on her shoulders.

"It's not your fault you know," he said softly.

Elria looked up from tending him, a brow raised questioningly, but she said nothing. She must have seen he was looking at Caerwyn. Caer turned to him. He wasn't sure if she'd heard him.

"It wasn't your fault, you know," he repeated. "The... bandits. No one could have seen that coming."

She sighed and shook her head. Her gaze flicked to Elria. "We can talk about this later."

Jais nodded.

Caer paced around the room a little more then finally spoke again. "I'm going out."

"Out?" Jais asked. "Is it not still night?"

"Yes, but I get the feeling that... the man we came to see? I think he is quite active at night. I figure now's as good a time as any to go talk to him."

Jais didn't miss the specificity of her words. 'Man' and 'him' suggested she already knew that the drahksan here in Cold River was male. How she knew, Jais had no clue.

"Have you made contact already?" he asked.

She quirked her lips. "In a way. I caught sight of him."

Jais sensed her need to be active, doing something. "Go on then."

Caer nodded. She put a hand on Elria's shoulder as she passed, on her way out of the room. "Take care of him."

"I will," Elria said and watched her leave. There was something odd in the way Elria made sure the door was shut and even seemed to listen for Caer's footsteps to recede down the hall.

"Good, now I can really get to work." She turned a smiling face on Jais. "But it will be easier if you be sleeping." She put a hand on his forehead and said, "Sleep."

A warm and relaxing sensation filtered into him from where her hand rested on his forehead. This was new. He felt it wash down over his face and instantly his eyes drooped shut. Yet a part of him did not surrender to the slumber. It watched and simply felt the sensations, curious and a bit amazed. No ordinary healer should be able to put people to sleep. His aunt had been able to, and often did, as part of her healing. It was a lot easier to work on a slumbering patient if she didn't want to explain her magic to them. It seemed Elria had a similar thought.

Jais felt the sensation move through his body, relaxing him. He went limp on the bed, his breathing soft and steady.

"That be better," Elria said, though her voice sounded a bit muffled and distant.

Jais didn't know how his mind had escaped the effects of the sleep even while his body hadn't. He was physically at rest, but he was still aware and partially awake. He didn't resist what had happened to his body, but instead he tried to feel it, observe it.

If this woman was like his aunt, then perhaps he could learn from her. He didn't know the finer points of healing and would be quite intrigued to know more.

Yet... Caerwyn seemed quite certain that the drahksan they were looking for was a man and was somewhere else.

How could that be? As far as Jais knew, only drahksani could be true healers. Humans could get close with medicines and herbs, which mimicked some of the effects of a drahksani healing, but they'd never be able to do the accelerated healing, the laying on of hands, like a drahksan.

But if humans couldn't then... what was Elria?

For the moment, he let that question lie as he felt her begin healing his shoulder. It was a different sensation than the sleep. That had been warm and relaxing, this was... soothing and more specific to his shoulder. He let his awareness simply observe and feel the whole process. It was slow, unlike the healings he'd done in the past. But he'd been under pressure, in battle. She didn't seem to use the same amount of energy he had. She was more direct and careful. It was like she was inside the wound, knitting together the muscle and flesh, unhurried and precise.

Amazing.

Once she was done with the wound on his shoulder, she reached across to his other shoulder. That was closed quicker. Then he heard her shifting down to begin on his side. He'd stopped the bleeding from where the arrow had cut him, but as with a stinging cut from a sliver or razor, the pain was acute and lingered.

Again, he simply felt what she did, soothing the pain, slowly encouraging his skin to heal and close the wound.

It was a little time later when she breathed a heavy sigh and he heard the scrape of something on the floor. Perhaps she was standing.

He was tired, nearly fully asleep now. Healing took a lot out of the person being healed. He saw that now. What he'd learned was that it didn't need to take as much from the healer. If a healer was careful and precise, the injured person's body could be encouraged to do most of the work, such that the one doing the healing expended little energy . It was a glorious revelation.

He needed to talk to her about this before she finished up with Barami and left.

He forced himself awake, using his own limited body-awareness to siphon energy from his limbs and other muscles to his mind, then punching through the fog of relaxation his body was under to force his eyes open.

"Elria," he said softly. His voice was a little hoarse and weak. He wasn't sure how much longer he'd be able to keep this up. He rolled his head to one side to look over at her.

Her brows were raised in surprise as she turned back to him. She had been about to work on Barami who was lying on another small bed across the room.

"How in the Sacred Breath are you awake?"

He grinned. "I'm tough, remember? Also, I'm a healer, like you."

Her eyes went wide. "You cannot be like me."

"I didn't think there were many like me either. My aunt was, but she never got a chance to teach me before she died." It still stung a little to say those words. His Aunt Sarelle had been like a mother to him for his entire life.

Her expression changed from shock and disbelief to one of sorrow and compassion. "I am sorry for your loss." She rose from her stool and came to kneel next to his bed. Her voice was hushed, a whisper. "Were you touched by a sacred being?" she asked quietly.

That was not what he'd been expecting at all. "No, but I guess you could say that my ancestors were?" He didn't really know how drahksani came to be. Perhaps it was a similar process. Though again, if she was a drahksan, or something similar, why hadn't Caerwyn been able to sense her? Yet if it had been a different type of 'sacred being' that had given Elria her abilities, perhaps Caer wouldn't be able to feel it.

Elria nodded as if that explained it. "I have never met one not of my clan who was touched. It is an honor to meet you." She put a hand over her heart and bowed for a moment.

"Can you find my sword?" Jais asked. He wanted to be able to at least sit up to talk to her, but that would require more energy. "The one with runes on the scabbard and gold on the guard."

She looked confused but nodded. She rummaged around near the bed for a moment then lifted his sword up and laid in on his chest. He lifted his hand, slowly. It took a lot of effort, like moving through water against a current. Then he finally set his hand on the grip. He struggled for a moment to pull the blade just a little out of the scabbard and touch the metal.

Father? I could use some more energy, just a little to revitalize myself.

As you wish, son.

Energy filled him. It wasn't a flood like he'd felt in the past, but a slow wave.

He sighed as he felt the heavy sluggish feel of his body slip away. "That's better." He put the sword aside and sat up, rotating to sit on the side of the bed. He smiled at Elria's slightly wondering look. To put her at ease, he said, "My companion probably didn't tell you that I can heal myself. I had already done so earlier today, but it had taken a lot out of me. It didn't help that I'd tried to heal Barami over there as well. It also doesn't help that I don't really know what I'm doing. That's why I was so happy to feel your healing touch. I... I was hoping you might show me how to use my healing."

Elria stared at him for a long moment before she nodded. He didn't know what she'd been thinking but she'd come to some decision. "Yes. I will teach you. Come over next to your friend."

She rose and crossed the short distance between the bunks in one long stride. She was tall for a woman, taller than he for certain. Her dress was pretty, a deep green, which matched her eyes. She was more rounded and shapely than Caerwyn, but there was a similar hardness—no that wasn't the right word. There was an intensity about her.

She sat on the stool, and he came to kneel next to Barami's bed.

"How much do you know?" she asked.

He laughed a little. "Let's assume I know nothing and start from the beginning."

She nodded. "Put your hand on him, flesh to flesh, like this." She leaned over and touched Barami's chest. His shirt had been removed already.

Jais did the same, his hand not far from hers.

"What do you feel?"

He quirked a grin. "Skin?"

She cocked her head to one side giving him an exasperated look.

He tried again. "It's warm. I think... I think I can feel his heart beating."

"Nothing beyond the surface?" she asked.

Oh!

He'd heard his aunt talk many times about 'reading the body,' but he didn't really know what that meant. Yet... now that he'd been so aware of what she'd done to him, perhaps...

He closed his eyes to shut out any distractions and concentrated on what he felt through his hand on Barami's chest. Beyond the flesh... was there anything? He felt the beating heart within, but... no... perhaps that was a place to start.

The beating heart. Was the pulse strong? Yes. Was there anything else?

He grimaced. "Can you help me? What am I looking for? How should I be feeling..." He didn't know how to explain it.

"Let your body connect with his. Let your awareness slip from you into him. Feel his blood flowing, the ease or contractions of his muscles. Hear the air moving in his lungs, see the messages flowing along from his brain to his body. You should be able to sense everything within him." She had to speak slowly, choosing her words. It was clear that the Northern tongue was a little foreign to her. He'd have to ask her where she was from... later.

He tried doing as she instructed. He'd been well connected within his own body while she'd been healing him. Now he tried to extend that awareness out to Barami's body as well. He knew what his own felt like and concentrated on the physical touch of his hand to the man's chest.

It was like a little bubble bursting as he pushed past the barrier of flesh and his awareness could 'feel' inside Barami as well. "I think I did it," he said softly. He was a little awed at this discovery. He explored within the man, sensing the various things Elria had mentioned. He could feel the blood flowing to muscles which flexed or relaxed. He felt the rise and fall of Barami's chest as the air was sucked in and expelled from his lungs. It was amazing. "Yes. I see it now!"

"Can you see the wound?"

"Yes, it's like... like some large area of... wrongness. It doesn't feel right."

She laughed a little. "That be not a bad way to say it, yes."

He opened his eyes to find her smiling at him. There was something in that look, something he couldn't fathom. Though... in a way it reminded him of how Alnia had looked at him. She broke off the gaze after a moment. "Now you keep your hand there. Feel what I do as I heal him."

She moved her hand down over the wound.

This sensation was much more familiar. He'd been aware when she'd healed him, and the sensation was the same. Though now, being so much more aware of the internal workings of another body, he could see the slow and steady flow of her energies and how they were not so much forcing the body to heal as encouraging the natural process to speed up.

She paused.

"Did you feel what I did?"

He nodded.

"Did you want to try it?"

"Yes."

They switched. He took her stool and she knelt on the floor.

Putting his hand over Barami's wound, he took a long moment to simply ready himself. Then he focused on the wound, seeing down into the 'wrongness.' He used his connection to Barami's body to 'speak' to it in a way without words. He sent a slow flow of energy into the wound, he didn't try to direct the healing but let the body reconstruct itself.

"Yes, doing quite well, you are."

He heard the encouragement and smiled as he finished up the healing on Barami. He lifted his hand away with a long breath blown out.

"That was... different." He nodded to himself. "You're an excellent teacher."

She smiled up at him. "I only showed you the way. You are the one who picked it up so quickly. You must have some training, no?"

He shook his head. "I'd done some healing before, in combat, when it was imperative, but nothing as delicate at this."

"Then you are a natural healer." She shook her own head, perhaps a little awed. "It took me years to master what you just did."

Oh.

"I'm sure there is still much more I could learn," he said softly. He thought for a long moment. "Can you heal diseases and sickness? I've never tried that."

She nodded. "I can, yes."

"Can you tell me about that?"

She smiled, leaning back against the wall. "I can."

6

BARAMI HOVERED AT THE EDGE OF CONSCIOUSNESS.

His mind, in a semi-feverish state, replayed the attack, those few moments of which he'd been aware. He'd caught a flash, an ever-so-brief flicker of light, then he'd heard something. It might have been the twang of a bow string, but he couldn't be sure. Well he hadn't been sure at the time, but he was now. Then pain exploding through his stomach, shocking his entire being. He hadn't been able to move, and his limbs had gone numb. He'd fallen but hadn't even felt himself hit the ground. He had a few flashes of color, movement, but then darkness.

But there was no pain now.

He considered for a moment that he might have died and gone to Erival, the gardens of the honored dead. But he'd always heard that that was a place of light, eternal day. He got the impression wherever he was now, was mostly dark, with a faint flickering light.

He opened his eyes, blinking for a moment.

He was in a room. Wooden walls and ceiling were his first sight. He was lying on something soft, probably a straw-stuffed mattress. There was a wall on his right side and one just next to his head at the top of the bed. To his left was a bit of an open space. He rolled his head to that side. He couldn't do much more, he was exhausted. There was a small table between his bed and the other in the room. It was a common enough layout to many tavern rooms, two beds with a chest at the foot most likely and a small table between them. He guessed he wasn't dead. He didn't imagine any place like this existed in Erival or Holn.

Also, Jais wasn't likely to be there in the room with him if he were dead, and the young man was sitting on the bed across the way, talking to someone Barami couldn't see.

"That be the hardest part. Once you know the sickness you are dealing with, you can start to see how it affects the body and work against it. It is hard to explain without experiencing it." The voice was unfamiliar, feminine with an odd cadence and sing-song lilting tone.

"If only I could stick around and learn from you. There is so much I don't know about any of this." That was Jais. He looked excited and regretful at the same time.

Neither Jais nor the stranger had noticed Barami was awake.

Jais seemed a little too interested in this woman. Wasn't he supposed to be courting Caerwyn or something like that? Where was Caerwyn? Who was this new woman?

"Caerwyn," he croaked, his voice rough. He coughed a few times.

That got their attention, and a moment later they were both next to him. The woman was tall, with flashing red hair and a slightly flushed face. There was an intensity about her Barami couldn't place.

"Hey, old man," Jais said in a friendly tone. Barami didn't

much like that moniker, but he was in no condition to refute it at the moment. "How do you feel?"

"Tired," he said. "No pain, though." He didn't know if that was a good thing or not.

Jais nodded. "We healed you. You should be fine, just rest."

"We?"

Jais nodded. "This is Elria. She's the healer here in Cold River, that's the town we were headed for when we were attacked... by bandits."

Bandits? That didn't seem likely. Before he could say anything though, Jais went on.

"Caer is out looking for that person we came here to see. She wanted us both to be in good shape to move on if needed. I was fairly hurt too, but Elria healed me. Good as new now. You should rest, though."

Barami got the feeling there was more to Jais' words, but his mind was a little sluggish and he didn't want to bring it up.

He simply nodded and closed his eyes, rolling his head back straight on the pillow.

He heard Jais and the woman move off, still talking, but he blocked out their words for now.

His mind drifted. Yet it went to the same place it always went these days.

Jais was right, he was an old man. He was over forty, which was ancient for a warrior. Those of the fighting trades who didn't die young, often wished they were dead by this time—tormented by old wounds and bad memories. Barami had his fair share of both, but he'd been privileged enough—as Caerwyn's protector—to receive the best healing the Afgenni Empire had. And those who had died before him haunted him less and less these days. No, what truly both-ered him was... his lack of a companion.

He'd followed Caerwyn north after her exile because he'd vowed to protect her with his life, but also because he'd held out a little hope that someday she might look at him differ-ently. Not as a constant friend and companion, but something more. That hadn't happened, and now it never would. She had Jais. Perhaps this new drahksan in town would be another possible mate for her. And he knew she didn't even really want a man to be with her, she just wanted the child they would provide. She was too strong and independent to need a man.

But what did that leave for him?

He could fight well enough still. Did that mean he'd spend his days chopping down enemies until one day they got him instead? Was that all there was?

His heart constricted at that thought. He'd passed up offers for bonding with many women from his tribe back in the Afgenni Empire. He'd been holding out hope for Caer-wyn. But now... he wasn't likely to get many more offers. He wasn't young like Jais, who already had Caerwyn and now seemed to be quite friendly with this new woman as well.

His mind caught a stray thought, a memory. That woman with Jais had flame-red hair... just like...

He shivered.

The full memory rushed back to him. The moment when he'd communed with the God Berem in that odd cave, before they faced the krolloc. He'd had a vision. Standing on a chilly plateau high up on a mountainside. There had been a woman, a redheaded beauty, but different from the one in the room now. The hair and eyes had been the same, flame red and emerald green, but the one in the vision had seemed more like Caerwyn, stern and hard, direct. Her face had been different too, a little longer.

Who was that woman?

It occurred to him that the woman with Jais shared similar traits. Perhaps they were from the same tribe or area. He could ask her... but what would he say? He was looking for a woman he'd only ever seen in a vision?

He sighed and settled. Sleep was coming on, he could feel it. His thoughts grew more and more muddled, harder to hold. Yet as his mind drifted from thoughts to dreams, that same woman from his vision stayed with him.

And his dreams with her were quite interesting.

7

VOLF FELT HER DRAWING NEAR.

He'd finished his nightly pilfering and returned to his hovel with his spoils. Some he'd eaten, some he'd stowed away for later. There wasn't much room in his small dwelling. It had once been a hall connecting two buildings across an alley. He didn't know why it had been created nor why it had been boarded up on either side. He'd found it and made his own door, then covered that with a large piece of scrap tin roofing he'd found in another alley. It looked like nothing so much as an end to the alley with a little refuse scattered around. He doubted anyone would suspect someone lived there.

Inside was a mattress he'd scrounged, a rough table he'd made, a chair, and then rough shelves he'd put in. It was cramped and confined, but he didn't need to be here all the time. It was a place to get out of the rain or sleep; otherwise, he was often out on the roofs, watching the town.

He was certain his pile of refuse would deter any average person wandering down the alley from finding his little hut, but her...

If she could sense him the way he sensed her then...

She was close, just outside.

He heard the scrape of tin as it was moved. He turned and there she was in his small doorway, ducking down to slip under and into his home.

The woman was tall and well built, square of shoulders and strong. Brown hair was tied back, revealing a kind face. There was a scar on her cheek, which tugged at one side of her mouth giving her a faint, roguish grin.

She looked around, taking everything in with soft brown, intelligent eyes. The single candle he had lit seemed enough for her to see.

"Not exactly what I expected," she said then shrugged. Her gaze met his. "Hello. Sorry to barge in like this, but I've been looking for you."

His heart raced. There was only one way out of here, and she was in his way. By her look, strong and sure, he doubted he could get past her to escape... but he didn't really think he wanted to. That's what frightened him so much.

He tried to make sure his voice was steady when he asked, "Who are you?"

"Caerwyn. You?"

"Volf."

"Volf?" She sounded out the word, tasted it on her lips and tongue, then shrugged again. "Volf it is." After a moment, she added, "Do you know why I'm here? Can you... sense me?"

His eyes widened just a little. He nodded, but he didn't know what to say. He'd known she could sense him, that had to be how she found him, but still... to have it said aloud.

"Are we connected?" he breathed. "Are we fated?"

She cocked her head to one side with an odd, considering look. "That's one possible way to look at it I suppose... but..."

She sighed. "I'm guessing you don't know what you are?" Her words now were tentative, questioning.

He blinked. What he was?

Was he something?

He'd known from his early teen years that he was different, not like other people. His skills at stealth, how light he was on his feet, his ability to go unseen... no one else could do that, and they all seemed surprised and afraid of him when they found out he could. He'd learned to stop telling people or asking about it. But did that mean he was something different? It seemed logical. But what?

He shook his head. "What am I?"

Her look became one of concern and compassion. "You've lived your entire life not knowing? What about your parents?" In an instant, her expression went through confusion to a sudden realization. "You're an orphan?"

He nodded. This was all a little much and his head was starting to spin, joining his already racing heart. What was happening? He had the feeling he was on the verge of something, some cliff with a gaping chasm before him.

He swallowed hard, remembering a rough childhood. "My parents left me with friends here in Cold River. I don't know why."

She pursed her lips at this as if she was trying to keep herself from saying something.

So, he went on. "I was a burden to them, this new family. I figured that out quickly enough. My... mother—the woman who raised me—she tried, but my adoptive father was not happy I was around. I was another mouth to feed in an already full house. I made my own way, on the streets, as soon as I was able."

She moved a half step toward him. "I'm sorry. I lost my

parents too, my birth parents, when I was very young. Luckily for me I found a family that accepted me." She quirked her lips. There was more she wasn't telling him. "But I know why your birth parents left you."

"You do?"

"Yes. It was for your own safety. They were saving your life. They were being hunted and wanted to make sure you weren't found with them."

"Hunted? By who? Why?"

She took another half step, which brought her to the edge of his little table. She crouched, leaning against the table for support. He hoped it would hold.

"Have you ever heard of drahksani?"

Drahksani?

"No." He shook his head.

She nodded. "Drahksani are humans with special abilities. I'm guessing you can do something, something no one else can do? That is because you are drahksani. No one knows how they came to be, but they were around for hundreds of years. Then humans turned on them, not trusting those who were different. Humans hunted down the drahksani everywhere. Only a few survived. Myself and a friend I brought with me... and you. We're the only ones I've found since I was a child."

He was... drahksani? What did that mean?

This was all a little much. But it did explain some things. "That's how we can sense each other?"

She nodded. "It's an ability some of us seem to have. My friend can't, but I sensed you a long way off and came here to find you."

"Why?"

That chasm before him oddly was growing deeper and

darker as more questions arose, and yet the other side seemed closer at the same time. The gap was closing, but it wasn't safe yet. He couldn't quite make the leap to the other side, to accepting what he was hearing.

"Because I... I think others like us need to know who and what they are. I want to reunite the drahksani." Again, there was something she was omitting, but her reason seemed sensible enough.

"I... don't know what to make of all this. It's a lot to take in."

She put a tentative hand on his leg. "I would very much like you to meet the rest of my group. Perhaps we can talk, tomorrow, during the day?"

He gave a short laugh. "That's usually when I sleep. I've lived my life at night for so long now... in the dark..."

"If you're not comfortable with it, that's fine. Perhaps I could come back tomorrow night?"

No. He needed answers now.

"I'll come with you now. I'll meet the others."

There was something comforting in that thought... others like him. He wasn't alone in this world, not strange anymore.

He smiled. "I am glad you found me Caerwyn."

She smiled as well, standing again. "As am I."

A thought, perhaps more of a distant feeling or question from the bottom of that black chasm in his mind bubbled up to him. It had been there, all his life, but he'd ignored it because of its constancy. He'd felt it keenly as a child but had grown so used to it he didn't think of it at all these days. Yet having felt her drawing near—knowing what the sensation was now... perhaps...

"Do you feel the other one?" he asked.

"The other one... of us? My friend in town?"

He shook his head. "No. There is another far away to the north. Do you feel it?"

She looked away for a moment, perhaps trying to concentrate and find her own senses. After a long moment, her eyes went wide. "I do, but it's unlike anything I've felt before."

Volf hesitated to say it, but he'd heard a rumor once, a long time ago. "I think I might know what it is."

8

GOSSE HAD MADE HIS WAY INTO COLD RIVER, FOLLOWING HIS prey. He hadn't known the name of the town at the time. He'd never been to this part of the North before. But he knew how to ask around and glean what information he needed. The town's name had come easily, but what he'd actually been seeking had taken a lot more work, most of the night.

He knew where his prey was. He could attack them now. Perhaps they were sleeping, perhaps he'd be able to kill both the drahksani before either woke, but he wasn't a man who liked 'perhaps.' He liked certainty.

His attack on the road had been carefully planned. It had been a test. He knew his one prey, the girl, but the other was new to him. He needed to know what sort of abilities he was up against. It had turned out the boy was a warrior, like Caerwyn. That he could handle... with the right planning and preparation. He'd never meant to defeat them that day and had been surprised how well he'd done. He was certain he could take the two of them... but it would require the right plan.

And for this plan, he'd need help.

That was how he'd ended up in a dimly lit tavern across the river from the main part of town. He'd heard there was a mercenary crew which frequented this place, a crew that specialized in darker deeds, the darker the better.

There were three other man around a small table, huddled together, drinking and talking quietly. It was quite late for anyone to be up. Perhaps these were the ones he sought. He shrugged. Might as well try.

He could take them if it came to a fight. He'd had another parrying dagger with his mount, several actually. He'd been fighting people with powers all his life; a few humans shouldn't trouble him much.

He did brush his hand by his side as he rose. The girl had cut him, but not deeply. He'd bandaged it, and it would heal just fine soon enough. It shouldn't hinder him tonight.

He approached the men with a hand on the pommel of his sword.

"I'm looking for Dathgar's crew," he said loud enough for them to hear, staying a couple steps back from their table.

"Who's askin'?" one of the men asked, his voice a rumbling, rough sound.

Gosse tossed a heavy coin purse onto their table. It was a gamble, but again he was certain he could get it back from them if they weren't the ones he wanted. "Someone with money."

One of the men laughed. "That'll do."

The three rose, each getting to their feet in the way of hardened warriors ready for a fight, slow and steady. They were big men, well two of them were, beefy and thick with muscle. The third was leaner and taller. The first had a sword, a big heavy-bladed thing. The tall one had a sword at his hip and a bow unstrung nearby. The last carried two axes and had a few smaller throwing axes on him as well.

"I'm Dathgar," the one with the axes and deep gravelly voice said. "What's the job?" They were all watching him closely. He didn't flinch or shrink under their stares.

"Murder. Two people. They're tough, both warriors. I could probably take them myself, but I want to be certain they die—ideally without me getting hurt in the process."

Dathgar nodded. "Only two?"

Gosse shrugged. The human who'd been traveling with the two should be dead. Few could survive an arrow through the gut. Just to be safe he added, "There may be a third with them. I don't care if he dies."

Dathgar sniffed. His eyes flicked away from Gosse to the money on the table. "How much is in there?"

"It's hard to gauge exactly. Most of it is gems. I'd say it's roughly equivalent to a couple thousand gold pieces."

Dathgar's eyes went wide, and he gripped the haft of one of his axes a little tighter.

Gosse could almost see the thoughts behind those eyes. Should Dathgar just kill this man and take his money?

Gosse should dissuade that thought.

There was a faint ringing, nothing more, and Gosse had his sword at Dathgar's throat. His dagger was drawn and ready in his off hand.

"In case you think me some easy mark you can steal from... don't. I'm no one to be trifled with." He withdrew his blade as quickly as he'd drawn it, keeping it in his hand, but at his side. "As, I'm sure, none of you are to be trifled with. So, do we have a deal?"

Dathgar glared at him for a long moment before breaking out into a smile and laughing. "You haven't even asked our price?" That with another glance at the money-bag.

Gosse shrugged. "I'm assuming that's enough. Am I wrong?"

Dathgar shook his head. "No. It's enough. You'll get me and my whole little band, all five of us."

"Five?" Everything he'd learned about Dathgar and his men had suggested there were only the three of them.

"Yes five," this from a soft, sibilant voice to his left.

Gosse started as two more men seemed to step out of the shadows in the dark room. He immediately reassessed his chances of taking these men... and didn't like them.

These two new ones were... dangerous, that was clear. Not in the way that Dathgar and the other two were. The first three were killers clear enough, they were dangerous, but in a predictable way. These two beside him. They were darker, more sinister and there was something else about them. Something he couldn't quite put his finger on.

The first was big and burly, a muscled lump of a man. He was built like Dathgar, but on a larger frame, as tall as the archer, which made him huge by anyone's standards. He probably outweighed the group leader by a couple hundred pounds. He didn't look smart, but there was a certain something, perhaps cunning in his eyes. Like he knew just how to kill Gosse in the most painful ways and was looking forward to it.

The second one, if possible, seemed even more dangerous. He was the one with the soft sibilant voice. He was reed thin and as tall as the archer or his burly companion. He had no weapons on him, holding only a staff. Gosse was always wary of those with no weapons. In a world like this, anyone who could survive without weapons, was either crazy or incredibly skilled in some other way... or both. But what was this man's skill set? It was the mystery that bothered Gosse. And there was a slightly different look in his eyes. It wasn't some expectation of painful death like his companion, but like he knew things, like he could control Gosse with a whisper of just the right word. It sent a shiver down Gosse's spine.

"Who are you, now?" Gosse said to the new couple, hoping he hadn't given away his apprehension. He was getting over his surprise, but still didn't like this situation.

The taller one spoke, hissing out his words. "I am Tyark." He placed a long-fingered hand on his chest. Then he moved the same hand to pat the other man on the shoulder. "This is my companion Gerhardt."

Dathgar laughed. "I think you're spooking our employer, Ty." Then, turning an affable grin to Gosse, he added. "These two are new to our team. We had some men... leave... a couple month back. These two seemed to fit well. Just as savage as the rest of us with a host of unique skills. Don't you worry, we'll make sure whoever you desire is dead." Dathgar winked.

Gosse wondered what 'unique skills' these two men possessed. They made him want to run away or run them through, he couldn't figure out which.

He shrugged. "Doesn't matter to me who we use, I just want to be there when it happens. I might even join you."

"Up to you." Dathgar seemed to ease a little now. "Who are the targets?"

"Names don't matter. They're at an inn on the other side of town. I can lead you to them." He considered for a moment. He wanted to get this done as soon as possible, but he would never rush things. "It's already late, might be dawn soon. I'll return tomorrow evening, and we can go in then."

Dathgar shrugged. "Up to you, boss."

Gosse nodded to them all and headed for the door.

He couldn't help but look back as he reached the portal. Tyark was looking at him intensely, still with that same gaze, as if he owned Gosse's soul. Gerhardt still looked like he wanted to twist the life out of him, wringing him like a wet cloth.

He left and only then allowed himself a shudder.

Never before had he met anyone who made him question what he had gotten himself into... until now.

9

It was near dawn.

Caerwyn was growing tired. Her drahksan nature meant she could often go for a couple days without sleep and function fairly well, but this past day had had its fair share of trials and she was hoping for a soft bed. Even just a short nap would help.

She didn't want to stick around here long. Better not to stay in one place for too long when you were being pursued by a dragon hunter. And now she had a direction to go.

North.

Toward... something.

The feeling wasn't like sensing other drahksan at all. It was a deeper, more primal thing. If sensing a drahksan could be compared to listening to someone speak and getting a better and clearer sense as you drew closer, then this was more like the beat of a drum. It wasn't distinct like a voice, but it seemed to beat within her at some primitive level.

She hadn't sensed it before because of its difference, but now that she had, she was certain it was calling to her. There was something up north and she would find out what it was.

Volf was with her as she made her way through the Setting Sun Inn to the room with Jais and Barami. She wondered if the healer had stayed around to tend them, but that seemed unlikely. Though... Elria hadn't asked for any payment, so perhaps.

As Caerwyn drew near, she heard voices through the door, Jais' and... the healer's. Apparently, the woman had stayed. That would make things more complicated. She'd have to get rid of the woman before they could talk freely.

Caerwyn knocked on the door then entered. Better to give warning than surprise them. The chamber was small, with a bed on either side of the room, and just enough space at the foot of each bed for two thick chests. There was a small window in the far wall. The shutters were open to let in the cooler night air, but the gauzy shades were drawn for privacy. Barami was sleeping and looked well healed, Jais and the healer woman Elria were talking, both sitting on his bed.

Jais looked over at her and smiled. It was the freest and happiest he'd looked since he'd lost his family and friends not that long ago.

"Caer, did you know that Elria was like us?"

That made Caerwyn stop for a moment. She blinked, trying to figure out what to say. Had Jais told the woman they were drahksani? That did not seem wise, but if he had, the woman didn't seem to be running screaming either.

"What do you mean? Did you tell her about...?" She didn't know how to end that sentence without sounding too suspicious but realized that just trailing off also sounded suspicious.

"She's a true healer, like my aunt and myself. She's been showing me how to use my abilities and telling me about hers."

"But she's not…" Again, Caerwyn didn't say the word and knew it sounded odd.

"No, I don't think so. She says…" He turned to Elria. "How did you come by your abilities?"

Elria looked a little put-on-the-spot. "Ah, it be not something we can talk about, but I can tell you that… I was touched by a sacred being and gifted these abilities." Though there was something in how she said it, as if Elria had already said too much.

So, the girl had secrets too.

Interesting.

Elria was looking back and forth between Caerwyn and Jais. She addressed Caerwyn. "Be you a healer as well?" Then she seemed to realize what she'd asked. "No, you couldn't be, or you wouldn't need me. Do you have other abilities?" The woman cocked her head to one side, obviously curious. Yet her curiosity didn't seem to be about whether Caerwyn had abilities, but of what sort they might be. Did Elria know of others with abilities? Could that be what Caerwyn was sensing?

…Yet, she didn't sense anything from Elria herself, so she couldn't be certain of what the woman was. And the woman's question was straying into dangerous territory.

Caerwyn smiled politely. "I think you understand very well that it is not always good to talk about such things openly. We all have our secrets. Shall we leave it at that?"

Elria nodded.

"How much do I owe you for your services?" Caerwyn asked, hoping that might lead to the woman leaving.

Elria smiled. "I have had a very pleasant night speaking with Jais." She smiled. "You owe me nothing." She rose and turned to Jais. "Thank you. It was a pleasure to talk with you." She turned and nodded to Caerwyn before stepping past her to the door. There she paused. "I would ask for nothing except..." She pursed her lips for a long moment, as if she didn't want to say more, then finally nodded to herself. "Be you heading north?"

Caerwyn froze. How could Elria know?

No, the girl didn't know... it was just a coincidence. Caerwyn saw that quickly enough, but it was still... odd.

"Why?" Caerwyn asked.

"I have family. My clan is far north from here. I have not seen them in some time and if that be the direction you were heading I might wish to travel with you?" It came out more as a question then a statement.

Caerwyn breathed a bit of a sigh. She gave Volf a quick look to make sure he wouldn't say anything. He was silent, keen blue eyes watching everything, taking it all in. "We are uncertain where we are heading next," Caerwyn lied. "Once we know, if we're going north, we'll let you know."

Elria nodded and left.

Caerwyn closed the door behind her and leaned on it for a moment. Under her breath she breathed a soft, "Well that could be a problem."

Jais' keen ears must have picked up her whisper.

"Why?" Jais looked to Volf. "And is this... who we were looking for?"

Caerwyn nodded. "Jais meet Volf." She turned to Volf and touched him lightly on the shoulder. He didn't flinch away, but she could tell from his reaction that he wasn't used to being touched. "Volf, this is Jais, my... friend and companion. He's... like us." Even with Elria out of the room, one couldn't be too careful

The two nodded to each other. She caught Jais sizing up Volf and nearly immediately rendering him as no threat. That seemed a bit premature since they didn't even know what the man could do, but she had to admit... she'd done the same thing when she'd first seen him.

In truth, he looked unobtrusive. He was tall and wiry, long and lean. His features were sharp, but not to the point of severity. His face was slender, with a large aquiline nose, making her think of him as 'hawkish.' Clear and keen blue eyes peered out over well defined, if slightly bony, cheeks. A small mouth completed his look.

She sat near Jais and lowered her voice. "As for why that girl might be a problem..." She looked up at Volf. "Well, we will be heading north, but we'll also have a lot to talk about. But perhaps I should let Volf explain." She looked up at the other man.

Volf ran a slender hand through his blond hair. His hair, like Jais' was shaggy and thick, unkempt, but generally cut short around the ears, not to the shoulders like Jais.

Volf looked around and spotted the stool, then pulled it up close to the bed. He then glanced over his shoulder at Barami.

"He's fine," Caerwyn said. "He's not one of us, but he knows about us. He's a dear friend of mine and has been for more than ten years. He can be trusted."

Volf nodded but kept his voice low all the same. His eyes darted between Caerwyn and Jais as he spoke, but mostly kept on Caerwyn. "It was long ago, when I was a child. I heard a rumor, but it was no more than that. There was a boy I knew who was the son of a merchant who traveled all over these lands. He said that when his father had been up north visiting the Dronnegir, he'd picked up a bit of their language, enough to suggest to him that somewhere even farther north than their home, high in the Thyrgran Mountains, there lived..." He looked around again. "...a dragon."

Caerwyn watched Jais' face as he heard this. She smiled a

little as he gaped. She'd done the same thing and wouldn't have wanted him to take the news better than she had.

"A true dragon?" Jais whispered.

Volf shrugged. "I don't know for certain. As I say, it was a rumor, overheard from a boy, overheard from his father, overheard from others."

Caerwyn still felt her pulse quicken. "This could be a chance for us to finally understand what we are. If we can find this dragon... if it exists... and speak to it. We could..." There were so many possibilities. "We could find out where we came from, and perhaps if it knows of others of our kind. Maybe it knows even more about what we can do than we do! I only had a little time with my true parents, my drahksani parents, and never really got a chance for them to teach me about who I am and what I can do. I've had to learn as I go. Like we all have. Think of the opportunity to know—"

"The truth," Jais finished. His voice was breathy, awed.

Volf gave a short laugh. "Here I thought you two would be more... experienced with... whatever it is we are."

Caerwyn shrugged. "We're all learning. Though I suspect we can at least let you know some basic things." She turned to Jais. "Volf didn't know what he was. I've informed him he's a drahksan, but perhaps there is more that can be said about that. There is a little I know from my studies." She turned her gaze back to Volf. "My father, my adoptive father, had a very extensive library."

"I would like to know more," Volf said and despite being a grown man he seemed like nothing so much as a boy in that moment.

"And I'll tell you what I can, but first..." She turned to Jais. "What do you say? Shall we go north?"

Jais shrugged. "On a rumor? I suppose we didn't have any other place to go."

It's more than rumor. "I'm guessing you can't feel it, but there's something up there. Both Volf and I can sense it. It's different than sensing another drahksani. It's hard to put into words, but I think maybe this could be what a dragon feels like. I don't know, but along with the rumor, I think it's worth investigating."

Jais smiled. "I'll trust you. I don't feel anything, but I can't feel you either so.... let's go north." After a moment, he added. "I don't think it would be that much of a problem to bring Elria along with us. We'll drop her off with her clan, then we'll be free to look for the dragon and speak as we wish. She did help us. We do owe her."

Caerwyn nodded. Jais was right. "I'll go find her."

"If you don't mind, can I go? I got some rest earlier and I'm... well there's so much I can still learn from her. I wouldn't mind talking a little more with her before we're on the road."

Caerwyn nodded. She was curious at Jais' intensity of interest in the woman. He was more animated and excited than he'd been in a long time. She wondered if there was more of a connection growing between him and the girl, than just a shared ability.

And what did it matter if there was? She'd made her choice when it came to Jais. She didn't need or want a man in that way. But still, she felt a little envious that this woman had been the one to bring such joy back into the man's life.

Jais sprang up and practically ran to the door. He turned back when he got there. "It was nice to meet you, Volf." He turned his eyes to her. "I'll catch up with you later today."

She raised her hand to stop him from running out. "I'd like to get moving soon. But I also want to rest. We'll head out after the noon meal. Let her know if she's coming with us, she'll need to be ready by then, as will you."

Jais nodded and was out the door.

Her gaze fell to Volf.

"When I first sensed you," Volf said slowly. "I was terrified. You called to me in a way no one ever had... and for a man who had spent most of his life alone, to feel something like that... I didn't know what to do." He smiled. "But now I am very glad to have met you. My life has changed forever because of you. I know what I am. Thank you, Caerwyn." He reached out for her and she found herself taking his hand in hers.

His rather intense blue eyes looked up at her.

It occurred to her only then that he wasn't an unattractive man. He could afford to fill out a little, everything on him seemed over-lean, but with his blond hair and those clear eyes, he had a charming look to him.

She hadn't been completely honest with Volf when she'd found him. She wasn't just trying to find more of her kind. There was still a deep desire within her to have a child. Jais... well things with him were just awkward now and she wouldn't ask him again. But perhaps now she had options.

She wasn't going to rush into anything, she'd just met this man... though she had been willing to propose mating with Jais even before she'd met him. Well she'd learned her lesson there. Taking her time would serve her well. She'd get to know the man then broach that topic later.

She'd not be so bold as she had been with Jais.

A stray thought crossed her mind: was she reluctant to approach this man about her child because she still wished to have it with Jais? Was Jais a better match for her than Volf?

No, that couldn't be it.

She'd made her choice about Jais, and he too about her: they were friends and companions.

Besides, it seemed he'd found someone new already.

10

JAIS FOUND ELRIA IN THE COMMON ROOM OF THE SETTING SUN Inn. She hadn't gone far.

She smiled when she saw him and said, "I thought I might wait here to find out where you be going."

Jais joined her at a small table. "We're going north, and you're more than welcome to come with us." He was excited, but at his words, there seemed a mix of emotions playing over her features. Mainly she didn't seem as happy or excited as he would have thought. "Is something wrong?"

She smiled again, though he wondered if that was just hiding her true feelings. "I have not been home in some time. It will be good to return, but..."

"What?"

She shook her head. "It be nothing," she said and Jais thought that would be it, but she spoke up a moment later. "My father be a hard man. I be liking what I do here." She shook her head. "But he may be wanting that I do not return to Cold River. Too long have I been away."

"You're a grown woman, you can do as you wish."

She shook her head. "That be not the way of our people.

We have duties. We are allowed to see some of the world when we are young, but then..." She sighed. "There are so few of us."

Jais grimaced. He didn't have a home to return to, so perhaps that was why he thought to encourage her to stay away. But if he had someone, a family waiting for him, if his uncle had needed someone to take over the hunting when he grew old, he might feel compelled to return.

"I understand." He laid a hand on hers.

She looked up at him and smiled. Cocking her head to one side, she looked into his eyes for a long moment. "Perhaps you do. Though there be other complications you would not understand. My people are... unique." She seemed to pick that word carefully. "But I thank you. It will be good to be speaking with you more about healing, as we go north."

He couldn't help but smile as he found himself held by her gaze. Something about her, the fall of that fiery hair, or the sparkle in those green eyes, just captivated him. Perhaps it was her smile and the way it rounded her cheeks.

"Will you be ready to leave by midday? That's when Caerwyn wants to head out."

She nodded. "I have little. I will be ready." She squeezed his hand. "Thank you again, Jais."

She rose and broke the contact, lifting her hand away. He rose as well and watched her exit the inn's common room.

He sighed. He wanted to be around Elria more, and he was looking forward to traveling together, but that might make things awkward. He didn't really know where he stood with Caerwyn. Did she still want a child? He'd told her he wasn't ready. They were friends certainly, but there was a lot that was unspoken between them, and that made things a little awkward already. Jais didn't know what adding Elria into the mix would do.

Perhaps he should have a talk with Caerwyn, but she wasn't the 'long talk' sort of woman, more direct and to the point, which made broaching the subject of talking even harder. He didn't know what to do. Perhaps she'd approach him?

He sighed and shrugged and hoped that's what would happen.

Maybe there would be time enough on the journey north to figure things out a little more.

He realized he'd been standing there in the common room gazing at the door for a long moment and took his seat again.

A serving woman came over asking if he wanted anything. He ordered a meal; he was famished. As he waited for it to come, he laughed a little to himself. All he'd wanted when he'd come into town was a soft bed and he hadn't really taken advantage of that. He'd rested for only a short while before being healed and staying up the rest of the night talking with Elria.

It occurred to him that he'd talked more with Elria this past night than he had with Caerwyn in the past month, if you didn't count his fighting practice with her. Elria was just that much easier to talk to and they had a shared interest and skill.

Life was complicated, that much he knew, he'd always known. He'd thought it might get better with time and age, but he was finding that it didn't. It only seemed to get worse.

He ate his meal when it arrived but tasted little of it. His mind was elsewhere, and his feelings were a jumbled mess tumbling around within him.

After a little while, Volf came down and joined him, saying that Caerwyn was sleeping. Jais wasn't in the mood to talk to the tall stranger.

Volf must have sensed this and after a while stood. "I should collect what little I have," he said as he rose. "I had never thought to leave this town, and now I will, in the company of those who understand me. Something else I never thought to find."

Jais smiled up at him but didn't really feel that happy. "Glad we could help."

Volf nodded to him and left.

Jais finished his meal but couldn't go back up to the room now with both beds taken. So he waited, feeling more and more anxious to be on the road. He went out and checked their donkey and wagon. All was in order there.

Even if his life wasn't.

GOSSE DIDN'T KNOW HOW HE KNEW, BUT HE KNEW: HIS PREY was gone.

He'd left the mercenaries outside; he didn't want to alarm anyone in the common room of the Setting Sun. He made his way to the Innkeeper, a matronly woman working at one of the hearths.

"Pardon me," he said with force. "Innkeeper?"

The woman turned and looked at him. She sprouted a smile. "Yes? How can I help you? Do you need a meal? A room?"

He shook his head and lowered his voice. He hadn't seen any of his prey in the common room, but that didn't mean that others might not be listening. "I'm looking for friends of mine who are staying here, I believe. Two men and a woman. They would have stood out: one of the men has dark skin and the woman carries a sword. Do you know them?"

The innkeeper nodded. "Indeed I do, but you missed them by a half a day. They left around noon."

Gosse put on a disappointed face. It wasn't much of an act. He was disappointed, but he was trying to appear to be a friend not a foe. "That's unfortunate. You didn't happen to overhear where they might be heading. I would love to catch up and travel with them if I could."

The woman considered. Even as she did, another younger serving girl stepped up. "Pardon," she said to the innkeeper, "I didn't mean to overhear, but if you were wondering where that odd group was going, I think it was north. I heard them talking to others about it over breakfast."

"North?" That was odd. What was north of here? The only thing Gosse had seen north of here was mountains. "What is north of here?" He figured it didn't hurt to ask.

"There are the Dronnegir. Strange folk who mostly keep to themselves," the matron said.

The younger woman piped in with more useful information. "One of them was speaking with that Dronnegir healer in town. I think she might have traveled with them."

Gosse smiled. "Thank you, that is very good to know." The girl blushed and bobbed a curtsey and scuttled off to her duties. Gosse turned to the woman. "Thank you. I'm in your debt." He tossed a few coins on the counter with a grin and left.

Outside, in a dark alley his vicious companions waited.

"Well?" Dathgar asked.

Gosse shook his head. "They've left, probably trying to keep ahead of me. Are we up for a little travel?"

"For what you're paying us, we'll travel as far as you need. Where are we heading?"

"North."

Dathgar shrugged. "Not much up there but mountains

and barbarians. Seems a strange choice, but we'll go where you want. We'll need a bit to gather supplies though. We'll meet at the west gate at the call of the midnight watch."

"Will there be issues with the gate's man?" Gosse asked.

"Nothing a little gold won't make go away."

Gosse nodded. "I'll meet you there." He left, glad to be out from under the glare of Tyark and Gerhardt. He still had a very uneasy feeling about those two.

As he retrieved his own meager things—he liked to travel light—he considered the strange feeling he'd had most of the day.

Somehow, he'd known the prey would be at the inn. Also, just as odd, he'd known they'd headed north. He'd always had an uncanny knack for tracking down his prey. He set himself a direction and would pick up their trail soon enough. He'd been eluded a few times in his youth, but now that he'd been doing this for fifty years, he had a good sense for things.

He'd never questioned it before, but now he wondered. His training as a dragon hunter had been extensive and he'd learned from one of the best, a legend, the notorious Elvar Siroc. He'd always thought that his ability to find his prey was because of that training, but if so, how did training make him aware that his prey had fled when he hadn't even started to investigate? He'd been more and more aware recently of his 'gut' feelings and how he followed them without thinking. They'd never led him wrong.

As he packed his saddlebags, a solution came to him.

It had to be his experience. After years of tracking down dragonborn, he'd gotten so good, that he just knew things. He had gotten to know their patterns of behavior so well that he knew what they did even as they did it.

Of course they would head north, there was nothing in

that direction. It didn't make sense to go north, and if they were trying to throw him off their tracks, then it made perfect sense to do what seemed illogical.

He grinned to himself, glad he'd worked out his thoughts.

He wouldn't question his gut again. It was only his great experience telling him what he would have found out if he looked into it anyway.

His grin widened. He knew his prey too well. They would never escape him. They were already dead... they just didn't know it yet.

11

CAERWYN WOKE EARLY BUT LINGERED ON HER BEDROLL, LYING down as she watched the sun rise over the low mountains to the east.

There were mountains all around them now, though those to the east and west were much farther away. Those to the north loomed higher and higher every day.

They'd been on the road for nearly two weeks, heading north. Even though it was still mid-summer, the temperature had been growing cooler. Not only were they heading straight north, but higher and higher into the foothills of the Thyrgran Mountains. She hadn't needed a blanket to sleep when they'd left Cold River. She did now.

Once the sun was fully up, she sat and stretched herself out a little. She rose to go kick Jais for his morning training, but before she did, she got a sense that something wasn't right. Something in her periphery.

She looked around and spotted it quickly. Elria was missing.

She kicked Jais, kneeling next to him as he roused. Something about this didn't sit right with her. She'd been feeling a bit of an itch she couldn't scratch at the base of her neck these past couple days and now it was getting worse. She kept her voice low looking around as she spoke.

"Do you know where Elria is?"

Jais sniffed, then perhaps as the question sank in, he perked up quickly. "She's gone?"

Caerwyn didn't answer but let him see for himself. Instead, she just said, "She wasn't there when I woke up."

"She could just be off relieving herself or..." He looked around intently.

"I don't think so, and I don't think you do either. All of her things are gone."

Jais was crouching next to her now peering into the long shadows of the new day. "Yesterday she said we were getting closer to her village. She might have... I don't know... gone ahead for some reason?"

"But why? And why wouldn't she say something before leaving? Something's wrong. I can feel it."

Jais seemed to disregard her apprehension. "I don't think there is anything amiss. She probably just wanted to get a start on the day and see her family. In some ways this makes our trek easier now, doesn't it? We don't have to talk in secret about what we are anymore."

She shrugged. "I suppose. But—" Caerwyn cut herself off. She was just repeating herself now.

"I know. I thought she'd at least say good-bye, but maybe this is where our paths fork."

Caerwyn rose slowly, still not feeling at ease. She couldn't help a bit of a jab at Jais. "You seemed to be getting quite close to her. Did you want her to leave?" She wasn't looking at him, still scanning the area around them.

"I..." He let out a long sigh. "If I'm honest, I don't know.

She was nice company, and I was learning a lot about healing. Didn't you find her pleasant?"

The woman had been good company, never complaining or shirking work. She didn't want to tell him that though. She just grunted.

"Fine, don't talk." Jais rose and stalked away. His voice had been hard, hurt.

She didn't know what she'd done. Somehow, he'd turned her accusation of him into one against her.

She shook her head. This was why she didn't want any male attachments. It always got messy and complicated and frustrating. She hadn't approached Volf about the possibility of helping her with a child, but the option was gaining some support in her musings. Over these past two weeks, Jais had seemingly grown closer to Elria and had seemed more standoffish with Caerwyn. She'd found it hard to talk to him with the other woman around and ended up frustrated more often than not. He just seemed... erratic. She couldn't believe how he was fawning over Elria, and not even two months since his previous lover had died. It vexed her and stung a little. She'd thought she and Jais had had a connection. Something deeper than just being friends. They were both drahksani. Didn't that mean something? But what did it mean? They'd never defined it. She just wasn't sure of where they stood with each other, and that bothered her.

So, she'd been spending more time with Volf, who was quiet and reserved. He seemed to be taking all the change he'd been going through in stride.

Men. She doubted she'd ever understand them.

She kicked the other two awake. "We're going to head out soon. Get ready."

"Are we training this morning?" Volf had joined them in their morning and evening combat training sessions. He had a long way to go before he'd be anywhere near competent, but gods he was light on his feet and agile. He could bend and slip out of the way of nearly any attack.

Caerwyn didn't want to stay, she wanted to be moving, but it would be good for all of them to get the training in.

"Yes. Once Jais gets back we'll run through things, but quickly, I want to be on the road." Not that they were on any road at all. They'd followed a bit of a road north out of Cold River, but after it had led to a few farms, it tapered off to a path, then nothing at all. They had sold their donkey and wagon at a small village over a week ago, for some provisions and supplies. They'd move quicker over the uneven terrain without it. Since then, they'd been trekking across rolling hills, higher and higher, with no sign of any one around at all. It was beautiful country, wild and lush, but as they rose into the foothills, the trees had noticeably changed. There were fewer, if any, of the trees with leaves. They had been replaced with tall pointy trees of the prickly leafless variety. Elria called them by various names, though the one word she'd used "evergreen" seemed to describe them best to Caerwyn.

"Where's Elria?" Barami asked as he started working on a fire.

"We don't know. We think she's gone off to find her own people without saying goodbye." Her tone was curt and hard. She didn't want to snap at her old friend, but just couldn't seem to settle herself.

"Doesn't seem right."

"I know!"

Barami looked up at her. "You doing well?"

She shook her head crouching next to him. "No. I can't put my finger on what's bothering me, and that's bothering me even more. Elria leaving just seems wrong, and Jais doesn't seem that worried."

"Certainly seems rude, and that's not like the young woman. She was always polite."

"Were you that fond of her too?"

Barami chuckled. "Oh, is that it?"

"Is what what?"

"You're upset with Jais for getting close to the girl?"

"I..." She moved her lips for several long moments with no sound coming out. Curse Barami. He knew her too well. Knew what she was feeling even when she didn't. "Perhaps."

"Perhaps? Just perhaps?" He chuckled some more. "You keep telling yourself that and maybe you'll believe it someday."

"Men!" She rose and stalked away.

Breakfast was a silent affair.

Training was rough. She was harsh on Jais and Volf, and neither appreciated it. Barami ended it after only a few bouts, and she was glad for that.

By the time they'd been on the move for a few hours, she was only just beginning to feel her anxiety ease. The movement helped as did the crisp mountain air.

That's when they encountered their first human life in over a week. They were following a river along a valley floor as the valley itself rose into the mountains. They came around a rocky outcropping, and three burley men stood in their way. It was clear from the surly expression on the men's faces as well as their weapons, out and ready, that they were not going to be friendly.

They were all brawny men with beards that were braided into several long ropes and hair which grew long and shaggy. One of them had hair similar in color to Elria, fiery red. The other two were blond.

The men called out to Caerwyn and the others as they drew close.

"This be the land of the Dronnegir!" the tallest of the three shouted. "You be not permitted here. Turn back now."

Caerwyn raised her hands, empty. "Stay here," she hissed over her shoulder to the others, then approached slowly. "I wish only to speak."

"Speak from there!" one of them responded. They didn't raise their weapons, which was a good sign, but they didn't look particularly inclined to talk either.

"We are just passing through. We are in search of..." Should she tell them? If she remembered correctly Volf had said that his rumor had started with this clan, the Dronnegir. Would they be willing to help Caerwyn find the dragon? It didn't look like it. She tried a vague approach. "In search of truth, high in those mountains."

"What truth?" This from the largest one again.

She sighed. "Our quest is our own," she said, her frustration from earlier that day returning.

"We care not. If you wish to head north from here... you cannot."

Caerwyn shrugged. This was going nowhere. She dropped her hands and returned to the others. It was Volf she addressed, her voice low. "Do you think it wise to mention to these men we are in search of a dragon?"

Volf looked a little stunned. He shrugged. I have only heard tales of the Dronnegir, and from all I've heard they are very private people. I don't know what they might accept or not. Sorry."

Caerwyn put the question to the group. "What do we think? Tell them of the dragon? Fight them? Go back?"

She didn't want to go back. Though that would be just the perfect way for this particular day to go.

"I wouldn't recommend fighting," Volf said. "One of the

things I have heard about the Dronnegir is that they are brutal warriors."

"Great." This from Jais.

Barami seemed the only one with a level head. "Tell them of the dragon. See what they say. Perhaps they know of it? If they do not, perhaps this is a fool's quest?"

The resonant beating of that implacable sense of something north of here in her gut told her this wasn't a fool's quest. It had only grown stronger over the past two weeks. But she took Barami's advice.

She turned back to the men.

"We seek a dragon! Do you know of one near here?"

All three men seemed quite surprised at the mention of a dragon. They muttered among themselves for a moment, which was the most activity out of the group she'd seen. The largest one, probably the leader, responded after a moment.

"No."

Well that ended quickly.

"Thank you for your help!" she called out to the men. It was mostly sarcasm, but she hoped they wouldn't take too much offence at that.

She returned to the others.

"So, what now?" she asked.

"I have an idea," Volf said. "For now, let's all turn around and leave before any or all of them get antsy."

"There are only three" She felt comfortable that her group could win an encounter with the brutes.

It was Barami who told her. "Take a look back, but up on the ridges on either side of the valley. We didn't think you'd seen them."

She glanced back, looking upward this time. On either side of the valley, just above where the three men stood, there were more burly men and women. Each side seemed to have a group of three or four or more; it was hard to tell from this angle. She wouldn't have seen them if she'd looked up from her previous vantage point, but the Dronnegir had a good angle down on all of them.

"It seems," Barami said softly. "They really do not want us to go past this point."

But Caerwyn could only wonder. Elria was of these people, that was obvious enough from the look of them all. Had she fled in the middle of the night to tell her people that Caerwyn and her group were coming? Was she the one behind them being blocked?

That itching at the base of her neck returned as did her surly mood.

This was not going to be a good day.

"THEY'RE HIDING SOMETHING. DID YOU SEE THE WAY THEY whispered to each other when you mentioned the dragon? They are trying to keep us away." Volf was adamant.

The feeling in his gut, the deep beating of some heady call, had only been growing as he headed north. It was too much now to ignore. He glanced at Caerwyn and he saw it in her eyes too.

"That did seem odd," Jais said.

They were all well out of earshot of the barbarians now, heading back out of the valley they'd been in.

"Exactly. I say we find another way around. Skirt this valley, give it a wide berth, and head north.

It was the dark-skinned human, Barami, who spoke next. "I don't know what you're all feeling but let me remind you that those men back there didn't seem the understanding type. If they find us in their lands again I doubt they'll be as... *friendly* as they were this time. I'm not saying we shouldn't go, I'm saying we should consider our next actions carefully."

Volf had to agree. He wasn't usually one to run in without

being prepared. Yet he did find himself anxious to get going, to find whatever was pulling at him.

"I have ways of keeping myself hidden, perhaps I could scout ahead and make sure the way is clear?"

"That's not a bad idea," Caerwyn said. She was smiling at him and he felt his whole spirit lift with that look. There was so much about her which was different from other women, and that spoke to a place deep within him. He too was far different than anyone he'd ever known. He felt a certain kinship with her and hoped she shared it.

"What is it you two are feeling?" Jais asked softly. There was something in his voice, a curiosity? No, perhaps more of a concern or uncertainty.

Caerwyn replied, "It's hard to describe, it's like..." She put a hand over her stomach. "A heavy feeling here. But more than heavy, it beats in time with my own heart, but stronger somehow. And it feels like it's pulling me... northward somewhere. Why?"

Jais stopped. "I think I might be feeling it too."

Caerwyn also stopped. "Really? But you've never felt any pull to drahksani before."

He grimaced. "I am well aware of that, which is why this feels so strange. I had to know what you both were feeling to see if perhaps I was feeling it too. I think I am, but it's still faint for me. But it's like you say, a throbbing... here, in my gut, pulling me." He too put his hand over his stomach.

Volf watched as something in Caerwyn's eyes gleamed to life at Jais' words. Yet those glimmering eyes turned to him just a moment later.

"Then we must be on the right track. If Jais can feel it, it must be something stronger than a drahksan. It has to be a dragon and with all three of us, I'm sure we'll be able to find it," she said, with an urgency in her voice which echoed what was in his soul.

"Yes," was his only reply.

Barami sighed heavily. "Well come on then, let's find another way around and see if we can't bypass these redheaded brutes." There was something in the man's voice. Volf turned to him, as they continued on down the valley.

"You almost sound like you want to get caught by these men?" he asked the man.

"Caught? No. And I don't want to fight them either, but..." He shook his head. "It's hard to explain. I won't bother you with the details. I guess I was just hoping they would be more welcoming. I'd thought..." He let out a long breath then grimaced. "It's nothing, don't worry yourself."

Volf shrugged; he wouldn't.

VOLF'S HEART WAS POUNDING.

It was late afternoon by the time they'd found another way north which they hoped would take them around the barbarian's lands. This time they were moving along a high ridge where the western side fell away steeply. Some spots were a sheer cliff, but most of the ridge was a grassy incline up to the tip. The eastern side fell away much more gradually and that's the side they traveled along.

They hoped the barbarians, which were to the west now, wouldn't see them moving along the higher ground if they stayed on the eastern side of the ridge, but that didn't stop Volf from worrying. He wasn't a fighter and if those men found them...

He wasn't using his ability to go unseen at the moment. It was always a little harder to do during the day, in full light.

He hoped that the ridge between them and the barbarians would be enough to keep all of them from sight.

The sun set in the early evening in the mountains, falling behind the jagged peaks to the west. Light still lingered for a while before full dark, as the mountains themselves seemed to glow from behind.

Caerwyn had said they'd keep moving until near dark and would forgo training, perhaps even a fire, so as not to draw any attention with noise or light.

The entire group was tense as they slipped farther and farther north. The mountains to the east seemed quite close. The eastern side of the ridge they traversed descended into a valley thick with evergreen's, then up the other side ascending to a gray peak far above them. From what Volf could determine the mountains around them seemed to be funneling them to a single point somewhere north and west of them now. And that was where he was being pulled.

Perhaps it was the pull, or the fading light, or his desire to glance over at Caerwyn when he could, but he was completely caught off guard when a tall woman rose from behind some large rocks to his right and grabbed him.

Even as it happened, he heard Caerwyn's voice behind him. "Ambush!"

Instinct, years of escaping and evading, kicked in.

The barbarian had a hold of his arm, her hand like a vice. He shrugged, shrank, and slipped from her hold. The 'shrinking' wasn't truly him entirely reducing in size, it was more a way he could move... within himself. He'd made his arm smaller for just a moment. He could do this to his entire body if he needed to fit into tight spaces, small places, but that took a lot of energy. Once he was out of her grip, it was easy to evade her.

He slipped into his shadow-self and she backed off with a

clipped yelp. Then he tumbled away to a small copse of trees, keeping his shadow-self extended around him.

When he turned back to the others, he saw them in a pitched fight.

Once he was safely at the trees, he dropped his shadow-self and hid normally behind a tree, watching his new companions.

"We don't wish to fight you or hurt you!" Caerwyn called out. The three of them were surrounded by eight of the barbarians, they were being compressed into a smaller and tighter space as they fought only defensively. Volf gaped a little at the battle prowess of his friends. He knew that he was a long way off in his training from being where they were, but that hadn't fully sunk in until now.

Barami made wide slashes with his long, thick blade, keeping the attackers at bay. That wasn't as impressive as the simple fluidity with which he wielded that large weapon with only one hand. He looked calm, relaxed even, and his motions were smooth and easy. Volf had the feeling Barami would be able to keep this up for a while.

Jais had less finesse. There was a certain flow and style to his twin swords, but he was more erratic and frantic than Barami. Perhaps that was part of that style or his lack of experience. Volf didn't know which.

Then there was Caerwyn. She was perfection in combat. Her sword was shorter than any she was going up against, but in a defensive action that seemed to work just fine. She wasn't trying to get in close and score a hit, only make sure their blades didn't get anywhere near her. And at that, she was masterful. Between her sword and shield, the blows raining down on her were shed like rain off a tin roof.

"Please! Stop!" Caerwyn called again. "We do not wish to fight you, but we will if you force us!"

One of the attackers shouted out. "You ignored our warning. You had your chance to turn back. You will see no mercy!"

So, these ones knew about the engagement earlier that day. Their communication between patrols must be impressive.

"Stop!"

This wasn't from Caerwyn, but one of the barbarians. The tall woman who had grabbed him initially had only just joined the others in the assault but hadn't even started to fight. She'd taken one look at Barami and called out to the others.

There was a pause in the fighting.

"What is it Hildr?" one of the men asked. Everyone was tense, ready.

Volf wasn't going to wait.

He slipped into his shadow-self once again and sprinted out to where the others were. Once there, he slipped up behind Caerwyn and touched her. Concentrating, he included her in his shadow-self, making her vanish within wisps of shadow, at least that's what the others would see.

There was commotion, shouting

"Trust me," he whispered to Caerwyn now that she could see him. "Come, this way!" He ran off again, and she followed. It did not take long to reach the copse of trees again. Once there he dropped the shadow-self.

"Can you go back for the others?" Caerwyn asked looking back.

Volf hedged. He could but... "I can only take one at a time. Also, if we wanted to flee farther from here while still unseen, I wouldn't be able to hide us all." He peered out past her. "I don't think they are in any danger now. It seems they're talking. We can keep an eye on them if we need to free them."

"Suur's sweaty sack!" Caerwyn swore under her breath.

Volf raised a single brow at the profanity.

"I only came with you because I thought you could get us all to safety. I should be back there with them. They won't last long against so many hardened warriors." Caerwyn was upset. He'd hoped she'd have appreciated saving her, but she was loyal to her friends. That was a concept he had little experience with having lived alone for so long.

He touched her arm. "I'm sorry." He didn't know what to say. "The fighting has stopped. Perhaps they will be fine."

She looked back at him, her face grave. "You saved me, that's something. But I'm not leaving them. I should be—" She shook her head then huffed out a heavy sigh. "I owe... both of them too much to abandon them."

He nodded.

They would have to wait and see how this played out.

13

BARAMI HAD NEARLY DROPPED HIS SWORD WHEN THE WOMAN from his vision had appeared in front of him.

She too had seemed quite surprised and called a halt to the fight.

Then Caerwyn vanished, probably the work of Volf. But after that, nothing changed. Perhaps Volf could only take one of them? Barami didn't know, and his mind wasn't quite working right. He was still fixated on the woman.

"They are servants of the gods!" the woman—whom one of the men had called Hildr—said.

He couldn't help but grin. That's what he'd said to her when he'd seen her in his vision. So, she must have seen the same things... or perhaps it had been less of a vision and more real? He didn't know.

Jais had inched next to him closing the gap left when Caerwyn had vanished. He whispered, "Are we?"

"Go with it," Barami said. Then to the others: "You saw my companion vanish! That is just one of our many tricks. Do not fear us... and do not attack us. We are here peacefully. We mean only to talk to your leaders." He hoped that would work.

He locked eyes with Hildr and nodded to her. She nodded in return.

All the Dronnegir warriors were looking at Hildr. Barami suspected she held a position of some weight in their society.

"We will take them to see The Egir. You have my word that they are not here to harm us or steal our secrets." That last bit she said with a sidelong look to Barami. He nodded solemnly. She returned the nod. "Everyone please put away your weapons. Light is fading. We should hurry."

Barami waited until he saw a couple of the Dronnegir put away their weapons, before he did the same, though he kept his shield handy.

"We're going with them?" Jais whispered.

"We are. Keep your mouth shut and your eyes open."

Jais nodded.

Light lingered for some of their walk then seemed to shift suddenly to the darker tones of twilight. Barami had hoped that he might get close the Hildr and speak to her, but it became obvious that she was the leader of this small group and was the one leading them back to wherever they were going. The Dronnegir had divided into two equal groups, with half walking ahead and half behind Jais and Barami. As much as the two of them still had their weapons, they were still in a very precarious position. They were outnumbered four to one now and would soon be surrounded by these people. He didn't want to think of them as an enemy, but it was hard not to think of them as a threat, what with their glowering looks and strong builds.

That was another thing. It seemed every one of these men and women were made of rather incredible stuff. They were nearly as thick with muscle as Jais, but all were taller than

Barami himself. They were rather ideal specimens of humanity. Though he wasn't sure about the pale skin. It made them
seem like ghosts once it grew dark. They were covered in
leathers and nearly all had long thick hair, so it was just their
faces, which bobbed along, eerie in the light of the two
torches which had been lit to help light their way.

They'd been nasty to fight as well, all that strength
behind their thick blades. Some of them even had swords
longer than his which they wielded with two hands, massive
things. It was only by the grace of Suur that the three of them
had managed to keep from harm as long as they had before
the fight had been called to a halt.

More lights came into view up ahead. From what Barami
could see, it was a whole village, though not a large one.
There were several long, odd-shaped buildings. The structures were low and long, several dozen feet from end to end.
As he drew closer, he could see that though it had at first
seemed like they were well spaced apart, that wasn't true. The
center-line of each building was well away from the center-
line of the next, but the wide low roofs stretched far to the
sides and where one roof hit the ground, another started. So
they were actually built immediately next to each other, a
series of triangles jutting up from the ground. The other
oddity was that those low roofs were covered in grass such
that each house looked like a long, sharp-ridged hill. The
shallow angle of the roof would make it quite easy for anyone
to walk onto the top of any of the buildings and indeed
several men and woman, perhaps lookouts, were doing just
that. The longhouses were placed in a rough square with six
to a side.

There was a high wooden palisade around the village,
which dominated a wide flat plateau amidst the heaving hills
of the lower mountains. Once within the palisade Barami

could see several pens where perhaps several hundred sheep were kept. There were a few shaggy-looking cattle as well and some chickens.

They were led between two of the houses, walking through the area where two roofs met. It felt like walking on normal grass and earth.

Amazing!

Once within the square yard in the center of the village, he was led to one longhouse, which looked no different than any of the rest. Though he changed his mind once he drew near. Each house had a different sigil, a rune of some sort, painted above its door. That was the only distinction. The wooden door was open. Just behind the door, several layers of furs were pulled back. As he entered, he could make out that the far end had a similar opening. There was a faint breeze blowing through the long structure, but the inside was still quite warm, near stifling. Perhaps that was because of the amount of people within, or the many fires being used to cook meals.

The inside of this odd house was even more fascinating than the outside. The fires were in special square boxes of field stone, perhaps three or four feet to a side. Each side of the box had a large opening for heat to blow out the sides, or perhaps for adding wood. The top was either left open or had a metal grate on it for cooking. The fire-boxes sat every twelve feet along the center line of the house.

The rest of the flooring was dirt, though there were many pots and other items scattered here and about. The aisle down the center of the house was about fifteen feet wide. To either side was a platform of wood, raised about two feet off the ground. Under the platforms was storage. Above were furs and mats, blankets and pillows which seemed to make up individual sleeping areas. Each was separated only by furs and leather hung from the many posts and beams which supported the low roof. About eight feet up was a mess of cross beams holding up the structure, from which other furs, perhaps those recently cured and drying, were hung. But even more items were stored on hooks all over the wooden structure of the house: personal items, food stuffs, weapons, and so much more. The whole place was jammed with people, stores, food, and so many other things it boggled the eye.

They passed a gap in the wooden sleeping palates on the sides. Instead, there was a man-sized hole sloping down into the ground, dug out, following the angle of the roofline, sloping down on either side of the house. Barami guessed this was an ingenious way to travel between huts, connecting them.

Finally, their group stopped before one of the sleeping areas. It was in many ways like any other in the house with two exceptions. The width was twice as wide as any other, and there were perhaps a few more pillows and mats on this one. Sitting cross-legged amidst those mats, though not reclining—very much erect—was a bear of a man. On one side of him rested a very large and impressive war-axe with a similarly sized shield on the other.

Hildr stopped and nodded to the man, then spoke in what must be her native tongue. She didn't say much. It sounded like a request. The large man nodded.

She quickly turned back to Barami, "Made sure, have I, that we will speak the Northern tongue. So you can understand."

He nodded his thanks.

Hildr addressed the large man on the platform again. "Father." Well that explained why others might defer to her. "Caught these men, we did, in the east hills. They are the same encountered at the Ice River valley. We attacked them. Routed or destroyed they would be, however..." She swallowed and drew herself up. She was putting herself out there for him. "Do you recall, several weeks hence, a vision I had?"

The large man nodded. Not one for many words. Barami knew the type—he was that type.

Hildr swept her arm back to indicate Barami. "I saw a man, with skin like twilight, who spoke to me as a messenger of the gods. This be he."

The intense gaze of the seated man locked onto Barami. For a long moment, he said nothing, his face solemn and hard, difficult to read.

"A messenger of the gods," the man said. It wasn't a question.

Barami nodded. He had been thinking on the trip here how he might approach this.

"Greetings," he said, putting as much gravitas and intensity into his voice as he could. "Indeed, I was sent by the gods to meet your most honored daughter those weeks ago. It was to herald my arrival today. The gods have chosen myself and my friends as emissaries." This was where he was taking a bit of a risk. "We are here to speak to the dragon in the mountains."

There was an audible and significant murmuring throughout the house at the mention of the dragon.

"The gods told you of the dragon?" This rumbled out from deep within the seated man, Hildr's father.

In a way... yes. "Yes." The God Berem had sent him to Hildr in that vision. So, in a way the gods had started this whole thing. It was a stretch. And one could argue that the feeling his companions were having was a form of message from the gods.

The man nodded slowly. "What say the gods?"

"That there is a great and wise being who could aid us in our quest." He hadn't worked out this bit and was winging it a little. "Have you heard of those called drahksani?"

The man nodded.

Barami swore internally. He'd hoped for some reaction from the man, something to indicate exactly what he thought of drahksani. Whether he was like the rest of humanity and generally against them or perhaps more enlightened.

Oh well, this was a gamble. "My three friends, they are drahksani."

He hoped for a reaction to that, but again the man was stone faced.

He pushed on. He hoped he wasn't digging himself a hole he couldn't get out of. "During the great purge the families of my friends were all slain. They have no guidance, no resource to help them. They are alone in the world. But we were told of this dragon by the gods." Which wasn't true at all, but he had to go with the whole 'sent by the gods' thing. "It could help us and guide us. We seek only its wisdom and guidance." He'd said 'guide' too many times, but he'd also run out of ideas and was scraping his mind for any way to make this sound noble.

A silence hung over the longhouse.

"It be true uncle!" The leader's gaze lifted and moved to somewhere behind Barami, where the voice had come from. Barami knew that voice. He'd traveled with it for long enough. He turned slowly. Behind them in a similar two-segment-wide bunking area was a large man who looked a lot like the leader. Next to him was Elria, kneeling serenely on the mats and blankets. She pointed to Jais. "That one is a healer like me. He is special. That much I know."

Barami nodded.

Jais' reaction was a bit more animated.

"Elria! I'm glad you're well! We didn't know what had happened to you." That got him a scathing glance from the leader's twin—perhaps his brother—sitting beside Elria.

Elria rose, a frustrated look at the man with her. "Be kind, Father," she said as she stepped down off the sleeping area and came to Jais. "Glad am I, that you are well. Apologies for leaving." Her shoulders slumped. "I did not know why you headed north. I had to warn my people. If you had told me..." She shrugged. "We all have secrets, do we not?"

"True." This from the leader again.

Barami turned to face him. The large man moved, uncrossing his legs and stepping down off the sleeping platform. If he'd seemed big sitting, he was immense when standing. He towered over Barami by a full head and was a bear of a man, more muscled than Jais despite probably being ten years older than Barami.

"It seems our secret is discovered," he rumbled, standing before Barami who had to crane his neck to look the man in the eye.

Their secret?

"I know not what to make of your story, man-of-the-gods. I make no judgments quickly. We shall discuss what to do and let you know."

Well they weren't being killed outright so that seemed like progress.

"Thank you." Barami nodded a bow.

"Take them to the Vierashal," the man commanded and Hildr nodded. "And take away their weapons. We shall take no risks with them."

Hildr nodded to Barami who handed over his sword and shield. Jais handed over his swords as well.

"This way," she said to Barami and Jais, and led them away.

Before they were pulled away, Elria whispered to Jais. "Come to you, I will."

They were taken out of the house back into the central yard, and the cool night air, which was a relief after the heady air inside the leader's longhouse. Hildr took them directly across the square to another structure. Again, the door was open, the coverings on the inside pulled away. It was empty, though several of the sleeping areas were made up with mats and furs and a fire was going in one of the boxes.

Once inside, Hildr put a hand on his shoulder, stopping him. Jais stopped as well, but she flicked her gaze from him to Jais.

"Go on, I'll be there in a moment," Barami said and Jais nodded. They'd been accompanied by four of the men who'd found them. At Hildr's nod they all followed Jais, giving him room, but clearly still watching him.

Hildr whispered. "Your story, be it all true?"

He lowered his voice to match hers, relieved that he finally had a chance to talk to her alone. "Mostly."

She gave him a hard, scathing look.

"The important parts. Yes, I was sent to you by the gods, that much I can say with perfect honesty. But I didn't know at the time we'd be coming here. I think the gods knew, which is why they sent me to you. I think they wanted to make sure we made it to this dragon. Their ways are hard to understand. But my friends *are* drahksani and they are in need of help. The gods, or something, gave them the ability to sense the dragon here in the mountains. We've been following their own pull to the dragon. I don't much understand it myself, but they feel it keenly enough.

He tentatively reached out to her and she met his hand half way.

He whispered, "I didn't know, when I saw you before, if it

was real. But here you are." Her hand was hard, calloused as they pressed palms together.

"Nor did I believe it real," she said softly. "But now." She interlaced her fingers with his.

Solid.

Real.

"We need your help, Hildr. Please." He looked her in the eye, those clear green eyes.

She nodded. "I should return to speak with my father and the others."

She let his hand go and motioned for him to join Jais.

He nodded to her and went in to the house.

"Well," Jais said with a shrug, lounging back on the furs. "Might as well get some rest. What were you and the tall one talking about?"

Barami didn't feel like talking. "Our lives."

"Your lives?"

"No." He indicated Jais and himself. "*Our* lives. Hopefully we'll still have them tomorrow."

"Oh."

"Indeed."

14

Jais didn't much like the sound of that. Though he liked the odds now. They were being watched by only four men. That was two each.

He whispered to Barami. "You think we could take those four?"

Barami gave him a hard look. "Could we? Perhaps. Should we? No."

"But what if they decide they don't believe your story?"

"I have faith."

"Why? And what was that woman saying about seeing you in a vision?"

Barami grunted. He was sitting, leaning against a support pole on the raised bedding area. One leg was off, foot still on the ground, the other was on the platform bent. He sighed. Jais got the feeling he didn't much want to talk, but after a moment, he spoke, keeping his voice low.

"You remember that cavern, the one with the statues of the gods. Where you summoned me before we fought the krolloc?"

Jais nodded.

"When I touched the statue of Berem... I never told you what I saw." He turned his head to look back out the door. "It was her."

"The tall one? Hildr?"

Barami nodded.

"Oh." But why would the gods show him her? Unless they knew the group would come here or if Barami was fated to —"Oh! Are you and she...?" He didn't know how to finish that thought.

Barami shrugged. "We're both unsure what we are and why we were shown to each other, but it's clear she remembers me. It wasn't just a vision. It was real for both of us."

"Oh."

Jais wished the gods would give him a nice clear sign who he was supposed to be with. If that's what Barami's vision had been. He was still quite uncertain. There were two women in his life right now, both of whom were more than a little confusing and hard to understand. And neither of them might be the right one for him. Perhaps Alnia had been it, and he'd lost her. He'd had one night, one perfect moment with her, before his life had been turned on its head, but now she was gone forever, and he was left wondering who was meant for him, if anyone?

Caer was more and more evasive and standoffish these last few weeks. Actually, she'd never really been that close to him. She was always a little prickly. As hard and... independent as she was, he found her quite hard to read. She didn't need him, and didn't really want him, except to possibly make a child. That's not what he wanted. The physical act of making a child—as interesting as that might be—wasn't what he wanted. He sought more. He wanted a life with her... well with someone.

Elria was exactly like Caerwyn in many ways: independent and aloof. Yet with Elria, he shared an interest. He'd thought they'd grown close, but if they had, then why had she run off to her family without even warning him of what lay ahead? Yes, family was important, but... Well, it just showed that they still had a lot of secrets from each other. At least Caerwyn didn't have any secrets. Well none he knew of. Yet with Elria, he felt like there was room to grow, to learn about each other, and have some sort of a relationship. He didn't think he'd ever have something like that with Caer.

"Gah!" He huffed out an exasperated sigh.

Suddenly being still, lying on the furs, wasn't comfortable. He got up and pushed himself off the sleeping pad, standing on the earthen floor. The four men all twitched a little watching him.

"Easy," he said raising an empty hand to calm them. "I just need to move around a little."

So, he paced around the fire-pit, though that only succeeded in making him hot and sweaty and more uncomfortable.

He moved a little away from the firebox. There was a cool breeze blowing through the longhouse which helped to cool him. But standing still just seemed to make him more fidgety and agitated.

"Jais."

He nearly jumped at his name. Turning, he saw Elria entering the longhouse.

His emotions did a strange dance within him, at the same time upset at her and happy to see her. Yet his agitation got the better of him and he snapped at her.

"What's going on here?" There was just too much he didn't know, and some certainty would go a long way.

She blushed, looking ashamed. "I be sorry, Jais." She spoke slowly trying to work through the words, breaking the usual cadence of her language. "When clear it was, that you be heading for the Dronnolund, my homeland, I had to warn my people. Not tolerant of strangers are they, as you now see."

"Why didn't you warn us... warn me?"

She grimaced. "I knew not what to say. You gave no reasons for coming north. If nothing serious it were, I thought you might turn back, when confronted with our Bariongurd." She sighed and looked away for a moment. When she looked back, there was an odd intensity in her eyes. "But, seeking the dragon! That... I know not what I would have done, had I known. Tried to prevent you, I might have. You do not understand—"

"No, I don't."

He heard movement behind him as he stepped in toward Elria. He saw her wave away someone. Probably those guards that had been watching him.

She spoke in what he guessed was her native tongue. "Voen Hiyvn, haan eya ol ukah. Antakaa meille hetki."

Jais glanced over his shoulder, uncertain what she'd said.

Two men had drawn closer, but then nodded at her words and returned to the others.

"Come," she said and took his hand.

He let her draw him away to the door of the longhouse. There was a stronger breeze here, and it cooled his body and his temper just a little. It helped that Elria seemed genuinely distressed at all that had happened.

She took a long moment before she spoke. He leaned in the doorway glancing at the new stars above. She stood outside.

"My people be Dronn Egir," she said slowly.

"Yes, I've heard that mentioned," he said. He wasn't sure what that had to do with any of this.

"It be more than a name. It be our title, our purpose. We

are Dronn Egir." This time he heard the separation of the words.

He repeated them. "Dronn Egir?"

"Yes. In our tongue it means Dragon Protector."

He sounded it out. "Dronn... Egir." He could see how that might translate. "So, you keep people from the dragon? Why?"

"It is what we do, what we have always done." That wasn't much of an answer, but he didn't interrupt in case she had more to say. She did, but it took a little time for her to begin in earnest. "Our stories tell of a time, long ago when we were a few families herding sheep in these hills. The dragon came to us and we bowed to its greatness. It had found a home in the mountains and wished to make a pact. In return for protecting it while it slept, it would grant us boons. We agreed." Her voice was wistful and distant. She turned back to him with a long breath.

"That was..." She shrugged. "Many many years ago. A hundred generations, or more, of our people. We know only that it be passed down to us from those who came before, that we must protect the dragon. It is our calling, our quest. Do you understand?"

He did.

He sighed heavily. "And we come seeking that very thing you wish to keep us from."

She nodded.

"The moot of elders meets now to discuss your fate. Before I came here, I tried to tell my father that you be... good people. I know not if he listened or if that will sway anyone." She stepped in and her green eyes looked up intently into his as she laid a soft hand on his chest. "I am trusting that you be here only to seek the wisdom of the dragon, not to harm it."

It wasn't a question. He got the feeling she didn't want it

to be a question because she didn't want to risk that his answer might be something other than 'yes,'

He nodded. "Yes. We seek only more information of our kind, and knowledge of what we are."

She cocked her head to one side. "Your friend called you..." She hesitated, perhaps trying to recall the word. "Drack—?"

"Drahksan," Jais finished for her. "Do you not know what that is?"

She shook her head. "My father and uncle know, but tell me, they would not. In Cold River, you said a sacred being had touched you? What does this word mean drahksan?"

He grimaced. "As far as I can tell, drahksan seems to mean that I have dragon's blood. My ancestors were born of dragons. Something like that. But that's the problem. We don't really know. It's one of the reasons we want to talk to the dragon."

She nodded. "But I have seen your abilities. You are a true healer. There be something special about you." She stepped closer, very close now. Her body brushed his, and he suddenly grew quite warm again despite the night's breeze.

He put a hand on her shoulder, partly to increase the intimacy and partly to keep her from getting any closer. He was so uncertain what he wanted in that moment and yet didn't want to lose the moment either. She felt both strong and fragile beneath his thick and heavy hand. There was more to her than to most women and he felt the not insignificant muscles of her shoulder move under his touch.

"Elria..." he began but didn't know what to say. "I..." He hoped words would come, but they didn't.

She seemed to sense his hesitation and apparently decided to act. It wasn't that quick of a move, he could have stopped it, but it was quick enough that he couldn't decide if he wanted to or not before she'd completed her action. She shifted in, just a little, lightly pressed to him and found his lips with hers.

It was a quick kiss, a chaste kiss, but it said volumes.

She withdrew quickly and instantly her cheeks flushed crimson. "I be sorry." He got the feeling she was apologizing for so much more than just the kiss, but everything happening. She looked down, away and shook her head. "Sorry," she repeated at a whisper and this time he felt a cold feeling in his gut.

He thought he knew what she was saying: that this 'moot' she spoke of would not go well for him. He was suddenly quite curious and afraid of what might happen if it didn't.

"Elria, if the others decide we are trespassing. What will happen to us?"

She swallowed. "Perhaps you will be expelled?"

He didn't like the question in her voice and his hand on her shoulder tightened just a bit. "Elria?"

She lifted her head, but still couldn't bring her eyes to meet his. Her lips pressed together for a long moment before she spoke. "You know of the dragon. That be a secret the others may not wish to be spread."

"We wouldn't tell anyone!" he hissed softly, but then wondered. Would they? If they met other drahksani, would those people not deserve to know of their... ancestor up in these hills?

"They would want to be certain." Her voice was choked up. Tears coming to her eyes.

Jais voice was hard, his hand falling away from her. "We would be killed."

She nodded.

Well that wouldn't be a particularly great end to his day.

The cold feeling in his stomach grew. He wanted to ask

how it would be done but couldn't bring himself. It was too much to contemplate. He was trying to be strong and not break down, begging for his life. He didn't know if she'd have any say in it anyway.

"Return I should, perhaps I can speak for you. I..." she shook her head and trailed off. "Goodbye," she whispered and turned to go.

She nearly ran into a large man heading their way from the leader's longhouse.

The man looked at her, then toward Jais.

His voice was even, unreadable. "The moot has decided."

15

CAERWYN KEPT HER BREATHING EVEN AND SLOW.

She and Volf were well hidden. The barbarian patrol passing only a few feet away had given no indication of having seen them. The three warriors walked slowly, glancing around themselves, but their gazes never locked onto where Caerwyn and Volf crouched amid some brush.

Caerwyn couldn't help but find it fascinating that this culture had women warriors. One of those in the patrol passing them was a woman, tall and well built, like Caerwyn herself. And there had been three in the patrol that had taken Barami and Jais.

Fascinating.

It was true that Caerwyn's experience of the world was limited, though much more encompassing than most. She'd lived in Domara, in the northwest as a girl, then Afgen, in the south, and now had traveled back north again years later into what was the central northern part of the continent. In all that travel, she'd never once encountered a culture that accepted women as warriors, at least not easily. The only reason she'd been accepted in the South was because of her superior skill and ability, but mostly because she'd been the adopted daughter of a prince, which had given her expanded opportunities.

Yet from what she could tell of this strange Northern culture, women were accepted as equal combatants. The one women—Hildr—had even looked to be in command of the party that captured Jais and Barami. Such thoughts were a distraction. She should be concentrating on freeing her friends, but she kept wondering what it would be like to be so accepted.

"They're well gone now," Volf said in whisper near her ear. She felt a slight thrill at his soft voice and warm breath, as one can only get from such near contact.

She nodded. "This way." She rose and looked quickly about for any other patrols before moving on quietly.

They had lost sight of their friends with the need to move more cautiously. Volf had said his ability to hide himself was limited, that he couldn't do it for an extended period of time, especially hiding both of them. If it had just been him... maybe.

So they'd had to move with care through the high rolling hills. They'd spotted the village on the plateau before it became full dark and it was easy enough to find now as it was well lit. They were still some distance from it however, moving strategically to avoid as many of the barbarians as they could.

In her mind, Caerwyn worked through the problems they'd face as they drew closer. First would be increased patrols. These people knew she and Volf were out here some-where. Second were the lookouts at the village itself. Third would be the wooden wall surrounding the area and its single gate—that she'd seen. She had to assume the gate would be guarded. That meant they'd need to most likely scale the wall at some other location while avoiding the patrols and the view of the lookouts. It was full dark now and that would make it easier, but by no means guaranteed. There might be a stretch of time where they'd need to use Volf's ability, though she didn't know how well it might work on them while climbing. She should find out.

She stopped to hide in a thicket of pine trees, which crowded close, filling the air with their fresh, tangy scent.

She took a moment to listen just in case any patrols might be near but heard nothing except the noises of night.

Volf had told them some bits of what he knew of his abilities in the days as they'd traveled north, but specifics hadn't been needed until now. "Your ability to hide yourself. How does it work, exactly?" she asked. She didn't look at him, keeping a wary watch out beyond their hiding spot instead.

"Ah... well I'm not sure I've really thought about it much."

"But you can use it when you wish?"

"Yes."

"Do you know how it hides you?"

"Ah... yes, I think. I've always called it my 'shadow-self,' I just thought I was being particularly sneaky, enough that others didn't see me even when I was close. I hadn't started thinking about how until just these last few days. I know that I can..." He harrumphed, perhaps searching for the right words. "I can flash it on and off and that seems to scare people. I don't know what they see, whether I'm there then not, or whether some shadow jumps over my form. I know that the world dims a little, as you perhaps recall from your time hidden as well."

This was easily solved.

"Very well, do it now and I'll tell you what I see... or don't see." She turned toward him. He was quite close. She'd known that from feeling the heat of his body near hers, but now she found his face surprisingly close to hers. She didn't flinch or fear the closeness, in truth he had rather pleasant features especially when he was grinning under that hawkish nose of his, as he was now. He'd been eating well since they'd met and his once 'bony' cheeks had filled out a little. It was still a little awkward being this close though, almost nose to nose.

"Very well," he said softly and then vanished.

It was hard to tell because she had only the dim light of the moon filtering down through the pines, but it had seemed like he'd been swallowed by the shadows around him. She reached up, tentative, and felt his arm where it should have been. He was still there, just not visible.

He chuckled softly, a sound from nowhere, then was back.

This time she did flinch at his sudden nearness, despite knowing he was there, despite her hand on his arm.

"Well?" he whispered.

"It—"

His fingers were on her lips, covering her mouth and silencing her as his head suddenly cocked to one side.

What had he heard?

She listened.

Voices, low and near.

She froze.

The words spoken by those who approached became clearer after another moment. "...think are in there? A few dozen? More?" someone asked.

"No one knows much about the Dronnegir. They're big, live secluded up here, and are fierce warriors."

"Do we think that's where they are?"

The voices stopped nearby.

"I..."

Caerwyn peered out through the pines as this person spoke and saw his face illuminated by the moonlight.

Gosse. Her hunter.

And even as she looked out he turned toward her. She ducked back behind the trunk of a tree, hoping the sudden movement hadn't given her away.

How could he have known?

"What is it?" one of the others with him asked.

"I don't know. I'm not sure if they're in there, but..." He grumbled a little bit. "Nothing, you're probably right."

There was a high-pitched sound, odd... like a laugh or chuckle, then from the same voice, "A stronghold of hardened warriors. I haven't had this much of a challenge in some time. This should be fun." The way the man said the word fun sent a chill down Caerwyn's spine. He wasn't afraid. He was actually anticipating this. What sort of man wanted the carnage of battle?

The sort of man Gosse had banded up with.

Yet from the little she knew of Gosse, he'd never been one for bloodlust. He'd never endangered others to get to her. When she'd been in the South, he hadn't threatened her family or the people there. Instead, he'd exposed her to get her to leave so he could face her alone. It had only been the anger of her father at losing his daughter that had saved her. He'd demanded Gosse stay as his 'guest' for several weeks. There hadn't been any debate.

What was the man up to now?

The men moved on, their voices fading away.

A touch on her arm made her flinch. The second time that night. What was happening with her?

"Who was that?" There was concern in Volf's voice. "You looked..." He fumbled for words for a moment.

It was only then that she realized her heart was racing, hammering in her chest.

"Scared?" she ventured the word.

She saw the faint nod of his head in the dim and dappled moonlight.

"I was." She sighed. It only occurred to her then, that she'd gotten Volf into a whole new world of trouble by involving him. He had a right to know. "That man... one of those men is hunting me... us"

"What?"

Suddenly she felt the need to move. She crept to the edge of the pines, feeling their needles scrape along the skin of her cheeks and hands, brushing over her clothes. She ignored that.

At the edge she peered out, looking in the direction the men had headed. The direction she'd been headed. She could still see their forms moving in the darkness, they weren't that far away yet. There were six of them.

They descended into a valley and out of sight, and she emerged from the trees turning back to Volf who'd followed her.

"I'm sorry, truly, but I can't abandon Jais to them. I'm going after them. I understand if you don't want to come with me." But she wanted him to. She could really use someone with her. Her heart was still pounding. She wasn't sure who she was more worried for, herself or Jais or these Dronnegir trapped in someone else's conflict.

Some part of her mind knew that six men against all these barbarians shouldn't stand a chance, yet she didn't believe that for some reason. Some instinct told her those six men were dangerous, far more than their limited number.

Volf put a hand on her shoulder. "I will follow you."

There was compassion and something else in his eyes, strength in his voice. It reassured her.

She gave a faint laugh. "Are you certain? There'll be a fight. You're still learning."

He grinned. "I may only be learning how to fight, but I've been getting out of danger all my life. I'll be fine. Don't worry about me. Do what you have to."

She nodded.

"Then let's be away. Keep a wary eye for patrols. We're going to be picking up our pace, I don't want to lose that group of men."

He nodded.

They moved quicker now and soon enough had the six men in view again.

Following carefully at a distance, they descended into a valley. This would be the last valley before they headed up to the plateau on which the village was laid out. A thick forest covered most of the floor of the dell. Caerwyn's keen ears picked up the burbling of a stream or creek somewhere in those woods.

The men disappeared into the trees at the base of the valley.

Caerwyn's heart jumped up into her throat, thumping harder. She couldn't help but feel like those men were simply waiting for her in the darkness of those trees, laying a trap.

But she moved on undaunted, hoping that wasn't the case. Hoping she wasn't leading Volf to his doom.

Yet no arrows were fired from the trees, no men struck from the shadows as they entered the woods. This did little to calm her. Instead, a sinking dread filled her gut.

"Wait," Volf hissed, grabbing her. She turned to him, wondering what he'd sensed. His head was cocked to one side, listening.

She too strained to hear what he was. There was something, a grunting? Rustling of clothes? It lasted a moment longer then more silence. She couldn't even determine what it was she'd heard.

"What was that?" she whispered.

He shook his head and shrugged. He didn't know either.

They moved on very carefully after that.

It was several heart-pounding moments later—dread filling Caerwyn at the thought of an ambush—that they came upon what had been the source of the noise.

"Gods!" Volf whispered.

Gods indeed. Caerwyn gaped as the scene before her. Bile rose in her throat.

Not far away the creek, perhaps ten feet across ran over its rocky bottom, babbling pleasantly. Where the creek split the forest, moonlight filtered down and illuminated a scene of carnage along its banks. Five of the barbarians were dead. Buckets were strewn around the scene. These people had been coming to get water and been slaughtered. Two of them were large men. One looked like he'd been stabbed through the throat, the other had no visible wounds, but lay splayed, a look of horror and pain on his face, stuck in death. Another, a woman, had had her neck broken, head horribly skewed—turned completely around—her face a mask of surprise. One of the men with Gosse had been a hulking brute and perhaps this was his work. The last two victims, both younger women, lay partially in the creek, blood from their wounds flowing out with the water, creating a darker flow as the stream moved on.

What amazed Caerwyn was that this had all happened in relative silence. She hadn't heard any serious fighting, just some faint noises.

"Who are these men?" Volf breathed. Now she could hear the fear in his voice as well, the trembling hesitation.

"Are you certain you want to come with me?" she asked again.

"Ah..." She turned to see him frozen in the shadows. She heard him swallow. "Yes." Though he didn't sound certain.

"Volf—"

"Go! I'm fine." He licked his lips and swallowed hard. "Please move on before I change my mind." After a moment, he tried to smile. "I'm fine," he repeated.

He wasn't. She was certain of that, but she nodded and led him onward.

As they emerged, cautious and wary, from the woods heading up the far side of the vale, she could hear the sounds of fighting above them.

The gates to the compound were perhaps two hundred feet away, and there were no guards visible, which did not bode well.

The time for stealth and hesitation was over.

She drew out her sword and put on her shield.

"Last chance," she said half turning to Volf.

His eyes were hard in the moonlight. He too had his sword out, something they'd purchased for him before leaving Cold River.

"Let's get these bastards."

She nodded.

Then they were running up the hill to help the surprised villagers and free their comrades.

16

Jais faced the Dronnegir leader. He was ready for anything, his face hard, stoic, calm... he hoped.

Everyone had gathered back in this main hall to see what the verdict would be. Barami stood next to Jais. Elria was behind them again in the alcove with her father. Hildr was with her father, before them. The rest of the village, as many as could fit, crowded around them. Jais got the impression this was a momentous occasion.

"Tend to our sacred duty, the Dronnegir have, for age upon age." The clan leader's voice carried well, deep and resonant as it was. He seemed to be speaking to everyone, not just Jais and Barami. "Never faltered nor failed, have we, in our task. Protected the Sacred Being, we have, keeping its secret... until now." The large man scanned the crowd around them. There was a certain accusing nature to his gaze. Was he blaming his people for others finding out about the dragon? That didn't seem right.

The leader then turned that disapproving gaze on Hildr and she, strong as she had seemed, withered under it. She flushed with embarrassment.

This didn't bode well.

"I doubt not that my daughter had a vision of this man." He indicated Barami. "But many magics are there in this world, other than that of the gods."

Jais' heart fell. Those words were clear enough. The man didn't believe their story.

"Drahksani possess many abilities, and one of them could have stolen our secrets from the mind of my daughter."

"Now, just hold on!" Jais couldn't listen to any more of this.

Yet at his words the chief's stony gaze fell to him and several men raised weapons toward him.

Tension hung in the room, hot and thick.

"Attack!"

Jais' heart stopped at the word, skipping a beat.

But the call hadn't come from anyone nearby. It was distant and behind the crowd.

"We are under attack!" the call came again. "Men at the gates!"

Jais couldn't quite make sense of these words. Was Caerwyn trying to free them? He didn't think she'd attack these people though. But if it wasn't her? Did these people have enemies? Where was Caerwyn? Was she safe? Would the chief think that this attack had been precipitated because of Jais and Barami's capture? Would they be blamed? Were they to blame?

He just didn't know enough.

He said the first thing that came to him in the instant of silence as everyone else tried to make sense of the call.

"Give us our weapons, we'll help you fight!"

"No!" The leader's voice was stern and sharp. "Take them away. To arms!"

Then everyone was moving.

Two men grabbed Jais. He resisted for a moment before a head shake from Barami stopped him, and he went with the men.

"What's your plan?" Jais asked the Southerner. He didn't care if the men around them heard.

"No plan. Just keep a careful watch. Wait for the right moment."

Jais nodded.

They were ushered out away from the fight, which as far as Jais could tell was in the main square of the village, or somewhere closer to the main gate perhaps. Jais and Barami went out the other side of the longhouse with the outer wall about twenty paces away. The four men with them turned them to the left but didn't get far.

Someone behind them barked out a command. Jais couldn't understand it. The four men stopped. All of them turned.

Elria and Hildr were running from the longhouse with several weapons each.

Hildr said something else in their language and the men around them muttered. There was a final command from her, sharper, before they all stepped away from Jais and Barami.

Elria tossed Jais his swords as Hildr did the same for Barami.

"Whether or not our fathers trust you, we do," Elria said as she drew out her own short sword and strapped on a shield. "I know you will fight to protect us. Perhaps that will help our fathers change their minds about you."

Hildr handed Barami his shield then she, too, readied her own sword and shield.

Jais turned to Elria. He couldn't quite reconcile the sight of her with weapons. "I thought you were a healer?"

She scoffed. "You're a healer. You fight."

He had no response for that. She was right. He shrugged.

Hildr said some final command to the four men and they were quickly ready for a fight as well. Then Hildr turned to them all with a gleam in her eye. "Shall we fight?"

They all charged between two of the triangular long-houses and into the square.

Nothing, not even his fight with the krolls and krolloc, could have prepared Jais for the carnage he ran into.

Blasts of fire exploded in the yard, sending men flying. Screams of pain and surprise echoed all around.

Jais and those with him came to an abrupt halt and simply stared in awe at the scene before them.

Several of the longhouses were on fire, men lay scorched and dying. The clash of steel on steel rang through the yard. It felt like the village was being overrun with enemies, but in truth there was only a small group clustered together on one side of the inner square formed by the longhouses. It was the one of them, laughing gleefully, as he hurled fire from his hands, that seemed to be causing most of the carnage. Guarding him was a brute, as tall as any of the barbarians, but built like Jais, broad and well-muscled.

"Gods!" Elria whispered. "I have to help them." The 'them' in question were the dozens of men scattered around the yard, burned and dying.

"Do so," Hildr said, her voice gruff. "We'll do our best to protect you and fend off these..."

Jais understood her lack of words. They were men, but he'd never seen any man do anything like what that tall one was doing.

Elria, perhaps the boldest of all of them, ran out into the yard, finding a man nearby and kneeling next to him.

That prompted Jais to action.

He followed her.

What can I do against that? he asked his father's spirit in his sword.

He must be drahksan to wield such magic, his father said, the tone analytical. *This blade was tempered with magic when it was created, it should stop those blasts. Unfortunately, the only way you'll know for certain is to put yourself in front of one. That choice is up to you, my son.*

Drahksan?

But one of the other man with him was the dragon hunter. Jais recognized him from the attack on the road to Cold River not so long ago. That made no sense, but he didn't have time to think about it. He ran out after Elria.

He got a chance to test his father's theory quick enough.

The man throwing fire must have seen Elria run out to help her fallen friend and he hurled a ball of swirling flames at her.

Jais slid to a spot between Elria and the bolt of fire.

Barami called out to him, but he didn't listen. He wouldn't let Elria die if he could prevent it. He didn't know if this would work, but he'd rather die trying than let the woman die alone and unprotected.

He lowered his sword into the path of the ball of fire. He'd closed his eyes for just a moment as the flames hit the blade. There was a blast of hot air, which blew past Jais, but beyond that... nothing. He opened his eyes to find his blade glowing with a faint reddish hue.

Oh, that is some potent magic. I can feel it. This from his father's spirit in the blade. *I don't know how many of those I can take. Too many might turn the metal to slag.*

Good to know. "I'll just have to end this quickly," he said to himself and charged at the magic-wielder.

The wizard threw another blazing bolt his way, perhaps uncertain what had happened to his first. Jais caught the fire on the blade once again, no hesitation this time. The blade grew brighter, a deep maroon.

The fire-thrower's eyes went wide with shock and fear.

Good.

Then a lumbering shadow stepped in front of the wizard, the brute of a man Jais had seen earlier. He wielded a massive blade, serrated like a saw, nasty and already dripping with blood. Apparently Jais would have to go through this one first.

That huge blade descended, intent on chopping Jais in two.

But this was a fight Jais had fought before. This was no mysterious magic. This was like his fight with the krolloc all over again... only this man wasn't half as big.

Jais grinned as he caught the serrated blade on his father's sword and threw it off to one side. His arm throbbed from the impact, but not enough to stop him. His other sword flashed out. The brute hadn't been expecting his attack to be thwarted. Thus, he was unprepared as Jais slid his blade into the man's chest. The brute's eyes went wide as he grunted and stepped back, off of Jais' blade.

Now it was Jais' turn to be surprised.

With the force of his blow, he should have plunged his sword into the other man nearly to the hilt, but the blade only bit a few inches, jarring Jais' arm. Now the brute was shrugging it off as if it were nothing. Any normal man should have fallen, but the brute shook his head and roared, attacking.

Another drahksan almost certainly. It was the only logical explanation.

Jais swore as he blocked another blow, this one sending him to his knees. Apparently, the big man hadn't put his full strength behind the first strike.

The brute put both hands on his sword and roared again, swinging the blade high in a great downward blow. Jais rolled away as earth was thrown up behind him from the force of the impact.

"Gods," he breathed and rolled to his feet.

Three quick strikes to the man's exposed side did seemingly little damage and had little effect. Though he noticed his father's sword—still glowing like embers—seemed to be more effective.

The brute roared again and leveled a sideways swing at Jais.

Jais leapt, his legs were strong enough to send him high over the other man's blade, and he let out his own roar as he hammered down on the brute's head with both blades. The big man was quick and jerked to one side. Jais still cut into the man's shoulder with his off-hand blade, but again, not deeply. He did however kick out as he descended and knock that huge sword from his opponent's grip.

He landed, thinking he now had the upper hand.

He didn't expect the punch to his gut.

The great fist sent him flying back ten feet, landing hard on his back with a thud that blew the air from him. He was dazed, but luckily, the man hadn't charged in to follow up on his sucker-punch. Jais got up as quick as he could, though it seemed likely he had a cracked rib from the throbbing sting mid-torso.

He drew in a long breath, despite the increase in pain this caused, and drew upon his healing ability, now well-honed from his time learning with Elria. It didn't take him long, just a moment to find the cracked rib and the area around it which was already swelling with a great bruise. He sent healing energies to that area and quickly the pain died. The rib reformed, and the other results of the punch dissipated.

Then he charged in again.

The brute had reacquired his sword.

Jais recalled something his aunt had done the day he'd met Caerwyn. Despite being a healer, she'd been able to affect the other woman's body in a way contrary to healing. Jais, reached out with his senses as he crossed the short distance to the large man. It was hard to do since he wasn't in physical contact with the man and most of the healing up to now had required contact. But he still managed to sense within the other man. He found the man's heart, beating like a drum. There was no way to describe what Jais did other than grabbing and squeezing the organ, except it was the brute's own body doing it at Jais' command.

The man grunted and doubled over.

Jais leapt again. He put one foot on the brute's shoulder to give him a little more range and height, then arched high up, to come down on that wizard. A wordless war cry came to his lips.

The tall fire-thrower turned. Eyes growing wide in the faint few heartbeats before Jais came down on him.

The man's mouth moved, saying some word or command—

Jais' swords swept through where the man had been as the fire-thrower vanished. Jais landed hard, his scream of fury turning into one of aggravation and frustration.

He spun around, but all the enemies were gone. The brute and the dragon hunter, they had all vanished with the fire-thrower.

Jais was left breathing hard as a heavy silence settled over the village.

"Jais!"

He looked up to see Caerwyn running toward him. She looked around frantically. "Where are they?"

Jais dropped to one knee, the fatigue of battle starting to weigh on him. He needed a moment. He wasn't truly weary, just... confused and frustrated.

"I don't know. They all just vanished." He had assumed she'd been talking about the attackers.

"Vanished?"

He nodded.

"Jais!" This call turned his head the other direction. Elria glanced over her shoulder at him. "If the fight is done, we need you!"

Yes, there were many men to heal.

He rose, at least now he had something to do, somewhere to direct his energy, even if he was still a little befuddled by the sudden disappearance of the enemy.

"I need to help," he said to Caerwyn and turned away to find the nearest injured man.

17

BARAMI HURRIED OVER TO CAERWYN. HILDR WASN'T FAR behind him. He'd been fighting one of the attackers, a hardened warrior with twin axes. Barami thought he'd struck a killing blow, but the man had vanished with the others before hitting the ground. Barami had no clue what had happened, only that that had been one of the most terrifying fights of his life... and he'd fought misshapen monstrous krolls. That man throwing fire had been horrific to watch.

"You're here." It was inane and obvious, but he couldn't help himself. His mind was still muddled from the fight. He threw his arms around Caerwyn in a bear-hug, releasing her quickly. "It's good to see you. I didn't know what had happened to you out in the hills."

"I was coming to free you, but then we encountered those men sneaking through the hills and followed them. We'd hoped to help in the fight, but they were gone before we even arrived."

"You come into the home of those who could be an enemy to fight another enemy?" This from Hildr. "Brave." The tall redheaded woman nodded to herself.

"Take them!" This from a familiar commanding voice: Hildr's father. "Throw down your weapons scoundrels!"

And with that, they were suddenly surrounded by a very angry looking group of Dronnegir warriors.

Barami sighed. He threw down his sword but turned to the clan's leader. He opened his mouth to speak but stopped himself and turned to Hildr. "What's your father's name?" He was getting tired of thinking of the man as just the Dronnegir's leader.

It wasn't Hildr who responded.

"I am Anubjorn, Egir of the Dronnegir!" the man roared. "How dare you bring war to my people! You shall all die for this!"

Die?

Barami's temper rose. Couldn't the man see he and Jais had been helping them? He opened his mouth again, but was interrupted as Hildr spoke, stepping in front of Barami.

"If you kill this man you must kill me as well!"

It was good to know someone was on their side.

Hildr addressed her father with all the fury Barami felt. "How dare you, father! Helped us and fought for us, these people did, and you sentence them to death? Where be your honor? Have you not eyes? Could you not see the enemies attacking all of us? That Barami and this friend were risking their lives for us?"

Anubjorn's face grew a bright red. Whether this was from being dressed down by his daughter, or being wrong, Barami couldn't tell. The man sputtered and blustered for a long moment before finding words.

"You cannot deny, my daughter, that these attackers arrived just after our... guests. That cannot be coincidence. Do you not think it so?" Barami noticed how the man spat out the word 'guests' as if it were foul tasting. "We are here for only one duty, daughter, and what be that?"

Hildr didn't back down. "To protect the Divine One. I know as well as any. But, by the sacred breath! When did that duty come before logic and sense?" That got her father even more enraged. The man's face went another shade deeper of rage-red.

But Hildr spoke before he could yell back at her. "Yes, the foes came soon after our guests, but see also how the others with Barami and Jais came on the heels of those foes. Why would they risk our wrath? They were safe, they had escaped. Why come and fight with us? Why run into our home if not to help? They did not disappear with the others, they are stuck here. They did not have to come!"

"They seek to trick us! This attack is a ruse. The others vanish, and these others arrive that we might be tricked into trusting them. You know we cannot trust any outside the clan! You know we cannot falter on our oath!"

Hildr began to speak, but it was her father's turn to cut her off. "What would you have me do? We cannot do as they ask. We cannot take them to the Divine One, and we cannot let them go, for they know far too much and could tell many of our secrets. So, what do we do? If we do not kill them shall we keep them prisoner here for the rest of their lives, feeding them out of our own meager stock?"

Barami could see the man's logic. But it was flawed by the view that he and the others couldn't be trusted. These people had lived so long thinking that everyone not of their clan was an enemy. He didn't know what to do against that sort of ingrained thinking.

"We can put them through the trial." Hildr said evenly.

The trial?

Anubjorn glared at her. "That proves nothing!"

"Now you spit on our ways? If the gods believe them worthy of our trust, they will survive the trial and prove their worth."

The man's face lost a shade or two of red and he harrumphed. "Be it so. They will undergo the trial and then we shall see if they be friend or foe. Until then they be prisoners."

The man spun away.

Hildr turned back to them. "Please leave your weapons and follow me."

Barami nodded to Caerwyn who relinquished her sword and shield. Volf dropped his sword.

Volf whispered something to Caer, but Barami was too far away to hear it. She shook her head and responded with a hushed. "Wait for now."

Volf nodded.

They were all led back to the hall Barami and Jais had been in before. Jais didn't join them for some time. Despite it being late, none of them slept.

They huddled together on the platform as guards stood vigilant nearby.

"Trial?" Caerwyn asked in a whisper. "Do you know what this is?"

Barami shook his head. "First I've heard of it."

"Great," Volf said with a heavy sigh. "It could be anything."

Barami agreed. He'd heard of people 'testing' for drahksan abilities when he was a child. They would throw the suspected person into a lake and if they drowned they were innocent, or burn them at the stake and if the gods kept the fire from them then they must be pure. It was barbaric and ill-conceived. He desperately hoped the trials here weren't as... deadly.

Jais joined them a while later, covered in grime and blood and looking exhausted.

He said simply, "We saved as many as we could." Then he collapsed and was soon sleeping. He didn't know about the trial.

DAWN CAME AND BARAMI, CAERWYN, AND VOLF HAD SLEPT little. Jais had slept, but still looked drained and tired when he woke. When told of the trial, Jais just nodded.

Barami had not slept at all and was bone-weary. He was too old to be missing sleep. But there would be no chance to rest now. They had been summoned.

They emerged into the light of day only the find the small village still smoking. One of the longhouses was half destroyed by fire and many others were burned along the side facing the inner square. The one which had taken the most damage was in the process of being torn down. It seemed the villagers would rebuild it from the ground up.

A pyre was being built in the middle of the large square. On it were far too many bodies, all bundled in white cloth. At a rough count, Barami estimated that roughly twenty were dead. Some of the forms were small... children.

He could only shake his head at that.

Jais beside him grunted. His voice was a little soft and hoarse with regret when he said, "We saved as many as we could. It wasn't enough."

"Were there other healers?" Caer asked.

Jais nodded. "Two others had the gift of healing. We all worked as fast as we could, but it wasn't enough. Many were dead before we even got to the fight."

Hildr drew near. She was somber, stoic. She glanced at

the pyre as she approached them but didn't seem to want to acknowledge it.

"This way," she said and turned to lead them away.

They were taken back to that same longhouse where the leaders lived. Once again Barami stood in the long hall before Anubjorn's area. Elria sat with her father looking as exhausted as Jais. Hildr took her place beside her father.

Yet they'd been led before a wizened old man, who stood in the center of the house. It was he who addressed them.

He began speaking, but it was in the Dronnegir tongue. A man of middle years next to him translated:

"In the ancient times, before lands and waters, there was only Mihonir and Helnir."

The names were similar enough that Barami recognized them. This was a creation story, or a tale based on the gods. Mihr and Holn were the names for them in the Northern tongue. He listened intently to understand what would be happening to them.

"The undying fire of Mihonir summoned forth lands and waters and the eternal darkness of Helnir be trapped away within Komir."

This was the same creation story he'd learned growing up.

"Komii, the waves, and Komir, the mountains made the world. After, Mihonir was so tired from sealing away the darkness, that he still had to relinquish his light to night, every day. Then came the creators, Suurn, Ylva, and Sova. Together these three created the Aedir, the ten greater beings. One of these be the guardian of the North, of ice and snow, Nosunir master of reason."

The names were all slightly changed, but the story was the same. Though why the elderly man was picking out Nosul, Barami didn't know.

"In the times of our ancestors, Steinn, a man of great courage and wisdom, sought Nosunir for his wisdom. This man had had three sons, but one had been killed. He feared one of his other sons had done the deed, but both of his remaining sons had denied it. So Steinn went to Nosunir. He pleaded with the god for a way to discern the truth, so that he might know which of his sons was a killer. Nosunir listened and told Steinn that the secrets of all men lay deep in darkness, as it be with Helnir. The only way to bring the truth to light would be to drag it up from the darkness. This would not be an easy thing. It might be painful. He asked Stein if he be willing to put his sons through such pain to know the truth. Steinn said yes, for he knew the righteous son would endure such pain to have the truth brought to light and the offender to justice."

The wizened old man pulled a chain out from under his shirt. It was of heavy links of iron and couldn't have been comfortable to wear. At the end of it was an amulet marked with a swirling sigil which was known throughout the world as the sign for Nosul, God of the North Winds.

Barami felt a shiver run down his spine as the man and his translator finished their tale.

"So Steinn was given this. The Talisman of Truth. With it, Steinn returned and placed it on the forehead of his sons and sought the truth from them. So as it was done in the ancient time, so let it be done now!"

Barami watched as the old man stepped toward Jais, the medallion in his raised hand.

To the young man's credit, he stood firm. He even looked calm as the aged man pressed the metal to Jais' forehead.

Then Jais let out a feral scream, eyes going wide as the amulet began to glow.

18

GOSSE'S HEART POUNDED A FRANTIC CADENCE, STRAINING TO get out of his chest. This was all so very wrong. He had made a grave mistake!

Tyark bore down on him, gaze burning with rage.

"Why didn't you tell me we were hunting drahksani!" the man hissed, his fury a near palpable thing. The tall, thin man radiated a great heat.

Gods!

Just remembering what the man had done in that village nearly made Gosse sick. He'd been hunting his entire life and knew well the carnage of battle, but what that fire had done to people. It was horrible

The wanton carnage the man had wreaked had shocked even Gosse, and he did not shock easily.

He'd known there would be casualties. If they wanted to get the drahksani, then some of the others with them would need to die. Killing those at the river getting water had been a necessity to avoid any alarm. He had assumed they would get to the village and call out the drahksani. Yet when they had arrived, Tyark had started throwing fire like a man possessed, eyes alight with a gleeful madness.

"I..." What could he say? That he was a dragon hunter? It was clear to him now that Tyark was a drahksan; most likely Gerhardt was as well. He should be fighting them... but he was too terrified. He needed space to plan. He needed to get away from these men.

"Are you a dragon hunter?"

It seemed the man wasn't an idiot. Gosse had to think quickly.

"No. Just a bounty hunter from the South. Those two, they are traitors down there. I sought only to bring them to justice. I didn't know they were drahksani!" He hoped with a dire desperation that Tyark believed him. The man looked like he wanted to roast Gosse. Gerhardt looked like he'd like to rip off a piece of roasted Gosse and eat it.

Tyark spun away, his every movement agitated and frenetic.

Thank all the gods, it looked like the man believed him.

He looked about for an escape or an ally, but he found little of use. Their three other companions had not fared well in the fight. Dathgar was alive but nursing a wounded leg. He wouldn't be moving far or fast any time soon. The sell-sword sat propped up by a tree. His leg was bandaged, and he was resting for the moment. The tall one, Regi, was unconscious and probably wouldn't wake up. He'd taken a few too many wounds in the fight and despite all the bandages on him was still losing too much blood. The last of their party, Magnor was, outright dead. He'd been dead before they'd mysteriously been transported to this clearing.

This is where they'd camped a couple days prior. It was just outside of the Dronnegir's territory and thus would be safe enough for now. Though Gosse didn't think he'd be safe anywhere near these men. Tyark was clearly a lunatic with incredible powers, and Gerhardt always looked like he was going to eat someone.

Gosse had come to trust his gut in all things, but he didn't know how he'd gone so wrong with this group. How did he not know these two were drahksani? He'd felt something when he'd met them, but not the 'knowing' in his gut he felt when he was around Caerwyn or the others he'd faced.

Oddly, he felt that 'knowing' now.

Sometime during the fight, he'd felt it and had nearly missed blocking a strike.

"It sickens me," Tyark said spitting out his words. "The very thought of dragon hunters... killing their own kind."

Their own kind?

"Dragon hunters aren't drahksan," Gosse said reflexively. That thought was appalling.

Tyark spun on him, brow lowered in suspicion. "Why would you say that? Of course they are! That's why I suspected you might be. You've got the right feel. What are you, half drahksan?"

Gosse's eyes went wide.

"What? No!"

Tyark's suspicion turned to confusion. "You don't feel like a full-blooded drahksan to me, and you haven't shown signs of any significant ability other than battle prowess."

"That's because I'm not a drahksan."

Tyark laughed a high-pitched and slightly crazy sound. "Of course you are, at least in part. I can feel it. Can't you feel me?"

Feel...?

Gosse's eyes went wide.

He could feel Tyark and Gerhardt. There was a definite

pull, that 'knowing' that he felt. He certainly didn't feel anything like that for Dathgar or the others.

Oh gods! "No!"

Tyark's suspicion returned. "You are, aren't you? You're dragon hunter scum!"

Gosse's heart raced, beating even faster, if that was possible.

"No!"

Tyark scowled, unconvinced.

"I'm a bounty hunter from the South, I swear. Of course I'm part drahksan." The words burned his mouth to say.

Oh gods! What was he? He'd always thought... he'd been taught from childhood that drahksan were evil, that they all needed to be hunted down and killed. He couldn't be one. Could he?

And yet...

It explained a lot if he was. He'd been told that dragon hunters needed to be exceptional in all ways to be able to defeat a drahksan, but in truth how could any normal human beat one with such abilities? It made sense that he'd need to be at least partially drahksani to be able to go toe-to-toe with one. But why... why hadn't anyone ever told him?

The question practically answered itself. If he was going to create a force to slaughter the enhanced drahksani, he'd not tell them they'd been created from the same stock. That must have been either a carefully guarded secret or one long forgotten.

Which meant...

He. Was. Drahksan.

Oh, by Suur! No, it still didn't sit right as much as it made sense now.

Far too much sense.

It was why he'd always known where his prey was. He'd

assumed it was his superior tracking ability, but it was clear now. There had been far too many times in the past when his tracking had failed him and he'd... guessed where to go. Guesses that had always been right. His gut's 'knowing' wasn't his gut at all, but a drahksan ability to sense others of his kind.

Then there was his age. He'd been hunting dragonborn for fifty years. Yet he was still strong and spritely with barely a wisp of gray in his hair. Drahksani aged slower than humans. He'd always attributed his lack of aging to his strict exercise regimen, but now he knew that wasn't the case.

Oh, by all the gods!

But then...

"Why didn't I sense you when I first met you?" he asked suddenly, not sure what had emboldened him.

Tyark scoffed. "I was masking my nature, and that of Gerhardt. It was a trick my father taught me, not long before a dragon hunter killed him."

"You can do that?"

Tyark drew himself up to his full spindly height. "Only the most powerful of drahksan can, yes."

That explained it.

"Just as only I can sense what you are," Tyark said with a sneer. "You must be only a quarter drahksan, or a mixed blood, perhaps. I can sense you, but I doubt if any normal drahksan could."

That was also telling.

Gosse nodded, but still didn't really understand what he was going to do.

He was drahksan... so did that mean he wasn't a dragon hunter anymore? Could he kill his own kind? And by extension... should he kill himself?

What was he to do?

He knew only one thing for certain. He needed to get as far away from Tyark and Gerhardt as he could.

"But there is something else," Tyark's voice was soft, his gaze distant. "I've had myself shielded for so long I was used to it, but now that I can sense again there is something... of great power, perhaps even greater than I..." His gaze drifted northward. "Up in those mountains." He seemed to lose himself for a moment, then, "Perhaps that's why the other drahksani were heading in this direction." He shook his head with what seemed like an expression of wonder. "I've never felt anything like this before. If it's a drahksan, I'd guess it's a first or second generation. One of the ancient ones." He pursed his lips in thought. "But even that doesn't feel right. This feels more... primal."

Gosse had no idea what the man was talking about. He was just glad Tyark's attentions weren't on him any longer.

"What's all this about drahksani now?" Dathgar perked up. He looked a little glassy-eyed and not fully comprehending what was happening around him.

Tyark spun on him. "Our employer had us hunting drahksan! At least three of the four of them were drahksani. I would prefer not to kill my own kind. There are so few of us. I'd rather recruit them if I could. If I can get enough drahksan together, we can have our revenge on humanity!"

"Humanity? What do you mean?" Dathgar was growing more lucid by the moment. "What's this about revenge?"

"You're the ones who hunted us, destroyed us! Humanity must suffer for its crimes against us!" Tyark's voice was soaring so high as to be nearly incomprehensible.

"You gonna kill me too?" Dathgar was indignant. He obviously didn't see the danger in his words.

"I don't know why I've put up with you as long as I have. It disgusts me to be working with human scum!" With that,

Tyark made a grabbing motion with his hand. At the same time Dathgar's expression went from indignation to surprise and he stiffened. Then Tyark spun his hand quickly. Dathgar's head wrenched around and, with a sickening crack, the man was dead, slumping to the ground.

Tyark was breathing heavily, whether from exertion or the passion of the previous moment, Gosse didn't know.

The man's killing of Dathgar on a whim however spoke volumes and only reaffirmed how much Gosse needed to get away from these men.

"I need to relieve myself," he said hoping he sounded calm. He rose and turned away.

"You're not going to get your prey."

Gosse stopped at the words. "Oh?" He wasn't sure what Tyark meant.

"I'm not going to kill those drahksan for you. Bounty hunter or no, we're done working for you."

Gosse half turned, he didn't like having his back to these men. "You can do what you will with them. My deal was with Dathgar and Dathgar is dead." He shrugged and hoped his next words weren't a mistake. "I'm no match for you and we both know it. So, do as you will."

Tyark drew himself up at the perceived compliment. "I'm glad you know your place."

Gosse nodded and waited a moment for more words, but they didn't come. He turned and walked into the forest... and kept walking.

He made sure to walk slowly, stay calm—despite the turmoil inside him—until he was out of sight of the others. Then he ran.

He just hoped those crazed drahksani wouldn't follow him.

19

CAERWYN TRIED TO REMAIN CALM, BUT IT WAS FAR FROM EASY.

Jais seemed to be recovering quickly. He still knelt where he'd collapsed after his 'trial' with the medallion. His breathing was returning to normal, as was his color, which had drained from him during the ordeal. He was still drawing long draughts of air, eyes wide. It was clear it had not been a pleasant experience.

Barami was undergoing the trial now, reacting in a similar manner. The man simply screamed, eyes clenched shut, body taught and tensed, every muscle flexed while that amulet was pressed to his head.

Then the high priest, as Caerwyn had come to think of him, drew back the sigil and Barami collapsed to the floor. Jais went to him, helped him to his knees, whispered something. Barami nodded faintly.

Volf was next.

He glanced at her with clear terror in his eyes. She nodded to the two others. "They're fine. It's a few moments of —" She had no idea what... pain? That's what it seemed like.

"You'll get through this. It may hurt, but we'll all come out the other side stronger."

Volf turned the other way and looked at Jais and Barami then back to her. He nodded, though he didn't look much calmed.

The high priest stepped before Volf and without a word pressed the metal to Volf's forehead. Volf's eyes went wide then clenched shut and he let out that same scream.

Now that the aged man was closer, Caerwyn caught that his eyes were closed as well. He seemed to be in his own trance. He would nod and sway and hum to himself.

It occurred to her, the man was most likely reading their memories and thoughts. He was searching for truth. That's what this trial was. That's what the story leading up to this had been about, the ancient man's search for truth in his sons.

But why would that be painful?

It took her a moment to answer herself.

Truths were not always easily admitted, even to oneself. Everyone hid some truths, and having them dragged to the surface might not be a pleasant experience.

Caerwyn searched back through her own memories. Did she have her own hidden truths? Did she have secrets she didn't want the world to know... well yes, but anything she'd not tell if she had to? She didn't think so.

Then Volf was collapsing next to her, and she had no more time to wonder. The aged Dronnegir man shuffled forward and met her gaze, then lifted the medallion.

It was like a light, far too bright to look at. With it came a dry cold which sapped the strength from her bones. The truth was an icy thing at times. It did not care about passions or family. It was cold and, at times, heartless. Truth was truth.

She didn't know if she was screaming. She only knew that everything in her life was being pulled out of her.

Every moment, even some she'd long forgotten, was exposed and brought forth into that harsh light. Her early childhood at her parents' small house in Domara far to the west. That was pleasant up until the harsh moment when her parents had been killed. That was replayed before her eyes, though in truth she'd seen nothing. She'd been fleeing into the forest. She remembered only the sound of fighting and screams.

Then her life on the run; for three years she'd lived as a wildling in the forests before stowing away on a boat heading south to the 'Firelands.'

There she'd met her new father, who'd found her stealing in a market and adopted her. He'd been curious at her strange appearance and tough nature. She'd made him a proud father, rising through the ranks of the Afgenni army, becoming a general. Then came the next most painful day of her life: being exposed as a drahksan before her family—and those she'd come to think of as 'her people,'—and exiled.

Then she'd traveled north with the one man who hadn't abandoned her, Barami. They'd found Jais, fought krolls and a krolloc, then made their way here.

The light vanished.

She drew a long breath, finding her legs weak beneath her, but oddly she didn't fall. She did have to reach out to a pillar supporting the ceiling and lean on it, but she stayed on her feet.

The aged man gave her a quizzical look for a long moment, then nodded to himself with a faint smile. He said a word: "Steinnhjartha"

She turned to the man of middle years following in the ancient man's wake. "What does that mean?"

The man smiled. "Stone heart. It means you are strong." The man glanced back at the three men who'd undergone the trial before her. "I have never seen anyone remain on their feet after the trial... until now."

Oh.

She nodded to the man.

It really hadn't seemed that bad.

She watched as the high priest shuffled toward Anubjorn. The old man spoke at some length in the Dronnegir tongue. The reactions on the faces of both Anubjorn and Hildr, as well as the assembled others, were telling.

Caerwyn guessed that the priest was telling everyone... everything about their guests. Well not everything or they'd have been there for ages, but the important bits.

By the time the man finished, all her companions including Volf were on their feet.

Volf leaned over to her. "That was not what I had expected."

"It didn't feel painful," Caerwyn said. "Did I scream?"

Volf grinned. "You did, yes, but I heard what that one said to you. I agree, you must have a heart like stone to resist that and stay on your feet afterward."

"Did it hurt you?"

"Yes, but not how I expected. It wasn't a physical pain at all, just a realization of so many things. It's odd though, now I can't even seem to recall those things."

Caerwyn had the same odd sensation. She'd uncovered some long-forgotten memories and emotions, but they were gone again now.

"I guess that's the nature of the magic in that thing. It drags everything up for the priest to see, but for us, we go back to normal afterward."

"Priest?"

"He's the one with a holy magical artifact and spouting off about the gods, what do you think?"

"Fair enough."

"Come forward." This from Anubjorn.

The leader, or Egir, of the barbarians surveyed them all for a long moment before he spoke again. "Havardr told us many truths. I was wrong to accuse you." There was little change on the stony face of the man, but Caerwyn was sure that had cost him to say. "You are what you say and came here meaning no harm to the Dronnegir and our ways."

Well that was a promising start.

"But, what should I do with you?" He raised a hand to forestall the words he must have seen forming on Caerwyn's lips. He spoke with care, slow and even. "Trust does not come easy for our kind. Especially for any outsiders. I know not if you can understand our oath; how it is a part of us. It is our life and to break it would be to break us. If we let you see the dragon, we would not be Dronnegir... I would not be Egir." His tone and demeanor changed as one: harder, harsher, stern. "What certainty do we have that you will not tell others of our secret here?"

Caerwyn waited to see if the man had more to say, but nothing was forthcoming.

"We helped you—" Jais said.

"Jais!" she said sharply. Jais had spoken first, and as usual his words were heated and passionate. That was not what was needed now. She moderated her own tone and spoke to Jais first. "Now is not the time for accusations or quick words. Please let me speak."

Jais looked a little put out but nodded.

She turned to Anubjorn. "Egir, you are right. You have no reason to trust us. We do not know your ways and customs. But, we have endured your trial. Does that not speak somewhat to our nature?" Caerwyn glanced at Hildr standing next to the Egir. She'd been the one who'd fought for them last night, who had suggested the trial. The woman nodded slightly. Caerwyn wasn't sure what to make of that except perhaps to push on with this line.

The Egir nodded. "You have, yes."

"And the purpose of the trial was to test our virtue, was it not? To see if we could be trusted?"

The large man pressed his lips together. He didn't want to admit it. After a moment he did. "Yes, but—"

"We came here today willing to undergo your trial. We have done everything you have demanded of us." Except leave when first asked, but she didn't bring that up. "What more do you need?"

The Egir glared at her. He didn't like this line of thought. Then his glare became something else and he grinned. "You ask what more? I say this. If you wish to speak with the dragon then you must become Dronnegir. You must become one of us... you must never leave this place."

She'd been about to agree to whatever it took to become a Dronnegir, but the words died at his last sentence.

Never leave?

That was impossible.

She spoke slowly, carefully. "We would gladly do what is needed to become one of your clan, but we cannot stay. Speaking to the dragon is but the beginning of our quest, not its end."

Even as Anubjorn spoke to righteously refuse their request, having found his perfect reason to deny them, Caerwyn's mind was churning through a plan. It was risky, very risky, but it might just be worth it.

"What if we appealed to a higher authority?"

The Egir stopped mid-sentence and glared at her again. "There is no higher authority."

"There is the dragon."

"But you cannot see the dragon without agreeing to stay," he said with a grin, thinking he had her.

"What if we let the dragon make that choice?"

"What?"

This is where the risk came in. She took a step forward to meet the Egir's eyes, not in contest, not to glare, but to make certain he knew she meant what she was saying. "You say we have to stay. I say we do not, that we can be trusted to keep your secrets because they are our secrets too. We are at an impasse. So why don't we go to see this dragon and both of us accept whatever outcome for us that the dragon decides. If he says we must stay... we will. But if he says we can go... you will let us leave. Agreed?"

"Caer, do you—" Jais started.

"I don't know—" Barami spoke at the same moment.

"Agreed?" she said more forcefully, cutting Barami and Jais off. Both had been saying variations on the same thing, questioning her.

The Egir considered her words for a long moment. He could say no, but that would be to block those who had helped his clan and had been trying to work within the rules of that clan for as long as they'd been here. He had to agree.

He finally nodded. "Agreed."

She nodded in return. "When can we leave?"

The Egir sighed out heavily. "Tomorrow at sunrise. It is a long trek up into the mountains. I shall send my best guides and my own brother." He nodded and that was that.

20

Volf let out a breath he hadn't known he was holding.

Had they just won or had Caerwyn just sold them into staying here for the rest of their lives? He didn't know.

All he knew in that moment was his intense admiration and respect for the woman who had just brokered a deal for them to go see the dragon.

He still didn't much understand the ways of these Dronnegir. They were just a little too foreign to him with their magic-mind-medallions and harsh living. But he could understand their lack of trust. Up until just a couple of weeks ago he hadn't trusted anyone. Caerwyn had changed all that for him... and for these people. She was truly an amazing woman.

"What does this mean?" Jais was asking Caerwyn.

She spoke softly, just to them. "I'm hoping that the dragon will see things differently than these people. The Dronnegir have been set in their ways for a long time. They aren't going to see reason, but the dragon might. I can only hope it will understand that we mean it no harm and aren't going to give away its secrets to all we meet." She lowered her voice further. "But that doesn't mean that if we meet other drahksan who need help that we might not send them this way."

"And put them through all this?" Jais asked.

She shook her head, "No, that's just it. What I'm hoping the dragon will say... to all of us... is that the Dronnegir have nothing to fear from drahksani, at least not those who come in peace to speak to the dragon. This is too valuable a resource to be left untapped."

"That seems like a long shot," Barami said.

Volf had to agree. These people did not seem so open to change. He wasn't sure if they'd take it so well, even if the dragon itself told them to do it, but maybe.

"I trust Caerwyn's judgment," Volf said. "If she believes it can be done, then I believe it as well."

She smiled at him and he felt his heart lift with that simple look. He returned the smile.

He didn't know why he felt like he did, but with her... it just felt like anything was possible, like his life had opened up and a whole new world was set before him.

They were being escorted out of the longhouse. The two women—Elria and Hildr?—approached, and for a moment Jais and Barami were drawn away as they spoke with the women.

Now was his moment.

Once they were out in the courtyard, he turned to Caerwyn. "I just wanted to say that you were amazing in there. I've never known anyone like you and when I'm around you I feel like the world is a new place filled with endless opportunities."

Her look was a little stunned. But she smiled and that gave him the impetus to push on.

"I just wanted you to know that if there is ever anything

you need... you just have to ask and if it is within my power to give it, I shall."

An odd look crossed her face at that point. She smiled faintly and nodded. "There just may be something you can do. Perhaps we can speak more about that... later."

He beamed and was so filled with impassioned joy he seized the moment. He stepped in and embraced her, kissing her fiercely. It was too much, and this would not be what she'd want, but oddly, she didn't push him away, but lingered in the kiss for a long moment before he finally withdrew.

"I just..." He had to say something to explain himself. "Thank you, for everything."

She still seemed a little shocked.

"Thank you too, Volf."

They continued on their way back to the longhouse where they'd been put the night before. Volf couldn't help but glance at her as they walked. He was rather pleasantly surprised that she too was glancing at him. There was something new in how she looked at him.

And she smiled at him.

He couldn't be happier.

21

JAIS COULDN'T GET THE IMAGE OUT OF HIS HEAD. HE DIDN'T know why Volf kissing Caerwyn bothered him so much. It wasn't like he had any special relationship with her. Yet that scene kept playing in his mind, and the more he thought about it the surlier he became.

Elria had pulled him aside only for a moment to say she'd speak with him soon. He'd hurried to catch up to Caerwyn and Volf only to see them... together.

The image grated on his mind. It didn't seem right. She hardly knew the man!

Though some part of him refuted that thought: *she's known him longer than she knew you when she proposed having a child with you.*

Barami had caught up to him soon after and they'd all returned to the guesthouse where he and Barami had been asked to wait that first night. Had it just been last night? It seemed like so long ago.

He didn't want to be around the others right now, though.

He left them and marched out the far end of the long-house. Twenty paces away, the wooden palisade dominated his view. On the other side of it, was a wall of mountains. Their gray sides reached high up to snowcapped peaks. It seemed like he was trapped by that wall and those mountains, and everything in his life.

He wanted to hit something, but everything he looked at seemed too fragile. This was the problem with having extraordinary strength, you couldn't take your frustrations out on anything without breaking it.

"Jais?"

He spun with harsh words on his lips. He was going to tell whoever it was to go away, that he wanted to be alone, but then he saw who it was.

Elria emerged from the longhouse. "Your friends said that, find you out here, I would. You seem upset. Are you well?"

She was beautiful and concerned and he didn't know why but right now, he wanted nothing more than to kiss her—with Caerwyn watching.

"I don't..." He just shook his head. Words were hard. His emotions were boiling within him and he didn't know what he wanted... who he wanted. "I thought I wanted to be alone." But the thought of her with him, comforted him. She was the one person who could comfort him. "I'm just so tired and I don't know... I can't..." He clenched a hand into a fist. Why couldn't he say anything that made sense?

She took a step in and laid a soft hand on his cheek.

Instantly, he felt a soothing warmth fill him from where her hand lay. He watched her grow wearier just with that little expenditure of energy.

He reached up and pulled her hand away. "Don't, please," he whispered. "I can't bear to see you suffer."

Where had those words come from?

He saw in her eyes the same concern for him that he felt

for her. "I cannot bear to see you suffer either." Her tone was soft, voice low and husky. She stepped in and was suddenly very close. His hand was in hers. He wanted this, to be near her.

He'd only ever been physically intimate with one woman, Alnia. She had died soon after, helping to save their village from krolls. He'd had only one night with her, one glorious night. Thinking of that now, with Elria overlaid in Alnia's place he felt his heart quicken.

She drew closer still, body pressing against his, lips coming to his. He accepted her advance and didn't move away. He wanted her closer.

The kiss was tender and inviting. It drew itself out in a series of brushing meetings of their lips, each growing deeper than the last until he pulled her tight to him, arms around her, and hers around him.

They stayed that way for a long moment before coming away breathless. They didn't separate far though. Jais kept her close, still in his arms. Their faces remained perilously near, tempting.

But his heart was still so confused.

"I don't know what I want," he whispered.

"I do," was her quiet response. She brought a hand up to the back of his head, tangling in his hair, before urging it forward, back to hers. She was making it clear to him what she wanted. Very clear indeed.

And he was starting to want her just as much.

When her lips finally pulled away, still so soft and sweet, she whispered again, "I must prepare for tomorrow, but I'll come to you tonight." It wasn't a question, and he didn't need to respond. He was certain she could feel his heart beating through his chest and that was response enough.

It still took her several long moments to pull herself away, the look in her eyes hungry. He was captivated by that look. Suddenly he couldn't wait for the evening. He pulled her back into a passionate kiss before letting her go.

She smiled, breathless, and turned away. But only a few steps away she looked back. The intensity of desire in her eyes filled a hole in him he hadn't known was empty.

She was padding away on the soft grasses and he watched her go for as long as he could.

Tonight.

He smiled.

"What are you doing, boy?" It was a harsh whisper from behind him, and he spun around flushing suddenly.

Barami stalked out of the longhouse. "What was that?" He was keeping his voice low. "I thought— Didn't you and Caerwyn...? Did you two talk?" The man seemed confused and angry and gave an exasperated shrug. "And now you're off making plans with another woman?"

At Caerwyn's name Jais' mood turned, spiraling down from the heights he'd reached moments before.

"Caerwyn has her own lover now!" he hissed. "She and Volf seemed to have bonded quite well yesterday. They were being quite friendly just now."

Barami tried to speak, but Jais' emotions had found a release and he spewed forth all his pent-up frustration and confusion before the other man could get a word in. "The only thing that Caer and I had was an agreement that if she found no other drahksani, then perhaps, maybe I would help get her with child. You know her better than I do, she doesn't want a man in her life. She doesn't want me. She pushed you away too. She doesn't need anyone. She's a strong woman. That's great, but it means she'll never feel for me how I feel for her." Realizing what he'd just said he amended it quickly. "Felt for her—if I felt anything. So why shouldn't I have a relationship that means something? With another woman who actually cares for me. Who wants me for more than just getting with child. Who wants me for *me*?" His voice had gotten quite loud and he hushed it instantly.

Barami opened his mouth, but Jais pushed on.

"You can't tell me you don't understand. I know you've wanted her since you first met her too. She's intoxicating like that." And she was. Jais knew that much. She was strong and certain and just drew others to her. "But we both know she can't give us what we really want. So, what do we have left to us, but to find another. You and Hildr seem to have hit it off well. Why can't I find some peace in the arms of a woman who wants me?"

"You owe Caer—"

"For what? For dragging me away from my life? For saving me from krolls? I think we all did enough saving of each other to be even on that score. I don't owe her anything!"

His fist was clenched, and he was shaking it, but he would never raise it against Barami. He couldn't stay here any longer, though, or he just might try. He turned and stalked away. He needed air, he needed to be away from the confines of this village. It was still early morning and there would be a lot of day to pass before tonight and Elria. Right now, he didn't want to be anywhere near his friends.

He headed for the gate to leave the village. There was an increased presence of guards at the gate, which was closed. Men stood on the tops of the longhouses all over as well. They were tense for an attack.

He asked to be let out.

The men hummed and hawed, until Hildr passed by and told them it was well to let him leave for a bit.

Jais then stalked down the hill to the river.

He stopped to drink, but then still felt too restless and kept moving.

For the entire morning and a good part of the afternoon, he wandered the hills around the village, always keeping it in sight so he'd know which way to go back. His anger and emotions had settled in that time, but he was still confused. He didn't know what he felt for Caerwyn or Elria. He knew only that one of them wanted him and the other didn't, and right now that want was enough for him. It was more than enough.

As the afternoon waned, he turned back to the village.

A shadow separated itself from a copse of trees and became a man who stood in his path. Jais knew this man well enough.

He reached for swords... that weren't there. In all his bluster, he'd left without his weapons!

"You," Jais said, fists up, ready for a fight.

"Indeed," the dragon hunter said softly.

22

BARAMI WATCHED CAERWYN PACING.

"Where is he?" It wasn't the first time Caerwyn had asked the question, nor was the aggravation mixed with worry in her voice a new thing.

They were in their longhouse, packed and ready for their trek up into the mountains. It was the twilight before dawn and they would be leaving shortly.

Barami shook his head slowly and muttered to himself, "Stupid selfish boy." Yet he couldn't help but feel a pang of guilt at Jais' absence. He didn't think he'd been overly hard on the boy yesterday. He'd said what needed to be said. But after their talk, Barami had recalled being young and how every rebuke from an adult felt like it was telling you how to live your life. And yes, Barami had been telling him what to do, but he'd thought it only common sense. What he hadn't banked on were those same overly excited emotions of youth. The boy was infatuated, and his emotions were out of control. Barami didn't think that was enough to make the young man disappear. He could understand a bit of a tantrum, but not returning for nearly a full day, that didn't seem right.

In truth, he was growing worried as well.

But there was no time to search for the boy now.

The Dronnegir woman, Elria seemed in a similar state to Caerwyn, anxious and concerned, but a little annoyed as well. Barami had caught some of her conversation with Jais yesterday, namely the part about meeting that evening. He guessed that hadn't happened and she was both aggravated and confused.

If anything, it was this which concerned Barami the most. Jais might have run off in a huff to spite his friends, but he shouldn't have missed his triste with the Dronnegir woman. That was truly worrying.

Elria spoke up. "Go to find him, I will."

"No, you'll stay here," Hildr said as she entered the long-house. The woman was bedecked in armor and ready for travel with a pack on her back. "Our fathers decreed it unsafe to venture beyond the tor. They be concerned about those attackers. No scouts have seen them. The council knows not where the foes may be nor what they plan. If the enemy finds a group beyond the wall—" She wet her lips nervously. "None might survive long against such magics. You be the only group allowed to leave." Hildr sighed and her gaze slipped to Barami. After a steadying breath she spoke again, slower, carefully. "I think my father would be glad if you and your friends were attacked. That would rid him of a great burden. So, I said I would go. Now he will be praying for the gods to save us, not kill you."

"A healer you may need, I will come too." Elria had already brought her pack. Barami was now uncertain whether the young woman had permission to do so.

Hildr shrugged. "Then both of our fathers will be praying for safe travels."

"My father will not be going?"

Hildr shook her head. "No. It was considered unwise for the Thunegir to leave; so the council decreed. They wish none of our kind to travel beyond the walls. They gave leave for a single guide, but since I am going, they will not send even that."

Caerwyn sounded a little annoyed and aggravated when she spoke. "This is some hospitality your father is showing us. I thought part of your duty was to guard the dragon. Should you not be out hunting that wizard and—"

Barami thought he knew her well enough to finish her thought: 'finding Jais,'

Hildr's shoulder's fell. "Protected the dragon we have, for thousands of years, mostly by virtue of its secrecy. We have never had to face such magic as this. I agree, we must fight the villains, but my father... be scared. We lost nearly two dozen of our kind fighting that wizard in our own village. He fears that any party he sends, will not return, and further lower our numbers. Despite the Dronnengyfr, it seems we are no match for such a man."

Barami quirked a brow at the new word. "Dronnengyfr?"

"Dragon boons," Elria said, though she didn't elaborate.

"Ah." Barami wouldn't push. It explained the healing and perhaps also why they fought like demons which was enough to know.

"So, are we leaving without Jais?" Volf said. He too seemed concerned. Jais' disappearance had affected them all.

Elria squirmed. "Perhaps, look for him, I should? Know the trails, I do, we could catch you up."

A stern look from Hildr quelled the younger woman. "No. The Thunegir would not forgive me for letting you go alone."

"Take care of myself, I can!"

"Against that wizard? I think not."

Elria fidgeted, perhaps trying to come up with some other argument. Barami was about to offer to escort her, his guilt biting him a little harder at that moment. Before he could, Hildr proclaimed: "We go together, or we wait together. But I will not let any out to search. It be too dangerous. So, what will it be?"

"You can't keep me here!" Caer had her hackles up, ready for a fight.

Hildr looked over, assessing Caerwyn calmly. Right now, it certainly seemed like the tall Dronnegir woman was in control. "Interesting it might be, to try. Few here have challenged me in a long time." Hildr sighed, relenting. "But you be right. I will not keep you here. The choice be yours: come with us now or leave and look for your friend. But if you go, I know not how willing my father might be to have another take you to the dragon. The season of storms be almost upon us. Soon the passes will be closed up into the mountains. Today be clear, but who can say what tomorrow will bring. The choice, as I said, is yours."

Caerwyn was trembling with a barely restrained fury at the choice before her. Barami had seen it a few times before in her. It was not in her character to be so distraught, but neither was it in her character to not get what she wanted.

"I'll stay and wait for Jais," Elria said softly, nodding to herself. "If he— *when* he returns I will follow you all."

Hildr nodded at that.

Caerwyn deflated a little. "That... works for me."

Hildr was all business. "Are we set?"

It didn't seem like anyone was happy, but they had little they could do about it now. Everyone muttered their agreement and picked up their equipment.

"This way, follow me." Hildr turned and led them out of the longhouse. Elria followed them as far as the doorway.

Barami certainly hoped Jais returned soon.

JAIS COULD ONLY SHAKE HIS HEAD.

He thought he was confused and uncertain about his life, but that was nothing compared to the man who'd captured him. He'd been forced to sit and listen to the man talk through the evening, and certainly, the dragon hunter had a rather fantastical story to tell, but Jais wasn't sure if he believed any of it.

And if he did, he had no clue what to do about it.

The dragon hunter was gone now. He had been since Jais had woken just a short while ago as the first rays of light had been cast upon his eyes. The sun was above the peaks to the east.

Jais had not slept well. He was tied to a tree, his hands manacled on the other side of the trunk with thick rope binding his torso to the tree as well. He was certain that had he been at full strength he could have broken out of these bonds, but he was drained. He still hadn't recovered from the massive amount of healing he'd done the night before. Nor from the trial he'd undergone. Also, he hadn't eaten anything the previous day, a fault he was regretting now. Well, he'd had a little food, provided by the dragon hunter. The man had shared a meal with him while he talked. But between two nights of poor sleep, not enough food and being generally weary, he hadn't been able to resist much when the man had found him yesterday, nor could he free himself now.

He tried to break his bonds once again, just to be certain. He felt the metal of the manacles bite into his wrists as he tried to pull them apart, break the chain holding them together, while muscles all over his torso strained to burst the ropes around him. He should have been able to break these bonds, but... He succeeded only in winding himself and causing more pain. He used a bit of healing to soothe his wrists, but that only weakened him further.

He gave up and sighed heavily.

He wondered what the others were doing. Were they searching for him or perhaps they thought he'd just left in a huff and were on their way to see the dragon. He couldn't imagine them leaving without him. He had to assure himself that Barami's tracking skills would lead them to him soon enough.

Until then, perhaps he'd humor this dragon hunter.

He had to give the man a little credit. For a start... Jais wasn't dead. The man had caught him unawares without his weapons. Their first fight had not gone well for Jais and the man could probably easily have bested him—as much as Jais wanted to believe he could beat the man. Instead, he'd only restrained him here and asked him to listen. Then there was his wild story.

"I don't know who I am," the man had said. "I think I'm drahksan, which... I don't know what that means. Have I been hunting and killing my own kind all my life?"

The man, Gosse, had seemed genuinely remorseful.

"Can you sense me?" Gosse had asked. "Drahksan can sense each other, can they not? Are you able to tell if I'm drahksan? If you can, then, I don't know what I'd do, but if you can't then the others must have been wrong or lying or something."

Jais hadn't known what to do, but in the end had told the man the truth. "I can't sense you, but I can't sense anyone. I seem to have missed that ability. I can't tell a human from a drahksan any more than any human can." He'd almost wanted to say he was sorry. The man had been so distraught. Then he recalled the man had tried to kill him and hadn't apologized.

A heavy sigh off to his right alerted Jais to the man's presence. Jais looked to see the man standing nearby, staring off into the vista of morning mountains and the rising sun.

"I've had a lot of time to think," Gosse said slowly. "I didn't sleep at all last night. I went for a walk as the sky began to lighten and I think—" He gave a hard single laugh. "Well I think I need more time to think."

Jais wasn't sure what the man was up to and kept a keen eye on him.

"All I know for certain right now is that I need some answers." Gosse looked down at him. "And you haven't been that helpful." It wasn't an accusation nor said with any malice. It was just a plain statement but Jais still was worried. Did this mean he was expendable now?

Gosse pulled out a long knife.

Jais squirmed and struggled. Gods no, he didn't want to die like this.

Gosse crossed the distance to him and crouched. He was eye level with Jais and held the knife up between their gazes. "Two days ago, I would have killed you without a thought."

The man's gaze moved from Jais' eyes to the blade then back several times.

Gosse sighed and put away the knife.

"Now I'm going to let you go." He chuckled to himself. "A part of me wanted to cut the ropes to be dramatic, but this is good rope and I could reuse it." He moved around behind the tree and Jais could hear and even feel the ropes being worked on. A moment later, they went slack.

He held still, the manacles keeping him rather attached to

the tree. But with the clink of a key, the manacles were released as well.

Jais sprang to his feet and turned, ready for a fight. Or so he thought before a wave of dizziness swarmed through his head and he had to go to one knee to avoid falling. He doubted he would have been any good in a fight anyway. His arms were near to numb from having been at an odd angle behind him all night, his shoulders sore. He could use up more energy to heal himself but then he'd just be more tired.

His head cleared a moment later and he looked up to see Gosse leaning on the tree Jais had been tied to.

"You're free to go."

Jais had to ask. "Why?"

Gosse's gaze lifted away from Jais off to that same vista behind him. "I'm done with killing for now." He shook his head slowly. "I've been killing all my life, and there were times when I grew sick of it, but I thought I was doing it for a reason, for a cause." His gaze drifted away, then down. He looked ashamed. "The things I've done." He was shaking his head again. "I thought I..." He looked up at Jais, brows knit, eyes asking a question Jais couldn't answer. "The goal was just. I was human. Drahksani were evil. These were things I knew, I believed. But if I am drahksan... Does that mean some human found me and took me from my parents and trained me to be like this? I know not all humans are good people, but I had to believe that those who trained me were right." Gosse's gaze shifted back to the mountains. "But none of that makes sense anymore. Until I know more about what I am and who I am—" He shrugged. "I'm done with it all."

Jais tried standing again and found he was still light-headed, but able to keep his legs under him. He was in no condition to fight even if he wanted to.

He turned and staggered a few steps before something stopped him. He turned back.

"You still looking for help? For answers?"

Gosse nodded.

"Are you willing to surrender to me? I can take you to the others in my group. They might be able to help you. If that's what you really want. But there is no way they're going to let you anywhere near them while still armed."

Gosse seemed to consider for a long moment, his gaze moving from Jais to that sunrise and back several times. Finally, he nodded. He drew out his sword and tossed it at Jais' feet; then did the same with several knives. He spoke as he did so. "In truth that had been my hope in letting you go." He even went so far as to go to where his things were and toss Jais his bow and quiver. "I am ready to pay for my crimes if that is what you wish. I just want to know the truth before I die."

Fair enough, Jais thought.

Gosse, still crouching next to his gear, looked away again and when he spoke next his voice was low. "I think I know the truth, and it's already killing me."

23

BARAMI MARVELED AT THE AMOUNT OF TIME AND THE LEVEL OF craftsmanship that must have gone into making these tunnels.

They were well below the hill on which the village was located, and the tunnel was running smooth and straight. He had no clue which direction they were heading, but he assumed it was north.

If he was honest with himself, he was more than just a little nervous at being so far underground in such a cramped space. It wasn't that cramped really, he could stretch his arms out to either side and still not touch the walls, but it sure felt small and tight around him.

They walked in single file. Hildr at the lead held a torch and Caerwyn, third in line behind him, had one as well. The red light flickered off the stone walls.

The tunnel wasn't carved from stone, but instead thick stone bricks had been used to form the sides and arched up to a curved dome above them. The floor was similarly paved with stone, flat and even.

The entrance, far above them now, had been concealed.

One of the large stone square fire-pits, in the middle of an empty longhouse—which seemed to be used mostly for storage—had hidden the way down. The grate on top had been lifted off to reveal the square was hollow within, a ladder leading down into darkness. The ladder ended at a platform beneath the false fire-pit and from there a winding stone stairway had spiraled down into the earth. Once they had all descended the ladder, torches had been lit. The last down had moved the grating on top back into place. They had descended those stone steps deeper and deeper into the hill. Finally, they had reached the bottom, and this straight tunnel.

Barami found the dark and the quiet a little too oppressive and needed to speak.

"Hildr, you had mentioned something about Dragon Boons? That even with them you didn't think you'd be able to defeat that wizard. What did that mean?"

Hildr didn't look back when she spoke, but her voice echoed along the hall. In some ways that sucked the power from her voice, but it also made it easier to make out her words... if she spoke slow enough.

"It was the deal our ancestors struck with the dragon. We protect it and it makes us... more. Normal people, our ancestors were, in a world with dragons, drahksan, and other strange things. The dragon gave us gifts, boons, to help us. Not physical things, not swords or spears, but magic, infused into our very beings. It be why Elria can heal. Stayed with us these gifts have, over many generations. Some Dronnegir possess powers from ancestors gifted long past. Others were gifted more recently."

"Recently?" Barami asked. Did these people keep getting boons from the dragon?

"Yes. The power must remain strong in our bloodlines.

Three are chosen every generation, to go to the dragon and receive new boons."

"Just three?"

"The dragon grows old. It gives only so much. The rest it keeps to sustain itself."

"Oh." That was news. Suddenly Barami wondered if they should be disturbing this beast at all if it was so frail. But he knew Caerwyn would insist. Even just talking to it would provide them with great insights he was sure.

"Did you receive a boon?" he asked.

"I did," she said evenly. "It be why I know the way to the dragon. It be not known to all in the clan. Only the chosen three are led through the paths and perils by one from the previous generation. I and Elria went, as did a boy named Sindr." She was quiet for a long moment before she went on. When she did her voice was low, soft. "Sindr died fighting with the wizard. Now only two from my generation remain."

Barami put a hand on her shoulder and squeezed. "I'm sorry for the loss."

She nodded.

"Here be the exit," she said, her voice still not having regained its full strength.

Barami glanced around her to see a heavy wooden door bound with iron. She opened it inward on hinges which made no sound. Beyond was faint sunlight filtering through heavy brush. "You three go first. I will close the door. Those bushes will part for you."

Barami was eager enough to get out of this dark place and pushed forward, moving sideways through bushes, which he guessed were cedar from their scent. The needles were softer than those in the South, flatter. They brushed around him before he stepped into full sunlight and had to shield his eyes, blinking.

He thought to move to one side as the next person, Caerwyn stepped through the bushes as well. After her came Volf then Hildr who spent a moment with the door before emerging from the bushes.

By that point, Barami could see well enough and glanced around to try to get his bearings.

Behind him, where they'd come out of the hill, was a craggy cliff-face stretching up about thirty odd feet before becoming a gentler slope up the side of a hill. In the distance above him smoke curled up into the sky from somewhere atop the hill. He guessed they were at the base of the hill upon which the village sat. Ahead of them was a very shallow decline into a sweeping valley filled with trees and bushes. He could hear the rush of water but couldn't see the source. Beyond this valley were other high-heaving hills and then the rather ominous sides of mountains.

"Most in the village know of that tunnel," Hildr said as she began picking her way down to a long stretch of trees. "It be our escape in case we are overrun. From here, only those chosen are shown the path into the mountains. That be how much of a secret the dragon's location remains."

Once at the trees, the sound of running water was much more prevalent and within the forest a short distance was a rushing stream.

"Is this the same brook which we crossed on the other side of the hill?" Barami asked.

"Indeed," Hildr said, flashing him a grin. "It runs out of the mountains and curves around the base of our hill. We call it Ice River." She chuckled. "Far south of here... it be called Cold River."

Barami looked at the little rushing watercourse and had to laugh. It was much more significant where it passed the town which bore its name. He said as much to Hildr who nodded.

"Many rivers join with it before then, making it much wider and deeper." She didn't cross but began following the creek. "We will follow the river for a while before the land becomes too difficult to traverse."

Barami grinned and drew in a long breath of air.

The day was warm without being too hot. The pleasant scent of cedars filled the air, and the stream made a relaxing burbling sound. He took in the trees around him, the clear waters, the blue sky, and the lithe, lean form of the woman in front of him as she picked her way along the rocky bank of the river.

"Barami," Hildr called from ahead. It was odd to hear his name in her accent, but he liked it. He wondered if she'd known he was looking at her backside. He raised his eyes and caught her as she glanced over her shoulder at him. "Join me."

He did, moving up to walk beside her.

"Told you, I have, of me and my clan. Tell me of the South, your home," she said softly.

He nodded. "Let me start with a question. How much hotter than this does it get up here in the North?"

She considered for a moment moving her head from side to side. "Not much more than this. Though one summer, when a child I be, there was great heat. All children of the village ran to the bottom of our hill, to play in the river and cool ourselves." She laughed a little. "But these waters be quite cold all year. Most times, we bathe fast."

He laughed. "My people would give a fortune for waters as chill as these. Drinking this water is refreshing. There is a great river which splits the Southern lands and most of those who live in the South live near its shores, or along one of its tributaries. The rest of the lands are ill suited for most. There are dried up deserts of blowing sand or cracked earth where only the hardiest of plants grow. Then there is the great jungle, wet and hot and full of life, but most of it is trying to kill you. Few people venture far from that great river to live in the dry lands or the jungle. My people, the Kigasi, call that jungle home. We are nomads, traveling through the jungle, knowing what is safe to eat and what animals and plants to avoid. We get our waters from the rains or roots when we venture far from the river." He heard his voice growing wistful. He laughed. It was far from an easy life, but he still missed it.

"It is hot all the time," he continued. "There is little relief from the heat, even at night." He gave a breathy laugh. "Only a rare night might be as pleasant as this."

"Truly?"

"Oh yes."

"It must be hard, enduring such heat. You must look forward to the winters!"

"We have no winters."

"You jest!"

"I do not. We tell seasons by the rains, not the temperature. What you call winter is simply a dryer season for us, but still incredibly hot. It might be a bit nicer on some days as the heat is not made worse by the oppressive moisture in the air which is ever-present in our summers or wet seasons."

"I can't imagine," she said in wonder. "So, have you never seen snow?"

"Snow? A little yes, but not in my homeland." It had snowed lightly a few times as he and Caerwyn had made their way north. Once there had been a couple feet of the stuff on the ground and they had stayed in a village for a week waiting for it to melt.

"We get so much snow here it buries our longhouses. Did you see the tunnels that connect our homes?"

"Are those the breaks in the platforms near the middle?"

"Yes, we dug paths to connect all the longhouses because some days we cannot leave through the doors. A few of the houses have ladders up to doors in the roofs. It be another reason for the tunnel under the village. Though even that can be blocked by snow."

Barami couldn't imagine it. He knew of floods, where water could cover things, but this did not sound like that at all. He'd found the very existence of the white stuff a little mysterious and magical. Yet that much on the ground, enough to bury a house, he had trouble seeing it in his mind. It made sense that there would be more snow farther north, but still.

"We come from very different worlds," he said softly. He was a man of action and not one to mince words. He had to know if this amazing woman was as fascinated with him as he was with her. "I like you. I would like to spend more time with you. Would you like that?"

She looked at him with a broad smile on her face, her red hair flashing in the sun. Her green eyes sparkled as she nodded. "I would like that very much, Barami." Her next words caught him a little off guard with their forward nature. "How many children would you like?"

"Ah...?" He might have found an answer if he hadn't lost his footing at that moment, perhaps from the shock of such a direct question, and fallen into the stream.

It was indeed quite cold.

JAIS RUSHED THROUGH THE GATES OF THE VILLAGE ONCE THEY

had been opened, ignoring the stern and disapproving looks of the men and women on guard.

"Jais!"

He saw Elria as she saw him and called out.

"Have the others left?"

She gave him a look which seemed to slip through a dozen different emotions from annoyance to relief and several others in between which let him know he should never have run off. "Yes, it be mid-morning! Where were you? We must hurry to catch them. I've packed a rucksack for you."

"Elria, I can't." he faltered not knowing how to explain this. He hadn't brought Gosse into the village. If any of the villagers had recognized the man from the attack, Jais was certain Gosse wouldn't have lived long.

She looked wounded and confused.

He did the only thing he could think of and embraced her, kissing her deeply, not caring if anyone saw.

"Jais?" She was confused and a little breathless.

"I'm so very sorry I missed our... night. It's a long story which I don't have time to tell now. I need to catch up to the others, but I have a... guest."

"Jais—"

He waved away her words, again not wanting to explain. "I'll take that pack you made up for me. Can you tell me how to catch up to the others?"

"I will take you myself."

Would that be wise? He didn't know how she might react to Gosse either. "Elria, I don't think that's best—"

"Jais, what be wrong with you? What happened?"

He was tired and at the end of his energy and somehow trusting the man who'd tried to kill him and Caerwyn multiple times. He didn't know what was going on within him at the moment, but he also didn't really want to stop and think too much about it. He didn't have time to.

"Fine. Grab my pack and come with me."

"With you? But that be not the way."

"It is now. I know I'm being evasive, Elria, but all will make sense once we're out beyond the walls. You may not like it, but it will make sense at least."

She didn't seem to like it now. She was frowning at him, but after a moment simply sighed heavily, shaking her head. "This way, you can grab your own rucksack, I have one that's just as heavy."

He followed her to the longhouse where he had been staying and plucked up the pack she'd prepared for him. It wasn't that heavy for him, even exhausted as he was. After he put it on he turned to her and she was laboring under the weight of hers.

Only then did he see the heavy bags under her eyes and the lackluster slouch to her shoulders. She was just as tired as he was. Had she slept at all last night? Had she been worrying about him?

He sighed. "Give me your pack."

"No."

"Don't be stubborn. I can carry it at least for a while."

"Perhaps I'll take you up on that later, but I'm not letting my own people see me walk out of here unable to carry my own gear."

He could understand that and shrugged. "Ready?"

She nodded, and they were off.

Soon enough they were out of the village and back down the hill where he'd left Gosse.

"Who's this?" the man asked as Jais returned to the spot he'd told the other man to wait, hiding just inside the forest on the slope of the hill.

Elria nearly jumped out of her skin with a clipped scream.

"Elria, this is Gosse." Jais hoped she wouldn't react too badly.

"Where did he come from? Who be he?" she asked a little breathless.

Jais was expecting other questions like, 'Is he going to attack us?' or 'Can we trust him?' Then it occurred to him that she hadn't seen the attackers during the fight. She'd run off almost immediately to tend to the wounded.

"Ah, Gosse is... a friend?" He probably should have tried to sound more convincing, but even he was a little uncertain of the man's status. What Jais knew was, "He needs our help. We need to get him to the others before they're too far gone... to... where they're going."

Elria seemed to catch Jais' hesitation and vagueness. She was a bit more direct. "He doesn't know?"

"I don't believe so. I didn't tell him."

"Tell me what?" Gosse asked.

"Nothing."

Gosse sighed with a shrug.

Jais just kept glancing back and forth between Elria and Gosse. He couldn't quite believe she didn't recognize him.

After a moment of this, at nearly the same time they both said, "What?"

He shook it off. "Nothing. We should be going," he said and nodded to Elria. "Lead the way."

Elria moved quickly through the forest. She seemed to be skirting the bottom of the hill on which the village sat.

"We need to hurry," she said picking up her pace.

"Why?" Jais asked.

She stopped only for a moment to take off her pack and hand it to him, which he took.

"Because of that." She pointed behind them.

Jais and Gosse looked to see dark clouds rolling in from the south. A storm was coming.

"There's another reason we should move faster," Gosse said slowly after a moment.

Jais turned to Gosse with a questioning glance. What was the man talking about?

There was a grim look on his face. "The more I accept what I am the more I can... feel things. And I can sense your friends north of us... but I can also sense my old companions. I don't know what that wizard is after, but he mentioned feeling something strong and primal up north. I don't know if he's going after your friends or whatever else is up there, but he's close behind the others. Your friends will need help."

Elria pulled Jais aside and whispered to him. "What be he talking about?"

Jais sighed. "That's a long story. I can tell you as we walk. But we need to move."

They all agreed to that.

24

A CHILL SHUDDERED THROUGH VOLF AS HE WATCHED THE FAST-moving waters plunge over the cliff to fall several hundred feet below them. Mist sprayed out from the high waterfall, casting the lands below in a shimmering haze.

Over the course of the morning, they had crossed hilly country, climbing higher. Eventually they had moved away from the river as it ran through a narrow gorge. They had climbed a steep hill to the base of one of the mountains itself. It loomed over them, stark and gray. The top of the mountain was now lost in clouds which had moved in over the course of the morning. They stood on a ledge which stretched perhaps fifteen feet out from the side of the mountain. They had followed this ledge up from the base of the mountain below, but now their path was at and end. They could go no farther because of the river. The ledge didn't even continue on the other side of the fast-moving waters.

The river rushed through a narrow cut between mountains, then over the edge to a pool in the gorge, far below. It would eventually become the creek they had followed earlier that day. Unless they were going to try to somehow go upriver, there was nowhere to go from here. Since they had brought no boat—and he was certain the water was too swift to paddle upstream anyway—he had to assume they were at their destination. But that didn't seem right. Volf could see no cave or other indication of any place for a dragon to live. There was nothing here but the ledge, the water, and the mountain.

"This next bit be a bit tricky," Hildr said removing her pack.

"Tricky?" Volf sounded a little incredulous to his own ears. "Are we going up the side of the mountain or something?"

Gods, he hadn't considered that option. He was an exceptional climber, but that was in a city, where houses and buildings had lots of places to grab and hold. This sheer mountain face next to them did not look like it would be fun to climb.

Hildr shook her head with a bit of a wild grin. "No, we walk on water."

That didn't sound much better.

Hildr laughed. "Don't worry. It be easy enough for the nimble, but we must be quick. There be a storm coming, and we'll want to be through before it hits. Rain might swell this river enough to make this passing much more difficult."

"What passing?" Caerwyn apparently shared his skepticism on how they might proceed from here.

"It's hard to see, so let me explain. There be several ropes here." Hildr was standing at the point where the ledge met the river, right up against the mountain. She reached around into the crevice carved by the river and seemed to be indicating the rock wall around the corner. "There be also holes cut into the rock here." With her one hand already around the corner, she kicked a foot around the corner as well and was only half visible. Then she slipped around the corner entirely.

Barami gasped and reached out for her as the three of them hurried over to peer up the river course.

Volf got there last and had to kneel to see around the other two.

"Gods," Caerwyn breathed.

He had to agree with that sentiment.

Hildr looked to be standing on... nothing. She was holding a rope which was tied between several iron loops somehow hammered into the rock wall. In truth, she wasn't standing on nothing. There were little holes with flat bottoms, into which she'd stuck her feet. But they weren't that deep. Only the first third of her boots, her toes really, were in the holes. She grinned at them then released one hand to wave them back away from the edge as she moved toward them.

Hildr swung herself back onto the ledge with a wild grin. "Your packs will weigh you down. They will be passed across separately. There be ropes to pull and hooks to hold the packs. I'll go across first, then you send the packs across. After that, you can follow. Always keep three points of contact: either both hands on the rope, or both feet in the holes. Understood?"

Volf let out a whistle. He understood well enough; he just didn't much like it.

"Barami, come here and I'll show you how to hook the packs." Hildr and Barami moved off.

Those two had been huddled close all morning, talking. Volf hadn't minded, it meant he'd had time to talk to Caerwyn. Though in truth, she hadn't been that chatty.

Even now, she was looking out over the hills to the south,

a great vista with everything laid before them. A distant look was in her eyes.

He guessed what was bothering her. "You're worried about Jais?"

She nodded wordless.

He sighed. Perhaps he'd have to accept that there was another man on her mind.

"About that... that kiss yesterday," he began slowly.

She turned, those dark brown eyes focusing on him. "It was nice," she said smiling. She looked away again and sighed heavily. "I think it's time I told you something."

"Oh?" Was this where she told him there was only one man for her and it wasn't him? He'd never experienced it personally, but as someone who crawled through the nights of a city, he'd heard it happen to others, men and women both. He'd wondered what it might feel like and now he knew. His heart constricted, tight. It became just a little hard to breathe.

"Jais is just a friend."

That was not what he'd been expecting.

"I am worried about him, but he is just a friend. In truth I am not looking for any man in my life."

Was that better or worse?

"I've never needed anyone but me. But now I want more. I want a child, Volf, a drahksan child. To be clear, I am not looking for a husband. I've never needed anyone to make me whole, well not a man anyway. I just want a child, and until I met you, Jais was the only one who could give me that."

Oh.

But she didn't want him to help raise it? Why had she brought him along then?

"So why am I here?" he asked softly. "Why did you find me and bring me here?"

She shrugged. "We drahksan need to stick together. We need to help each other. I thought..." Another shrug.

He nodded. "So, you don't need me at all except to possibly help you have a child?"

"You're a very useful man to have around. To say we don't need you—"

"Not *we*," he said being precise. "*You*. You don't need me."

She grimaced and shook her head. "No, sorry."

But she didn't need Jais either.

Could Volf live with that?

He wasn't sure.

She was still the most fascinating woman he'd ever met. To make a child with her would be an honor.

And if he stuck around, perhaps she might change her mind. There was a lot he couldn't predict, but if he was certain she was the woman for him then staying close to her was the only way to find out if she ever might change her mind.

He forced a grin. He wasn't feeling particularly happy, but the prospects for the future weren't all together dim either. "I can appreciate that. And if you wished to have a child with me, I would be willing to help in that way."

"Truly?" She seemed surprised.

He was surprised she was surprised.

"Of course. It would be an honor to help you have a child."

She gave a short laugh. "Jais was a lot more reserved about that. He seemed to think a lot of feelings would get in the way if we just went ahead and did it."

Jais' loss.

"I don't see it that way at all." He shrugged. "You are an amazing woman and if I can help you in any way, I will. You've already done so much for me."

A soft and genuine smile spread onto her face. "Thank you." She stepped over to him and gave him a peck on the cheek. "When this is all over we'll talk about that."

He hoped he hadn't flushed too much at her attention. He cleared his throat and nodded. "I look forward to it." What wasn't there to look forward to?

"You two ready for this?" Barami called over. "Take off your packs. Hildr is across, and I'm sending them over now."

They both removed the packs they carried and handed them over to Barami, who hung them on heavy hooks attached to a rope. This was a separate rope than the one used to move across the rock face. This rope was a couple feet above the other and seemed to be strung around a metal wheel rotating around a spike in the rock wall. Each pack was carefully put on a hook—not wanting to drop it into the water—then the rope was pushed along, turning around the wheel and moving smoothly along the rock face to the far side where Hildr waited.

Even leaning as far out as he dared, Volf couldn't see the other landing on which Hildr must have been. The wall curved just a little and the path of rope and footholds went on for some time before disappearing around the bend.

Perhaps in answer to his unspoken question Barami said, "I don't think Hildr is far around the bend. It didn't take her long to get across. Once the packs are all over, we'll give it a go ourselves. I can go last if you both wish."

"No, I'll go last," Caerwyn said softly, still staring out over the great valley below them.

"Don't wait too long." Even as Barami said this, fat rain drops started to fall. "Remember what Hildr said about rain. We'll want to do this quickly." He turned to Volf. "You first? Or shall I?"

Volf didn't really want to go across at all, but the temptation of the dragon was too much. This close he could feel the call resonating in his soul.

He could be brave if he needed to be. "I'll go first."

That way if I fall in, someone might be able to grab me before I go over that waterfall.

So he wasn't thinking brave thoughts. No one was perfect.

Once Barami gave him the signal, he went to the edge. The rain was still only falling sporadically, but looking back, he could see much darker, thicker clouds quite a bit closer than he'd like.

He reached around the corner and found the rope after groping around for a moment. Making sure he had a solid hold on that he dared to lean out a bit to check where the first foothold was. He saw it and tentatively pushed a foot out until it slid into the hole.

The water rushed by about two feet beneath him, frothing and white.

He leaned out to put his other hand on the rope... and immediately saw a problem.

He'd put his foot in the first foothold, which meant he had no place to put his other foot.

He looked down searching and saw the solution quickly. There were actually two footholds quite near each other. He moved his first foot out to the second hold then could easily move his other foot into the first.

He called back to the others. "Careful. Make sure to put your leading foot into the second spot when you first go out!"

There were shouts back of acknowledgement, but in truth, they probably had no idea what that meant... or wouldn't until they tried it.

He moved slowly.

The rain picked up.

The footholds were placed close together, so he could play it safe and shuffle along one at a time or stretch a little and try two or three if he'd had longer legs. He had no wish to fall into those cold waters and moved slowly, keeping steady and safe. Earlier that day, when they'd stopped for a quick break, down where the stream was just bouncing along the rocks, he'd drunk from its waters. It was frigid. It had been refreshing then, but now he shivered at the thought of falling into those waters, especially as fast as they were here. He'd be over the waterfall before he knew it, still shocked from the cold.

So Barami caught up to him quickly.

Barami yelled to him over the noise of the rushing water. "I hate to tell you to go faster, but this rain is starting to come down."

Indeed, the rain was making the footholds slippery, and the rope slick, but since he'd found it easier to slide his hands along it, that worked for him.

He tried to move faster. Barami remained close behind him.

"Almost there," a voice to his left said, surprising him and making him miss a foothold. Luckily, he had a death grip on the rope and saved himself from falling for the half-a-heartbeat it took him to regain purchase. His pulse raced, thumping in his throat, but he drew in a long breath to regain himself.

Hildr chuckled. "Sorry."

He looked over to find her not ten feet away on a landing. The rock wall curved around onto the landing with the rope and footholds continuing over the landing to make it easier to dismount or get on again.

Seeing the end so near, he found he could move a little faster now.

He was soon hopping off the wall with a heavy sigh of relief. Barami was right after him.

"Where is Caerwyn?" Hildr asked peering down along the wall.

Volf looked back as well and couldn't see her.

Barami grimaced and grumbled. "I think she was waiting for Jais." He shook his head. "I told her not to wait."

The rain was coming in sheets now and Volf could see the water starting to rise. Where it had been a couple feet below the footholds before the storm, now it was eighteen inches, perhaps. It hadn't taken him that long the come across the wall—despite feeling like an eternity—which meant the water was rising fast.

And still Caerwyn was nowhere to be seen.

They were all getting drenched just standing here and his heart began to pound a little harder as his mind ran through scenarios of her slipping from the wall.

Then he blew out a heavy breath as she finally came into view.

She, too, was soaked, her dark hair matted against her head. She seemed to be struggling a little, or perhaps she was just trying to move quickly in the storm. She wasn't following Hildr's instructions to keep three points of contact, going hand over hand as she shuffled her feet along.

Then she slipped.

Her foot slid out from the wall, but her other foot hadn't yet found purchase and one hand was off the rope. She yelped a cry as she fell, one hand clutching the rope, pulling it low. She was in the middle between two anchor points, her feet dipped into the waters. It was a testament to the swift current that her feet were thrown out again, tossed to one side.

She pulled up with her one hand until the other could

grab the rope, then hauled herself up the rest of the way to ensure her feet were placed in holds once again.

There she clung for a long moment, breathing hard.

Volf had nearly leapt into the waters, ready to save her. He didn't know if he would have, but the way his heart had lurched at the sight of her falling made him wonder just how brave, or how stupid he might have been.

Then Caerwyn was moving again and not long later, she was on the landing with them.

"That was fun," she said a little breathless. It was clear she was trying to make light of the accident, but none of them laughed.

"We should move on. It still be some distance to the cave," Hildr said sternly. "The storm makes rockslides much more likely. We should be quick."

Rockslides? "Where do we go from here?" Volf looked around and saw no path.

Hildr pointed up the mountainside.

Far above them was a large cave. They would have to climb part of the mountian to get there. It wasn't as steep as the sheer cliff on the other side of the wall-walk, but it wouldn't be a simple climb either. Ropes were already in place, knotted to help climb in some of the steeper spots, and there were a few landings along the way where they might be able to rest.

Volf sighed. He'd been wondering if things could get worse than that wall-walk.

Now he knew.

25

JAIS' HEART WAS POUNDING. FEAR WAS A LIVING THING FOR HIM now. He'd never been faced with great heights back home. He didn't know if he was terrified of the drop below them because of any innate fear of heights, or just the danger inherent in their current situation.

The ledge itself was running with water and treacherous. They all kept as far from the edge as they could, skirting along the mountainside as they climbed higher on the rocky path. It didn't help that water was sheeting down the mountainside, making it hard to support himself, as his hand slid along the mostly smooth stone. It also meant there was an ever-present little rush of water pushing their feet out toward the edge.

"We should not go on," Elria called back over the high winds and thrashing rains.

"We have to!" Jais shouted up to her. She was leading them. With a glance back to Gosse, the other man nodded. Everyone had gone ahead so far, which meant the crazy drahksan wizard was probably close on the heels of his friends.

He didn't like this any more than Elria did.

They came upon a small cave, not much more than an alcove in the stone, but large enough that the three of them crammed together could get out of the rain for a moment.

Elria turned to him, soaked. Her hair was plastered to her face and covering much of her expression. What Jais did see was at least one stern eye and a frowning mouth. "No farther shall we go, until you tell me everything," Elria said.

As she waited for a response, Elria motioned for him to drop her pack. Once he did, she fished around in it for a moment, coming out with a long piece of twine. She pulled her hair back and tied it.

Now Jais could see both eyes and was certain she wasn't impressed.

How to best say this.

"Gosse is a drahksan like me... at least we're fairly certain of that. One of the abilities of most drahksani is to sense other drahksani. I can't, but he can." This was the tricky part. "That wizard who attacked your village. It seems he was after us, not you. It also seems he was a drahksan, which means Gosse can sense him as well as my friends. They're all up there, heading for the dragon. We need to warn them or help them or something."

Elria had listened intently, eyes darting from Jais to Gosse and back. They narrowed as they settled on Gosse. "Where did you come from?"

Gosse looked to Jais. His gaze said it all: 'should I tell her?'

Jais sighed. "It's a long story that we don't have time for now. We need to catch up to the others and help them."

She nodded to that. "I will get the full story from you at some point." It wasn't a question.

"Yes, I promise."

"Good." She shook out some tension then moved close to

Jais and kissed him quickly. "For luck. This next bit gets a little tricky," she said by way of explaining her actions. She didn't smile. In fact, she seemed a bit grim. She nodded to herself then stepped back out into the rain.

Jais followed.

She spoke—raising her voice in the torrential rain—as she moved carefully up the path.

"Ahead there be a river. It be probably quite swollen by now. We need to move next to it. It be very precarious. I will need your full attention to walk you through it."

She went on to explain some odd path along a wall, which Jais didn't quite understand. He got only that it would be hard with the storm and was very dangerous. He hoped it would make more sense when he saw it.

It was hard to tell where the path ended and the river began. The raging waters burst from the narrow crack in the mountain and spilled over the ledge before cascading down in a wide waterfall. It was clear that the water swirling around their feet would only get deeper and more forceful as they reached that crevice so they all stayed as close to the mountain's wall as they could.

Jais' feet were soaked, his boots now just vessels for water. He assumed it was the same for the other two. Despite being summer, the waters were cold, and his teeth were chattering before he reached the river.

"There be a rope, just around the corner." Elria was having to yell to be heard over the storm's winds and the rivers rushing roar.

She turned herself so she was face first into the rock, then edged to the corner and reached around once she could bend her elbow.

The waters swirling around her feet were nearly as high

as her tall boots, mid-calf. The push of the river must have been too much. Her feet were swept out from under her.

Jais was quick and caught her one arm. The other still seemed to be holding something around the corner. She regained her footing but didn't let go of Jais' arm.

Her eyes were a little wide as she gulped in air. "Thank you!"

He couldn't tell, but he thought there were tears in her eyes. There was too much water everywhere to be certain. She was breathing hard though and took a moment to recover before going on.

"You will have to push your feet against the river. It won't be easy. Trust the rope and your hands. Hold tight because the river will be trying to push your feet from under you." She took a moment to simply breathe before going on. "Usually we'd send our packs across separately, but we don't have time. We'll just have to go along with them." Her eyes met Jais' and there was something desperate and dire in her gaze. She couldn't lower her voice that much and still be heard, but she managed. "I think I love you, Jais. So, don't die on me, please."

His heart lurched at those words.

In the heat of the moment, as uncertain as he might have been, he could only reply with. "I love you too, Elria."

She nodded with a quick, faint smile then was edging toward the corner once again. Jais moved with her, still holding her other arm.

She moved one foot around the corner, the river doing its best to try and push it back. Finally, she nodded. "I need you to let my arm go now. Follow quickly."

Jais nodded as he released her.

Then she was gone around the corner, and it was Jais' turn to face the wall and search for the rope.

His fingers touched something but slipped off. He tried again, and his hand curled around a thick rope.

He barely heard her shout. She sounded distant over the cacophony of water around him. "Move your foot out, feel for a gap in the rock. Then move that same foot along to the next one, it be close. Then swing around."

He did as instructed, finding one notch, then a second one. He glanced at Gosse and nodded before slipping around into the river. The water swirled around his knees here.

Despite having sounded far away, Elria hadn't gone far at all. She'd been waiting for them. He moved over a couple notches toward her, gripping the rope hard, making room for Gosse.

But as he turned to her to smile and reassure her he was safe he saw a great surge of water rolling down the river to them. He hurried to her, placing his hand over hers to make sure she was secure as it hit them.

She stayed where she was.

He didn't.

Only one of his feet had found a foothold in his rush to close the gap between him and Elria. When the surge hit him, he was pulled off the wall. His hand on hers wasn't a solid hold and it slipped off first, his other came away with the force of his body being turned in the river.

Then there was only the shock of icy water over his head. Spun around, he didn't know which way was up. He flailed wildly to find a rock or something to hold to keep himself from plunging over that waterfall.

Then his hand hit something, a death grip on his arm. He was pulled from the waters and half tossed back onto the ledge, sliding down but not out or off.

Whatever had caught him still held him and after the shock of his icy trip wore off, he looked up to see Gosse's hand clutching his arm. The man was half around the corner and half braced against the rock holding Jais. The look on his face was frantic.

"You alive?" It was a silly question in most circumstances, but much appreciated now.

Jais nodded.

"I got him!" Gosse yelled back in the other direction. "Keep going, we'll catch up!"

There was a response, he could hear the sound, but not the words.

Gosse's reply was simply, "Go!" Then he turned back to Jais. "You ready to try again?"

Jais nodded.

However, a problem became quickly apparent.

He was too cold.

He'd been shivering before, but after his ice water bath, he was trembling violently. The rain was cold, but the river was frigid. He could hardly stand, he felt so weak. The first time he tried to grab the rope he couldn't make his fingers wrap around it.

"I can't," he yelled to Gosse and slid back around the corner.

He sat down and shook violently, teeth chattering. Tears mingled with the rain on his face.

Gosse yelled around the corner for a moment then returned to him.

"Come on, big guy!" the man said, picking him up and helping him back down along the ledge.

They found that same cave where they'd stopped on the way up and huddled together.

"We'll wait for the rain to pass then try again," Gosse said.

Jais could only nod. He couldn't form words with the chattering of his teeth.

There wasn't room for a fire, so they waited, cold and miserable.

Jais could only pray Elria made it through.

But with that fire-crazed wizard and his vicious bodyguard, he feared what awaited her on the other side.

26

THEY'D BEEN MOVING THROUGH THE CAVE FOR SOME TIME NOW, and Caerwyn's clothes were nearly dry. It had been a grueling day. After the wall-walk had come a steep uphill climb, sometimes using knotted ropes, anchored and left behind by previous Dronnegir who'd blazed this harsh trail. Hildr, always amazing in her capabilities, had climbed up free-hand to help speed along their ascent.

The storm had been lessening somewhat by then. All in all, it hadn't lasted that long, but it had been intense.

She still wondered what had happened to Jais. If he had come after them, she hoped he'd waited until the storm passed to attempt the wall-walk.

She'd been sure she was going to die when she'd slipped off the wall. Of all the most terrifying moments in her life, that ranked up there with the worst.

But they were safe now.

Once within the cave, they'd brought out lanterns and lit them. Everyone had one as the cave floor, though mostly flat, was still not entirely level with many catches and bumps.

Caerwyn kept one eye on the ground ahead of her and the other on Hildr, who led the way.

The cave was wide, and they didn't have to walk single file, so Volf walked next to her. He'd seemed different since their conversation on the mountainside. If anything, he was more attentive, yet without being intrusive.

Barami walked ahead with Hildr, which had become a thing with them now. They chatted in low tones as they walked, occasionally laughing or gasping at something the other said.

Caerwyn felt a bit of a loss watching Barami find someone. She shouldn't be upset. She'd been pushing him away for years, knowing how he felt about her. She was glad he'd found someone. But now that he had, Caerwyn was losing something as well. She'd seen it often enough growing up. Friends would find lovers or mates and suddenly had less time for their friends. She was mourning their deep friendship, even though it was far from over.

The question that plagued her was simple: what if Barami chose to stay with Hildr and not continue with Caerwyn when she left? It seemed likely. She wasn't sure what she'd do in that instance. She'd soldier on, as she always did. No man would ever define her and eventually all her male friends would probably find someone and leave her.

Suddenly she felt very alone. She'd been walking in silence for too long.

"Tell me about yourself," she said to Volf. "What was it like growing up in Cold River?"

"I've already told you all the interesting bits." He had gone over much of his life on the way up north, seeming quite happy to have someone to talk to.

"Then tell me the not interesting bits."

He laughed. "Well, I spent most nights on the roofs of the town."

"That's fairly interesting."

"Perhaps, but all I was doing was watching and listening. I wanted to know how others lived. What a normal life was. I came to have certain families I'd watch over. There was the smith's family living over the forge. They had three sons and one daughter. The smith, Nyordin by name, wanted his sons to take over the forge after him, but they each had their own ambitions. One left to be a traveling minstrel. Another joined the Forest Walkers—"

"What are they?"

"The Forest Walkers? They are the protectors of Cold River and the surrounding area. They patrol the lands like the Dronnegir patrol their lands and keep wild men and wild beasts out."

"Oh."

"The third son learned a little smithing but was always more interested in the horses that came through for shoeing and eventually became a teamster. I think he even went on to become a horse merchant."

"So, the smith was left alone? No one took over his forge?" That resonated a little too deeply with her at the moment.

Volf Laughed. "No, you forget there was another child. And you, better than most, should know a woman does not have to be demure and soft."

"The daughter? She took over the forge?"

"Indeed she did, and is a darned good smith to hear her father boast of her in the pub."

Caerwyn had to laugh a little. "I'm glad. Does she like doing it, or does she do it only because there was no one else?"

Volf drew in a long breath. "I think she always wanted to

do what her brothers were doing, and when she saw that they were going elsewhere she seized that opportunity. I believe she is quite happy. Though in recent years there's been some trouble."

"Oh?"

"She has grown quite strong and stout. Her mother worries that she won't find a husband."

"Does she need one?"

Volf sighed. "The daughter wants one. She wants a family... children... and..." He gave Caerwyn an odd look.

She understood his hesitancy. "You don't need to be afraid to talk about such things with me. I know I am odd in my desires." She gave him a warm smile to help hide her own insecurities.

"Well then, yes, she does want a husband and children. She'll need someone to take over the forge from her when she grows old."

"But she's too manly?"

"Or so everyone thought. But just earlier this year, her brother—the one in the Forest Walkers—brought home a friend from a village to the east. He was a large man and looking for a large woman apparently. He and the daughter are now courting."

"That seems like an ideal match."

"Oh, why do you think so?"

Caerwyn shrugged. "He will be away much of the time guarding the villages and she will be left to her work. They can have a few children but otherwise keep to themselves."

Volf hedged a little. "That may sound ideal to you, but to others it sounds lonely. I do not know what will happen with that smith's daughter and her new beau, but I think perhaps they may want to see more of each other than that."

"Oh." She shrugged again. It just showed how much she

didn't really know or understand other women, or men, or anyone really.

They walked in silence for some time.

Thoughts bounced around in her head until she felt compelled to speak them. "I wonder if my upbringing is causing my desire to be alone and independent." She'd never discussed this with anyone before—never one to delve into her emotions too deeply.

"Oh?" Volf prompted.

"Well I was raised in a prince's house. I had many people around me, but no one really on my level. The prince had no other sons or daughters—he was a widower and never remarried—that's why he'd adopted me. But I was always enough for him, and he enough for me." She shrugged. "I never needed anyone else and it came to the point where I didn't want anyone else, not in that way anyway." She laughed. "I only grudgingly accepted Barami as a friend because he stuck to my side and would never leave. I saved his life, had I mentioned that?"

"I think I'd heard it somewhere."

She smiled at the memory, despite it having been a horrible day. It was long ago, and she had a different view on it now. "He and his unit were escorting me to a meeting in Uluantu with some Chieftains who wished for imperial support in dealing with some Imbuti rebels. On the way there, those same rebels attacked us. They thought to kill a princess. They had been quite surprised to find out I wasn't some soft royal; that I could fight." She sighed. "Still, most of my men were killed, outnumbered two to one. When I could see that we were falling, failing, with only a few remaining, I charged into the enemy ranks." She shook her head slowly. "They did not expect that, and it gave me an edge. I knew then we could win. Yet even as I did, I saw a raider sneaking up behind Barami. With one throw of Davlas I slew the raider just as he struck. Barami took only a glancing blow instead of a fatal one. After that, we finished off the foes together."

"Davlas? What is that?"

Another sigh. "That was a magical weapon. A spear. Davlas was its name and when I called it, it would appear in my hand. It always flew true and never failed me."

"Where is it now?"

"It was broken by a krolloc."

"A krolloc? Those are only myths are they not?"

"They most certainly are not. Jais, Barami, and I fought one not much more than a month ago. We defeated it, barely, but it destroyed Davlas." She felt a little odd hearing the intense loss in her voice. She really did miss that spear, but it was just a thing.

"It sounds like that weapon meant a lot to you."

"It did. It was a gift from my father." That's what it was. Not the thing itself, but what it had meant to her... that's what she'd lost.

"Ah," Volf said, then a moment later, his voice changed dramatically when he breathed a quiet, "Oh!"

She looked at him, but he was looking ahead of them.

She followed his gaze, and her eyes went as wide as his as she too let out her own breathy, "My gods!"

They had come to the dragon.

27

Volf couldn't take his eyes from the majestic beast ahead of him.

It lay in a massive cave, so large he couldn't see the far walls and so tall Volf could see no top, only darkness. The grand surroundings did nothing to minimize the magnificence of the dragon itself. It was curled around itself but still took up an area forty to fifty feet across. He had no clue how large it might be when stretched out, but he guessed several hundred feet given the long serpentine neck and tail. The wings were folded away, but they too seemed massive. He'd seen a great eagle once with a wingspan of perhaps five or six feet. Its body was so much smaller than those great wings. He had to assume that wings would scale with size meaning if this creature was several hundred feet long then its wings would be probably double or triple that. Yet it wasn't really the creature's size—at least not that alone—that astounded him.

First, there was its glow. He'd thought it a trick of the lantern light, but as he stared at it, he could tell that the cave was being dimly lit by the dragon itself. The scales were an odd shade of rusty red-gold, but luminescent and somehow still vibrant.

Then there was the heat. He'd been cold since the rain had started and the cave itself had been chilly, but now, as he inched closer, he felt a warmth radiating off the beast along with the light. But more than the heat itself was a strange warm feeling inside him. Once, in his youth, he'd heard tales of the dragons of old and how they could inspire a wide array of emotions from awe and peace to fear and submission all depending on how the dragon itself was feeling. For the longest time—in ages past—dragons were the rulers of human-kind and now he could understand why. He would easily submit to such a creature, quite willingly.

He realized now that the odd feeling in his gut, the pull he'd felt to come here, was that same sense of emotional inspiration but at a much more primal level.

Last, though in many ways mixed in with everything else, was the sheer feeling of power that the dragon gave off. Perhaps it was just some mixture of the light and warmth and emotional pull, but Volf couldn't help but feel small and insignificant compared to this creature. More than just its size it felt like it was... on another level of creation. It wasn't a god, but it wasn't a mortal like him either. It was somewhere in between and still far above the comprehension and control of humanity.

"Oh," he said again quietly. "Wow." No other words seemed appropriate.

"It be amazing, yes?" Hildr said and though she'd seen it before there was still a level of awe in her voice equal to what Volf felt.

"Gods," Barami breathed.

"They were the mounts of the gods," Hildr said evenly. "This be as close as you will probably ever get to a god."

Now Volf understood why the Dronnegir referred to the dragon as a 'divine being,' He also understood why they would have devoted their lives—generations of lives—to it. He was quite willing to do so now.

"Set up camp here," Hildr said indicating a level spot of the cave. "There is a ritual I must perform to wake it. It will take some time."

Volf had to work to tear his gaze away from the dragon and even as he helped Caerwyn and Barami set up a simple camp he—and they—kept turning to gaze at it for long periods. It wasn't a choice really, the creature demanded attention even in this dormant state.

They did not speak loudly, that would defile this place, but communicated in hushed voices.

Once the camp was set, they waited and watched as Hildr performed a sort of dance, murmuring to herself in her tongue. It was mesmerizing to watch, but still not as entrancing as the dragon itself.

When she finished she stepped over to them and seemed rather fatigued.

It had been a long day, but Volf no longer felt that sense of tiredness. Being near the dragon energized him.

Then the dragon began to move and Volf's heart nearly stopped.

It was a slow process. First one wing unfolded and stretched out. It was indeed long and massive, straining upwards several hundred feet. The glow from the wing illuminated the shadowed area above the dragon. This cavern seemed to be a wide cylindrical space within the mountain and even once the wing was fully extended, Volf still couldn't see the top. One of the immediate things he noticed about the wing itself was its poor condition. The leathery flaps, stretched between sinews, were full of holes, large and small, like moth-eaten cloth. Volf wondered if a wing in such a state would still be able to make the creature fly?

After the wing came the head and tail, uncurling from the mound of scales. The head had been partially covered by a wing when he'd first arrived and seeing it now caused him to forget to breathe for several long moments. As large as a small house, it was blocky yet smooth.

He'd seen drawings of what people thought dragons looked like and they were usually covered in horns and spikes. This one had none of that, only smooth scales. The back of the head was roughly a large cube with the eyes set into the front and leathery flaps for ears at the back. In front of that was the snout, boxy and long with several long teeth protruding from the top jaw to hang out next to the lower jaw as it tapered near the end. Thin tendrils of smoke drifted up from its massive nostrils as if they were the chimneys for some inner fire. Here again Volf could see scales missing, leaving gaps with discolored areas beneath.

It stretched out its long neck, weaving from side to side as if working out kinks from its long sleep.

The tail was so incredibly long, even longer than Volf had imagined. It tapered slowly with a great diamond-shaped tip, which not only looked like it could cause great damage but was currently doing so. The tail had also been stretched out and, as it swayed from side to side, the tip carved lines into the stone walls like they were butter.

Then the dragon began to lever itself up onto its legs, but here it seemed to have some trouble. It took several attempts to get its feet under it and stand.

More and more Volf was seeing the effects of its probably vastly long life on this being. Apart from the missing scales and the physical anomalies, it moved like an old person, slow and deliberate. Great creaks of ancient bones echoed through the cave

But despite the signs of its ancient heritage, once it was standing, unfurling the other wing, Volf was still stupefied for several long moments gazing at it. It let out a long bellowing roar that shook the mountain, causing dust and small rocks to tremble loose and fall around them.

Then, with a final couple head stretches—which cracked some bones in its neck, sending shudders down Volf's spine —it looked down at them.

"Your dance is beautiful young one," it said, and the sound reverberated through the cavern and even within him.

Hildr bowed low to the beast. "Your praise be gracious, divine one."

"Is it time for yet another generation to be blessed?" the dragon asked. "It doesn't seem like it's been that long?"

"No, divine one. But I bring travelers from far lands who have sought out your wisdom and guidance. They are drahk-sani, but many of the drahksani have been killed, hunted during the great purge many years ago, so they have no fami-lies or others to guide them. They felt your presence here and hoped to speak with you." She hesitated only a moment before continuing her tone a bit repentant. "We have failed to keep your secret from them. The Dronnegir apologize for this intrusion."

The dragon's gaze swung up to look at Volf and the others.

Volf swallowed hard under that fiery glance. The dragon's eyes burned with an inner fire, glowing red like metal fresh from a forge, much more so than the ever-present glow from its body.

"Drahksan." It said the word as if recalling some distant memory. "Hunted?" It shook its head and seemed to deflate a little in what seemed like the dragon equivalent of a sigh.

"Why would humans hunt their protectors?" It shook its head again. "Such short memories." Then it focused on Volf and Caerwyn again. "How may I help you, my children?"

It was Caerwyn who spoke first, perhaps recovering a little quicker from her shock. "Hello great one," she began, her voice strong. Volf didn't think his would be. "We seek only knowledge of who and what we are. Much has been lost over time, and if drahksani were meant to be the protectors of humanity, then we have all lost our way. So many have died that those of us who remain hardly know what we can do, or how to do it. There were none to teach us. We are lost and hoped you might guide us, provide us with your wisdom and knowledge."

The dragon peered at her for a long time. Volf wasn't sure how she endured it. He'd be shrinking away from such a gaze.

Then the dragon did turn its attention his way and he felt it connect with him in a way it was hard to explain or even fully understand. The dragon was a part of him. It knew him explicitly; every shadowed corner of his soul was exposed. Yet unlike the truth-medallion the Dronnegir had used on him, this was more like a warmth that filled him, driving out the shadows. He didn't scream, and he didn't flinch, because he couldn't. At that moment, he wasn't in control of himself.

Then the gaze left him and with it went the intensity of the dragon's being within him.

"Oh," he breathed out quietly.

"I can see the truth of your words. Your lives have been hard. I shall tell you what I know and what I can see." It let out a great gust of a breath, sulfuric and hot. Smoke billowed out from its mouth and dissipated as it ascended up the great shaft of the cave.

"Caerwyn, approach. It will be easier to do this through touch. Words are always a clumsy medium."

It knew her name.

Of course it would. If it had looked into her the same way it had into him—and he guessed it had—it would know her name as well as so much more.

Caerwyn strode forward, unafraid. She stopped directly under the head of the gigantic beast. It lowered its great head slowly until the tip of its snout touched her forehead. It was there only an instant before drawing back.

Caerwyn staggered as if struck before catching herself and drawing several long, deep breaths. Even as she recovered, the dragon spoke again. "For your loss I grant you this boon."

The dragon moved one leg—thicker than any tree-trunk Volf had ever seen—forward. A claw the length of a man emerged to cut a trough into the stone. The dragon then backed up and lowered its head to that trough and breathed out a gust of fire. The short burst of flame roared through the cave then was gone. When the smoke cleared, what remained was a glowing line in the stone trough it had carved. "For you. It is safe to take it now."

Caerwyn looked oddly at the item. Volf couldn't see more than the glow it let off. She stepped forward and picked it up.

It was a spear, and she gasped as she touched it. Volf thought this might be because it was still glowing hot, but she didn't drop it reflexively, so perhaps not. After a long moment, Caerwyn nodded and moved away. She came out from under the dragon and turned again to meet its gaze.

"Thank you... thank you. There are no words."

The dragon nodded. "I know, my daughter. Take these gifts and may your life be a blessing to all creatures of this world. That is all the thanks I ask."

She nodded and retreated back. Once she got to their

little camp she sat with the spear in her lap and simply stared at it for a long time.

If she did much else, Volf missed it as the dragon then called him forward.

He was terrified, yet somehow also at peace. The feeling from the dragon was one of calm awe. Yet still it was so massive he couldn't help but be afraid.

He stepped up before it and closed his eyes. He didn't want to see that massive head descending toward him.

He felt it.

Odd for something so large, but it came as no more than a brush against his skin, the sulfuric smell that clung to it rolling over him for a moment before it too was gone.

But he wasn't thinking about the smell.

No, his mind was whirling with revelations.

CAERWYN NEEDED TIME TO PROCESS EVERYTHING SHE HAD JUST learned. That one touch from the dragon had conveyed so much information, her mind was still reeling to catch up and assimilate it all.

First and foremost, was a detailed inventory of her abilities. Yet it would take some time still to fully understand how to use some of them. She was physically strong and tough, that wasn't anything new, but the power to surge her strength and endurance... that was. She felt like perhaps she'd done this before without knowing what she was doing. Now she knew how, and what it would cost her—fatigue and lethargy that would follow. She had known of her enhanced senses, hearing and sight beyond human levels. Yet she hadn't known just how intense they were: she could hunt by scent alone, isolate sounds thousands of feet away, or focus on a single point to see details at a similar distance. Even the ability to—in a way—see in the dark by having her own voice echo back to her to tell where walls were, to the point of knowing all details of the enshrouded space. The most astonishing ability of all, was her ability to simply ignore and make herself immune to the magic of others. It was something she could use at will and she knew with a certainty she'd used it in the past. A specific memory came to her of fighting the krolloc and it trying to pick her up with its magic and not being able to. She was glad she'd be able to turn it off though, otherwise Jais' healing wouldn't have affected her.

All of this would take time to integrate and master.

The second most fascinating thing that had come with the dragon's touch—what might have been just a whim for the creature—was a detailed knowledge of the creation and history of the drahksani. This, even more so than her knowledge of her new abilities, would take a lot of time to understand and fully comprehend.

Dragons had sacrificed themselves. She knew now that dragons didn't reproduce in any normal sense. They ended their existence to create an egg. This egg usually held only a single dragon within which would have all the memories of its predecessor. It was a rebirth of sorts, which kept them effectively immortal. They could produce two or more dragons in an egg, and each would have the memories of the parent, but each would be lesser in some degree, the total power of all within the egg would never be greater than the one who died to create them. To create the drahksani, dragons had died and instead of creating dragons within their eggs, they'd created this new race instead. Usually dozens or more at a time—each powerful, carrying a fraction of a dragon's power within them.

The drahksani had been created at the end of the age of dragons when the great beasts were fading from the realm and they wished to leave something of themselves behind to help and protect humanity. There was more, so much more, but that's what had sunk in first, and it was wondrous to know.

Finally, the dragon had somehow imparted knowledge of her own specific bloodline. She could trace it back, well over a hundred generations, to the first of her line. She didn't care about that so much as the knowledge of her parents. She knew them now as if she'd lived with them their whole lives. She had a permanent picture of her mother's smile and her father's piercing blue eyes. She knew what they had been able to do and who they had been, their likes and dislikes, their quirks and habits. This more than anything, as important as it all was, affected her the most. She was meeting her parents for the first time, truly getting to know them, and it was bringing up emotions she'd locked away for so very long. Tears cascaded from her eyes, over her cheeks and around a sad smile.

Then there was the dragon's gift: Davlas remade... but so much more than her other spear had been. It had the same name and qualities: unerring accuracy at incredible distances and would return to her when she called its name. But this one was unbreakable, forged of dragon's breath, the purest and rarest of magic. She didn't even have to hold it to throw it. It would float on its own, and she could control it with a thought, recalling it without saying a word. It was more than she could have ever asked for.

"And you, human, do you wish for anything from me?"

Caerwyn looked up to see the dragon addressing Barami.

Volf was staggering away from the beast carrying something she couldn't see cradled in the palm of his hand. If his experience had been anything like hers, he'd need some time to take it all in.

Barami stepped forward. "I require nothing from your greatness. I am here only as a friend of these drahksani and seek nothing in return.

"You ask for nothing, but I shall give you something still. Lay your sword on the ground before you."

Barami, probably thinking it best not to upset or refuse the gift of a dragon, took out his large sword and laid it down.

The dragon moved forward a bit and lowered its head, breathing on the blade of the weapon. Once done, it drew back. "Your blade will never falter, never break nor dull. Use it wisely, great warrior."

"I will, my thanks are eternal." Barami bowed.

"And I know you seek nothing from me, my child," the dragon said to Hildr. "Yet I sense something new within you and will give you this one additional boon. Come to me."

She stepped forward, seeming surprised. The dragon did as it had done with Caerwyn—and she was guessing with Volf though she hadn't seen it—and touched her head with its snout. Hildr drew away a little confused. She said nothing but her furrowed brow spoke volumes. Either she had no clue what the dragon had done, or it had thoroughly baffled her.

"Thank you," she said backing away.

"May your life be bountiful and long," the dragon said. It let out a great gust of smoky air and seemed to shrink a little, losing some of its luster. The one odd thing about the dragon that Caerwyn's mind had trouble reconciling was the intense sense of power it gave off versus the great feeling of age and wear. The more she looked at it the more she saw past the aura of power to all the missing scales and the slow movements. She had to wonder how old this dragon was. Supposedly, the age of dragons had been... well, she knew now. From the knowledge the dragon had given her, she could discern that it had been a hundred centuries since dragons had ruled this world. That was along life.

"I grow weary," the dragon said its voice losing some of its presence. It began to sit and settle and curl back in on itself. "I must save some energy for the next generation of your people."

It was settled not long later, and the smooth even movements of its torso suggested it had fallen asleep quickly.

Hildr was joining them. Her voice was a little sad and lost when she spoke. "We have been thinking for some time now that the dragon may not live much longer." She sat folding her legs under her. "The past three generations who have come have all noted how it wanes and grows weary a little sooner each time." A heavy sigh. "I and my father believe its next generation of boons will be its last."

Caerwyn's heart broke a little at such news. It was impossible to believe that a creature of such power could die, and yet it seemed so very likely.

"I'm sorry," was all she could think to say. She had to wonder: if she hadn't come, if it hadn't helped her, would it have lasted still another generation for the Dronnegir?

Volf sat nearby. He was looking at something on his hand, a ring?

"Is that your gift?" Caerwyn asked. She had to ask again before he realized the question was for him.

"Yes. And I learned... so much."

She nodded, understanding the wonder and awe she saw on his face.

"What a magnificent beast!" This voice was new and unknown to Caerwyn. "It shall be mine!" The words and tone were arrogant and incongruent with the peace and power of this place.

She should have reacted faster, but she was still too consumed with the gifts of the dragon to move quickly.

Barami let out a grunt.

Caerwyn turned to see the man being held by...

Her eyes went wide, and she suddenly knew what was happening. The odd thing was, she'd known there were drahksani following her. Somewhere in her mind, she'd registered feeling their presence, but this entire trip that sense had been overwhelmed by the sense of the dragon ahead of her.

She'd ignored the little warning within her and now it was too late.

Of the band of men she'd seen with Gosse, she knew now that two of them were drahksani. Barami had told her of a wizard—a tall lean man—and a brute who'd tossed Jais around like he was nothing. She guessed it was the wizard who stepped around a column of stone. He held no weapon but radiated a sense of power not unlike that of the dragon. The brute was the one holding Barami in a constricting grip.

The large man had one long arm wrapped around Barami pinning the Southern warrior's arms to his side. The other hand clutched him under the jaw, around his neck. Barami's eyes were bulging from lack of air as he struggled to be free.

"If you wish your friend to live, you will surrender yourselves to me now," the wizard said in a soft sneering tone. "I have a proposition for the drahksani among you."

29

VOLF ACTED TOO LATE TO DO ANYTHING USEFUL.

So, he did what he'd always done when threatened. He slipped into his shadow-form—the true name of what he had called his shadow-self—and vanished.

A tap on the smooth, round, glowing red jewel in his new ring and he'd make no sound as well as he ran from the threat and abandoned everyone. There was more the ring could do, but he'd not had time to assimilate all its powers.

He hated himself for leaving.

He was working so hard to show Caerwyn he was a man worthy of her, and here he was running from a fight. She would never run, he was certain of that.

Even though he still didn't fully understand everything the dragon had shown him, nor did he fully understand the powers within the ring he'd been gifted, he seemed to be able to use some without too much work.

He wrapped his shadow-form around him tighter as he ran and the world around him blurred. This was 'shadow-walking,' He'd learned of this new ability from the dragon.

He'd be able to traverse more distance now than he would if he'd been running normally. It was all still new, and he wasn't even sure how he was doing what he was doing. Perhaps, once he had time to take in everything the dragon had shown him, it would all fall into place, but for now, he was just glad it worked.

It had taken them some time to walk from the entrance to the cave to where the dragon lay, but he traversed that distance in a matter of minutes.

There he stopped and dropped his shadow-form.

The storm had passed, and the sky was clearing. It was still day, but the peaks around him were so high that the sun was already well behind them, casting long shadows. He tried to catch his breath and recover himself.

Looking back into the cave, he sent his senses out. This was another new ability—or perhaps one he'd always had but never knew of. He cast his awareness back into the dragon's cave and was able to see and hear what was happening in that place without being anywhere near it. Again, the how of what he was doing eluded him, but he was aware that it was easier to do this to a place he knew well or had been recently.

Sight came first, and he saw that the situation hadn't changed much in the short time since he'd left. It looked like Caerwyn and Hildr had surrendered themselves, their weapons piled in one spot as they stood together, a little distance from the other two men. Barami was still held, but he didn't look like his life was in danger anymore. The tall, thin man was talking.

Volf's hearing came a moment later.

"...with me and we can crush the scum of humanity under our heels!" The lean man lifted a hand and clenched it into a fist. "They do not deserve our help! They are the ones who befouled our kind to create those who would hunt us.

They are the ones who destroyed us in the great wars! Humanity sought dominance and caught us unawares, but we can take back our power and be the dominators! We will rule this world!" Spittle flew from the man's mouth with the vigor of his words.

"I will never join with you," Caerwyn said defiant and brash.

That's how Volf should have been instead of fleeing.

"You are in no position to refuse me. You will come willingly, or you will come unwillingly, but either way, you're coming with me." The man sneered, and Volf felt a strong urge the punch the look off the man's face.

"How will you control me?"

The man laughed. "For now, I simply have to threaten this one." He nodded his head toward his companion holding Barami. The massive man gripped Barami's throat once again and began choking him. "Shall I have Gerhardt kill him slowly? No, killing him would only incite your rage. But I can have him cause great harm and pain to your friend." He turned back to Gerhardt. "Stop. Pull an arm out of its socket to start."

"No!" Caerwyn said taking a step forward, but a look from the wizard caused her to stop.

"Do you not wish him harmed?"

"No, please."

The wizard stalked over to her, standing before her unafraid, taller than her by a head he glared down at her. "I shall keep him in one piece for now. But you must see that I am in control. What I do now can be undone. But if you question me further, other things might happen to your friend... which cannot be undone." He tore his gaze from Caerwyn and nodded to Gerhardt.

The big man kept his hand on Barami's throat but

released the arm around the other man's torso. He lifted Barami by his throat rather easily as if the aged warrior were nothing but a doll. Then he wrapped a meaty hand around one of Barami's arms and gave a slight, quick tug.

Barami's face contorted in pain and he probably would have screamed if his air had not been restricted. Caerwyn and Hildr gave twin cries of alarm.

Gerhardt brought the other man back in toward him and wrapped his arm tightly around Barami once more, releasing his throat. Barami gasped and panted with pain.

The lean one turned back to Caerwyn. "Do you understand now? Are you willing to comply?"

Despite the defiance clear on her face she nodded. She apparently couldn't bring herself to say the words.

"Say it!"

"I comply!" Caerwyn shouted harshly.

The man smiled viciously. "Good. Now it is time for my —" He cocked his head to one side. "Hold!" He called sharply reaching out a hand in a grasping motion. The lean man then stalked away from Caerwyn. Volf's magical vision followed him until Elria came into view.

"No!" Volf found himself breathing the word.

He must have run right past her and not noticed.

Gods! How many had he doomed with his cowardice?

Elria was frozen in mid-step as she'd crept around a rock pillar. Her eyes were wide with surprise as the lean man came into view. She looked like she wanted to move but couldn't. Volf guessed from the tall drahksan's grasping motion, the man had done something to hold her in place.

"What do we have here? Another human who thinks she can threaten her superiors? That will not do. Gerhardt!"

The large man lumbered into view a moment later.

"Take her."

Gerhardt nodded and put his free hand under one of her slightly outstretched arms and picked her up. Elria remained in her pose, stuck as the brute carried her to the other two women.

The lean one laughed. "Now, my young drahksan acolyte, I give you a choice."

Volf couldn't watch anymore and withdrew his extended awareness.

He drew in a sharp breath as he blinked and looked around him to recall where he was.

He had to find help.

Looking out of the cave and down the mountainside he nearly cried with relief.

Two shapes were clambering up from the river landing far below.

———

"Who shall live?" the wizard said with a curling grin, making Cearwyn's skin crawl. "Pick one of these two humans. They shall die gloriously for our cause. The other can remain alive, for now."

"I could never!" Caerwyn had no words for this man's vileness. It made her sick, but what made her even more ill was her own inability.

Her heart was pounding. This was all too much too fast. She still hadn't had time to clear her mind of the dragon's gifts and was reacting too slowly.

Volf had vanished, but she didn't know what that meant. Was he trying to help, or had he fled? She didn't know and couldn't count on him. She just didn't know him well enough to have any sense for what he was doing. Barami she could count on, but he was injured and restrained.

Hildr was giving her a stern look. Caerwyn got the meaning clearly enough: 'let's fight,' But she couldn't, not while Barami was at the whim of that brute of a man. She locked gazes with Hildr and then flicked her eyes off to Barami. Hopefully, the other woman got the hint. If they were going to do anything, freeing him would have to be a part of it. Hildr followed her gaze discreetly and gave a nearly imperceptible nod.

She'd rather fight than be this man's puppet. Barami would understand that.

Elria wouldn't be able to help. Gerhardt had set her down near the wizard and she still seemed frozen. It was just Hildr and herself against these two vicious men.

She screamed and with three quick steps reached the wizard, punching him hard in the face as he stared at her, stunned. Then she dove for her new spear... remembering only now she didn't need to hold it to control it. She came up ready and glanced at Hildr who was trying to tear that brute's arms away from Barami and free him but having no luck. She was having to dodge his other heavy fist as he swung lazily at her.

Caerwyn flung the spear at the brute's head.

It would have hit.

"Halt!" The wizard's command echoed around the chamber. Caerwyn wasn't quite sure what he'd done, but the spear wasn't moving. It hovered a hair's breadth away from the brute, quivering.

She tried to push it onward with her mental control, but such control was still new to her. She was able to push it forward, but only after the brute had moved out of its path.

"Stop or she dies!"

Caerwyn glanced at the wizard who now held Elria, knife to her throat. The woman's eyes were darting about, but seemed the only part of her able to move.

Shades and Shadows!

She let Davlas drop to the floor with a mental command. Better it stayed near the enemies just in case.

"Gerhardt, stop playing!"

Caerwyn heard a muffled scream and turned to see the brute with a hand over Hildr's face, grasping her skull like it was some child's ball.

"Last chance, drahksan!" the wizard called out. "Either you surrender now and choose one of these women to die, or they both die, and I'll let Gerhardt tear your friend apart... slowly! What will it be?"

She was outmatched. She had one weapon and could probably take out one of the two men, but not both, not fast enough to avoid someone dying.

Years of experience as a warrior, a general, a leader, meant Caerwyn could easily see and assess tactics. Her mind flashed through so many now. There were options open to her, but none of them were good. Plans came and went, discarded because none of them would get everyone out of this alive. Too much was stacked against her. If one of the enemy hadn't been holding someone hostage, if even one of her allies had been free, there might have been a chance, however slim to win this fight.

But she quickly realized, that every plan, every tactic would mean death for someone.

For the briefest of moments, she limited her plans to those where she would be the only casualty. There weren't many of these options, and still in most of them, another ally would perish as well. But the simple and honest truth was... she didn't want to die.

Which left her nothing.

No options to get out of this. There was no fight she could bring to the enemy to save everyone. Someone was going to die.

The choice before her now was simple: would someone die in a fight, or would she surrender and choose one of Elria or Hildr to perish?

Fights were inherently unstable. If she chose to fight, something unforeseen might occur. Yet she didn't want to give up, didn't want to have to choose someone to die.

And yet... if she did fight, she'd seen all the possibilities, she'd essentially be choosing someone to die anyway, and the fight might not turn out as she'd hoped. She didn't know enough of her enemies to be completely certain of any outcome.

She wanted so much to fight, to resist, to go down swinging... yet she couldn't.

And with that realization... something within her broke and crumbled.

She screamed and fell to her knees, head in hands. She buried her fingers in her hair and clenched tight. The pain helped to clear her head. But she knew she'd lost.

"Will they both die, or will you choose? Last chance!"

"I'll choose!" she shouted through restrained tears. "Gods, I'll choose," she whimpered.

But how could she?

Hildr had been growing so close to Barami. By all the gods, Caerwyn had heard them talking about children and other things domestic! They were practically planning a life together. How could she do that to Barami? How could she take away the woman he'd finally found who was a match for him?

She couldn't.

But Elria was an innocent as well. Caerwyn had seen how Jais had looked at her. There was something between them, and even if Caerwyn did perhaps wish a child from Jais, she wouldn't want him to be deprived of a possible relationship with another. Then there were the women's father's. Neither would be happy to learn their daughter had died, chosen by her. Those staunch men were already sorry enough for letting any of them come here. She'd never be able to show her face to the Dronnegir again.

"Now!" the wizard demanded.

A word slipped out. She didn't know how or what mechanism in her mind had already made the impossible choice, but it had. "Elria!"

Oh, gods!

Laughter flooded around her. "See how easy that was! Now get up and bind that other human while I prepare for the ritual."

Ritual? "What Ritual?" She'd already proven she was no threat to him.

More laughter.

She looked up to see him sneering as he chortled at her weakness and ignorance. "Why, the ritual where I kill that dragon and take its power." His laughter changed pitch and flew into a wild cackle.

Elria's eyes were still wild. The look the other woman gave Caerwyn was one of sheer horror and reproach. She knew she was going to die and that Caerwyn had picked her over her cousin.

Caerwyn had to look away, tears filling her eyes.

Gods... please...

Her heart was breaking, torn. She'd endured so much in her life, and this was what she'd come to. All her powers, all her skills as a warrior, and she was powerless to stop this madman.

Her mind raced, trying still to come up with some desperate plan to save everyone, but she couldn't. Every action she thought of led to the death of Barami or one of these women.

Her teeth were clenched, jaw aching from the force. But if she opened her mouth she'd scream, or weep and she wasn't the type of woman who did either.

She rose slowly, moving sluggishly, over to Hildr. The slow steps were to give herself time. Perhaps in these last final seconds she'd think of something, but she reached the woman with no plan, no action, nothing.

She had truly lost.

The brute Gerhardt released Hildr's face and the woman dropped to the ground gasping great gulps of air.

"I'm sorry," Caerwyn said through tight teeth as she tied the other woman up, binding her hands and feet. Caerwyn leaned her against the rock wall to try to make her comfortable.

"He'll kill us all," Hildr said in a hushed tone.

"I know!" Caerwyn hissed back, but that expended the last of the fire and fight within her. "But what can we do?" She heard the limp spirit in her words and hated herself for it. She wanted to cry at her own impotence, but clenched her jaw instead. "He's too powerful. If Jais were here and we were all ready for a fight, we might have a chance, but with Barami already subdued..." She couldn't go on. She shook her head. "I'm sorry." Her voice cracked, and she went back to clenching her jaw.

Hildr's eyes darted about, as if searching for some idea, some plan, but she only shook her head slowly. It seemed she had no ideas either. Her lips were tight, angry, and perhaps she was feeling just as powerless as Caerwyn.

The wizard bound Elria—still held by his magic, helpless —with rope and laid her on the stone floor a few dozen feet from the dragon then knelt next to her, speaking to himself in low tones.

Caerwyn should be attacking him. He wasn't looking. He'd be easy to strike down, but Gerhardt stood near his master with Barami still clutched like a doll in his arms. The big man wasn't that smart, but he had wits enough to be watching Caerwyn as his master worked. If she tried anything, Barami would suffer.

It was just another impossible choice. No, not impossible. She'd choose Barami over nearly anyone in this world. But still she hated herself for not being able to help Elria.

Wait!

Perhaps...

She glanced over at where she'd dropped Davlas. It lay a few feet from Gerhardt and it had been the wizard who'd stopped its flight the last time.

She connected to the spear, and using her mental commands, she flung it at Gerhardt's head.

Despite his bulk, the man wasn't slow. He saw the spear coming and moved: head tilting, hand rising. It wasn't enough to fully get out of the way. The spear took him just beside his eye and tore along the side of his head just as his hand grabbed the shaft. He threw the spear to the floor and stepped on it. She wouldn't be able to move it now.

That was it. She'd done the only thing she could do, and it hadn't been enough. Gerhardt was injured, but the bloody gash hardly seemed to inconvenience the brute. He still held Barami, perhaps squeezing him just a little tighter now. She could still try to charge the man but crossing even the short distance between them would give Gerhardt more than enough time to crush Barami, or otherwise kill her friend.

She was out of options. It ate at her soul. Here she was, unbound and watching this evil transpire. But if she acted, Barami would die.

Yet if she did nothing, Elria would die.

30

JAIS RECOGNIZED VOLF JUMPING DOWN THE CLIFF-SIDE AT them. The man must have been crazy. This wasn't a sheer cliff by any means, but the slope was steep enough that one couldn't just walk up it.

Once the rain had stopped, he and Gosse had gone back to the waterfall and waited for the water level to go down. That had taken far too long, and they'd still gone across the wall-walk with water swirling around their feet. Once across, they followed the climbing path up the side of the mountain. Ropes hung in places, knotted and easy to climb, leading up to ledges which could be traversed for a short stretch, then more ropes and more ledges.

They were wet and cold and tired. Jais especially hadn't slept well or for very long in three nights and was nearly delirious with fatigue. He kept forcing himself onward through sheer force of will as each step or pull on a rope became a little slower, a little harder. Their progress was slow. The afternoon had stretched as the clouds cleared and the sun set behind the peaks around them.

They were perhaps two thirds of the way up the climbing trail and Jais was starting to wonder if he could even go on.

And then Volf appeared, nimbly jumping down the mountainside at him as if he were some weightless sprite with boundless energy.

He had to be imagining this.

He nodded to Gosse at Volf rapidly coming down to them. "Do you see that?" he asked.

The other man looked, and his eyes widened. "See it, yes. Believe it? No."

He wasn't seeing things, but that didn't explain how Volf was practically running down the side of a mountain.

"Thank all the gods!" Volf called from the ledge above them. "You need to hurry. The others are in trouble!"

Hurry? Jais could feel his muscles cramping and stiffening. He wasn't sure he'd be able to maintain the pace he was going for much longer.

But if Caerwyn was in trouble... or Elria. Oh, gods!

"Anything you can do to get us up there faster?" Jais shouted. Even the energy put into yelling seemed too much for him, leaving him a little breathless.

"I have my own way of getting up and down, but I can't help you any. You need to hurry!"

Gosse turned to Jais and shrugged. "I guess we hurry then." The man grabbed the next length of rope, this one was only perhaps a dozen feet or so up to the next ledge, on which Volf stood. Gosse began hauling himself up.

Jais grabbed the rope, feeling his shoulder muscles jump, twitch, and tense. His arm was trembling.

He wouldn't— He *couldn't* fall. He had to help the others.

He put one arm over the other and pulled his not inconsiderable weight up another length of rope.

By the time he clambered over the lip of the next ledge, Volf was already above them, urging them onward.

Gosse was staring at the man. "I've never seen... he just jumped up there like it was nothing. A hop over a fallen branch, no more."

Jais didn't deign to respond. It was clear, something had happened to Volf since they'd last seen him, but there wasn't the time—nor did Jais have the energy—to ask. He grabbed the next rope and continued climbing.

"Right, sorry, got distracted," Gosse said behind him.

It was full-on evening by the time they finally completed the climb and were at the mouth of a cave. The first stars were starting to blink into existence as the sky turned from azure to indigo.

Jais was breathing heavily and leaning against the cave-mouth, practically asleep on his feet.

"How much farther?" he asked between breaths.

"Perhaps a half mile. The cave is rather long."

"Gods." Jais' shoulders fell. "I don't know how far I can go. I'm exhausted."

"You have to. Caerwyn and Elria are in there. That crazy man has them all at his mercy. He seems to have magic that I don't understand."

"Tyark," Gosse said as if that meant something. Wait... it did mean something. Gosse had mentioned that name in his long-winded explanation of why he was switching sides. Tyark was...

Jais' mind was working about as fast as his body.

...a drahksan with magical powers. He'd been the wizard throwing fire around the Dronnegir village.

"Great."

"Now that we're all on level ground, I might be able to get

us all there quicker," Volf said, but he didn't sound certain at all.

"How?" Gosse asked.

"I don't have the words to explain it. I only just learned how, but I believe I can do it if you're both willing to try."

"I'm not sure I'm willing to do anything." Gosse was indignant. "You're a drahksan, yes?"

Volf seemed a little surprised at the question. "Yes."

"And can you sense me as drahksan?" Gosse asked.

Volf looked at the man oddly. "Of course."

"Of course." Gosse's gaze jumped to the steep valley. "Gods! Of course."

"What's with him?" Volf asked Jais. "And who is he? Never mind, doesn't matter, we need to get going now!"

"Long story. He's having a bit of a crisis of faith and you've just confirmed he's drahksani. He didn't really know before. And I agree, if the others are in trouble we need to go. Gosse?"

Gosse spun on him. "What?"

"We need to go. You have your confirmation. Now it's time to help some people for a change." Jais was being hard but was too tired to care.

Gosse pushed onward. "Help? I..." Gosse's face snarled into a sour look. "I'm a monster, how can I help anyone? All I know how to do is kill my own kind! You can't know what that's like!"

"You're a monster who has a chance to redeem himself," Jais said. No matter how tired he felt, they had to keep moving. "From the sounds of it, there are people, drahksan and otherwise, in these caves that need help. Are you willing to help them?"

Gosse seemed self-consumed for a moment then shook his head. "Let's go."

"Good," Volf said a bit uncertain himself, it seemed. "You'll have to both be touching me. Take my hands." Volf held out a hand to each of them. Jais grasped one hand as Gosse took the other.

Volf turned so he was facing into the cave. "When I tell you to walk, do so. Nice and slow should be fine, but we need to be making forward motion. Just give me a moment to figure this out in my head. This is going to require a lot of concentration."

"What are you—" Gosse began, but was cut off.

"Hush!"

Jais would do as instructed.

"Now. Walk." Volf took a step and the other two followed.

The cave blurred around them as they were plunged into an odd semi-darkness. It only grew darker as they made their way deeper inside remarkably quickly. Each step seemed to be taking them farther than ten strides, perhaps farther than a hundred, and the world sped past them despite their leisurely pace.

Jais only hoped it would be quick enough to help the others.

And that he had the strength to do so.

BARAMI COULDN'T MOVE. HE'D GIVEN UP STRUGGLING AND kicking at his captor. It didn't seem to affect the large man and he wasn't going to escape Gerhardt's grip any time soon. The one arm around him was thicker than most men's legs and bunching with muscles on muscles. He reminded Barami of Jais, only bigger. Barami's strength, considerable as it may have been, was nowhere near what was needed to escape. So, he bided his time.

Then there was his arm, a splitting pain in his shoulder as the limb hung limp. Currently, it was only slightly more useless than his other arm since both were pinned, but he was sweating from the pain and his vision swam occasionally as he threatened to black out.

He wasn't in good shape.

But in some ways, he was better than Caerwyn.

It was like the fighting spirit—what made her who she was—had just drained out of her, leaving an empty husk of a person, shocked and trembling, with a lost look in her eyes that pierced his soul.

He couldn't fathom the choice she'd made. Though a selfish part of him was so very glad she hadn't chosen Hildr.

He too was torn in his own way. There was a part of him, the part that had always been willing to sacrifice himself for her, that wanted her to attack. If he died, perhaps it would be a fitting cost to save everyone else here. Yet another part of him, one he'd only recently discovered, wanted desperately to stay alive. He had something—a budding relationship with Hildr—to live for. As much as he might be willing to die to save everyone here, he wanted so much to see what would happen with Hildr. They'd talked a lot over the last day and he felt they were making a solid connection. They'd practically been planning a life together. He didn't want to lose that.

It was his desperate, selfish hope to live, that had prevented him from calling out to Caerwyn to fight no matter what. But that choice was taking a greater and greater toll on her, and on him as he watched her.

There had to be some way to defeat these two villains. He'd been praying to Suur and Lansus for some insight, some strategy, some hidden strength to escape and put these evil men in their place. Yet if the gods were listening, they were not acting today.

The wizard seemed to be finishing up his ritual. It had been quite involved, drawing sigils on the ground around the dragon in his own blood and another symbol of some sort in Elria's blood on her own forehead. He'd then knelt next to Elria for some time simply muttering to himself.

The wizard's hold on the woman had wavered a couple times during the ritual. She'd tried to roll away, struggle, but always he'd stilled her with his magic once again and continued on.

Now he drew out a long, curved dagger.

Elria screamed but couldn't otherwise move.

Perhaps it was a reaction to the scream or perhaps the big man just expected trouble now, but Gerhardt's muscles flexed and held Barami even tighter. His chest was constricted farther, forcing him to take shallow breaths.

"Hush now, my dear." The wizard's tone was mockingly soft. Then he laughed. "This will be painful, but not for long," the wizard said to Elria putting a hand over her mouth to stifle her protests. "You will be part of a great moment in history. The first mortal to kill a dragon on his own." The man chuckled gleefully as he lowered the dagger to Elria's neck.

He muttered some final words that Barami could not understand, then slid the dagger across Elria's throat drawing a gurgled gasp. Blood sprayed around her and showered the wizard.

Elria twitched then went still.

The others shouted and screamed. Barami thought he did too, but he couldn't tell. He was growing faint, darkness clouding his vision as it grew harder to breathe. He was losing sense of himself.

The wizard stood, bloody dagger held aloft. His tone was exultant as he bellowed. "Witness ye gods and demons! I take your power for my own!" This was followed by more mysterious words as he slid the bloody dagger across his palm, then pressed the flat of the blade into the wound.

There was a terrible sound, a high-pitched whine, which hurt to hear. It grew in intensity and volume, slowly lowering in pitch until it was a great roar. It sounded... painful, the rending of a soul, and Barami shuddered to hear it even though he was nearly delirious himself.

The form of the dragon began to glow brighter and brighter, the light increasing in intensity with the awful noise until it was near blinding. Gerhardt turned away then, and Barami could only see the effects of the light, casting the immense cave in brilliance before flashing several times and fading to nothing.

Then... darkness.

Some torch flickered somewhere in the massive cave, but they had not needed other light with the dragon's glow before now.

He was nearly lost in unconsciousness, but before he slipped away he heard two very disparate noises.

One was an arrogant cackle of triumph, grating and a little mad. Over this, he heard a heart-rending scream of a single word. Barami thought perhaps he knew that voice, but he was losing any sense of memory now. He heard only that soul-shredding cry...

"Elria!"

JAIS ARRIVED IN TIME TO SEE THE KNIFE LIFT AWAY FROM Elria's throat and her body twitch then still. If he hadn't been disoriented from the strange distance-eating walk and nearly incapacitated with exhaustion he'd have run or done something. He didn't know what. Perhaps he would have tried to tackle the wizard or save Elria. His mind spun with the options as the dragon flared out of being, halting him with its brilliance.

He'd seen the beast—the most glorious and wondrous of creatures—for only a moment before it exploded with light and that ear-piercing shriek.

Now the cave was plunged into darkness, and he could only scream, falling to his knees, then his hands as the wizard now seemed to glow with the same light the dragon had a moment before. He didn't know what had happened, but he was certain Elria was dead and that something great and beautiful and powerful had died with her.

He heard the echoes of his scream die out in the sudden silence, his throat raw from the shout.

"Oh, hello!" The voice was almost cheery as the wizard spoke. "Who have we here? More drahksani to join with me? Wonderful!"

A fury flickered to life within Jais, and he stood slowly, feeling it bloom then blaze within him. Despite his hoarse voice, he shouted once again.

"I will never join you!"

He charged and threw himself in a flying tackle at the man, but as had happened the last time he'd tried to kill the man, the wizard simply vanished, and pain exploded up Jais' arms and head as he crashed against the stone floor. He used that pain as energy and sprang to his feet again. There wasn't much light, but now the wizard glowed and was easy to spot.

The man was crouching next to Caerwyn who knelt on the floor. He had a hand under her chin pushing her face up to look at him. "Defend me, or I'll have Gerhardt squeeze a little more life out of your friend there."

"No," she whimpered, through clenched teeth. "I can't."

Jais had to blink. The sound of her voice, so powerless, threw him for a moment. What had happened to her? He caught sight of the brute he'd fought the other night holding Barami in a death grip.

So that's the game the wizard was playing. Holding the Southern warrior hostage to make Caerwyn do his bidding?

Jais had trouble believing that Caerwyn or Barami would allow themselves to be used in that way, but it seemed that's what had happened.

He turned toward the brute. If he could free Barami, Caerwyn wouldn't be in the clutches of that vile man anymore either.

A voice close to his ear whispered from the darkness. "No, get that wizard. We'll fight the brute." It was Volf.

Jais glanced around but couldn't see the man anywhere. Volf and Gosse were nowhere to be seen. Gone.

But if they were going to free Barami, he was fine with that.

He stalked toward the wizard.

"Fight for me, woman, or the puny humans die!" the wizard hissed.

"No, please," Caerwyn whispered, but still got to her feet as she did so.

"Fight him, Caerwyn!" Jais shouted. "Kill him!" She was so close she could have easily grappled the man.

"Davlas," she said halfheartedly.

Jais was confused, her spear had been broken over two months ago in the fight with the krolloc. Yet one appeared in her hand now. It was near obsidian in color infused with lines of dark red, like veins in marble.

As he drew near, she stepped in front of him. "Jais, please. If I kill him Barami dies."

He opened his mouth to tell her Volf and Gosse would free Barami, but he couldn't. Then the wizard would know what was happening as well. He'd need to wait for them to act. That grated on him as he felt an intense drive to kill the man behind Caerwyn.

He tried to move around her, but she wouldn't let him.

"Attack him. Kill him!" the wizard shouted.

She poked at him with the spear, her attacks slow and easily deflected. She was shaking her head, tears streaming down her cheeks.

"Caerwyn, what are you—? You don't have to listen to him!" Jais tried to get through to her but didn't know what to say. What had happened to her to make her like this? She seemed... broken.

"Kill him or I'll kill your friend!" the madman shouted.

Caerwyn trembled, her face pale and without hope, something Jais thought he'd never see. He swore he would make this wizard pay.

31

GOSSE BARELY HAD TIME TO BREATHE AS THE WORLD SHIFTED and grew lighter around him. Volf was dropping... whatever it was that kept him hidden. He hadn't realized he'd been holding his breath. It was only as he charged Gerhardt that he realized he needed air.

He gulped in a breath, then struck at the large man's arm.

Volf had made his goal very clear. Gosse was to do everything he could to keep the brute occupied, and Volf was going to do something sneaky.

The brute was surprised, that much was clear. He tried to move, but Gosse was too quick and his sword bit into the other man's arm, though not nearly as deep as it should have. The man had an incredibly tough hide. The wound trickled blood as Gosse withdrew his sword and the cut hardly seemed to affect the man.

By the Deepest Shadows, this wasn't going to be easy.

Gerhardt drew forth his axe, holding the large weapon in one hand, and swung at Gosse. With the attack made more awkward because Gerhardt still held Barami, Gosse easily ducked under the blow and danced to one side, much nimbler than his foe.

He came up and stabbed the other man low in the side. His sword bit deep enough, but still the wound seemed to bleed little when he moved away, dodging another of the big man's blows.

Gosse danced around the man with all the grace of his newly realized heritage and all the skill he'd learned over forty years of fighting drahksani. The other man's body bled from a dozen cuts, but still he wouldn't go down or release his prisoner.

Then Gerhardt screamed. None of Gosse's attacks had elicited such a violent verbal response, but the big man dropped to one knee, eyes wide. Gerhardt released Barami, who fell to the ground, limp.

Gosse took a risk, thinking the big man incapacitated, and lunged in to strike at the man's throat. He drove his sword through the man's neck and had the satisfaction of seeing the life go out of the big man's eyes... even as a swing from Gerhardt's giant axe caught Gosse in the side of his head.

Then there was nothing.

VOLF TREMBLED. HE COULDN'T STOP HIS HAND FROM SHAKING. The hand that had driven his knife into the large man's back.

The knife still stood there. Rammed to the hilt into the man's large form. It had taken all of Volf's strength and a little of his drahksan-enhanced speed to thrust the blade in. It had bounced around a little. Volf was on the verge of being sick recalling it. But he must have hit something vital. Yet he couldn't retrieve the knife, couldn't bring himself to touch it.

This was the first man he'd killed. Even though the man

was a brute and a villain—and in truth it had been Gosse who had struck the killing blow —that didn't stop him from regretting the loss of life.

He tried to stop himself from shaking, but everything around him was death and chaos. Yet he needed to do something.

He stepped around Gerhardt's hulking form to see Gosse's head... not attached to his body.

Bile rose in his throat.

"Gods," he breathed in a prayer of mercy.

He ran to Barami and found the man alive, if unconscious.

"He's alive!" he shouted at the others, his voice sounding shaky even to him.

Hopefully now the tables would turn on the last villain.

CAERWYN FELT SOMETHING HARDEN INSIDE OF HER AS SHE SPUN and threw Davlas with all her might at the wizard. She let out a feral scream as she did, releasing all her pent-up fear, anger, and frustration.

The man's reactions were amazing, and the spear only just brushed the side of his head as he flinched out of the way at the last moment.

She commanded it to spin around and skewer him from the back, but Jais was also charging in on the man and a moment later the wizard was gone, vanished once again.

"Coward!" Jais screamed, hoarse.

She summoned Davlas back to her hand before it hit Jais, then fell to her knees again, shoulders slumping as the energy went out of her.

Gods...

She'd been so weak.

How could anyone ever forgive her? How could she ever forgive herself?

"What have I done," she whispered to herself.

Jais knelt beside her. She knew it was him, the feel of his essence to her spirit-link was familiar after having traveled with him for weeks now. He set a hand on her back.

Spirit-link... it was odd knowing what her abilities were called now. This was the sense she had which pulled her to other drahksani.

Yet Jais would never get to experience the gifts she received. The dragon was dead. Jais had been the one—more so than any of them—who'd wanted to know about who he was and what he could do. He'd never get that chance now because she'd let that wizard kill Elria and the dragon.

"Caer? What happened?" Jais' voice was soft, tentative and caring. It was far too much. He should hate her, and perhaps he would once he knew the truth. She couldn't take his kindness and was overcome with sobs, loud and embarrassing and in no way cathartic.

"Caer?" Jais was rubbing her back. "It will be well," he said in a hushed tone.

No, it wouldn't be. It could never be. She'd always been so strong, able to handle anything life had thrown at her. It hadn't been an easy life by any means, not with having had to flee from two families, but she'd always faced the future with determination. Now she saw only darkness ahead.

Jais reached around to embrace her.

She flinched away. She couldn't—wouldn't let him comfort her. "Don't!" Her tone was harsh, scathing. He started back. Good. That's what he should be doing, recoiling from her cowardice and uselessness.

"Caer?"

She barely had any energy, but she rose and strode away from him. She tried to speak through her sobs, but her words were slurred and came out in odd tones and cadence. She didn't know if anyone would understand her, but she had to keep them all away. "Stay away from me! I don't deserve your— I don't deserve anything from any of you! Just stop it!"

She reached a wall and collapsed to her knees at its base, her head tilting forward to rest on its cold surface.

"Stay away," she repeated with much less vigor through her tears. She needed to be alone. She deserved to be alone. She hadn't done her job, hadn't protected those who needed it. She'd failed. She was a failure. Her entire life had been a failure. She could see that now. She had been too young and weak to help her parents. She should have died with them, but she'd run away. She should have stood up to Gosse when he'd accused her of being drahksani to her adoptive father, but she hadn't, she'd fled yet again.

She could see now the thread of cowardice in her life. How useless she was. Now she'd sunk so low as to let herself be used by an evil man. What redemption was there for that?

No one approached her this time.

It was for the best. She deserved to be alone and cold, miserable.

———

JAIS STARED AT CAERWYN. IT WAS ALL HE COULD DO. THIS wasn't her. It couldn't be. He'd never seen her like this before and couldn't have even imagined it. He'd never seen her weep, not like this. She seemed... broken. Yet she was a rock. She was the rock that kept their group together. Without her...

"Jais!" He turned at the sound of his name. "We need you!" Volf was leaning over Barami. Next to them was Gosse.

Oh, Gods!

Jais ran over to the scene. He'd been too distracted with fighting the wizard and then Caerwyn's odd breakdown, that he hadn't noticed what had happened in the rest of the room.

For a moment, he simply stood staring down at Gosse's decapitated form. It didn't seem possible. The man had only just come to know what he was. He might not have even had time to figure out who he was. His impulse was to heal the man, but his mind told him it wouldn't be possible.

"I'm sorry," he said softly to the corpse and turned to Volf and Barami. "What's wrong with him?"

Volf's eyes were wide with fear and concern. "How should I know?"

Of course, Jais had to stop thinking others could know what was wrong with someone just by touching them. He hurried over and knelt by Barami, skirting around the massive form of Gerhardt. He only wished he'd been able to help take down that demon of a man. In truth, he'd been mostly useless in this past fight.

Kneeling by Barami, he put a hand on the man's forehead and searched for the wounds and pain within him. Almost instantly he caught the dislocated shoulder and a couple of fractured ribs, other than that the man seemed to be mostly well, just unconscious.

He turned to Volf. "I can handle this. Go free Hildr and..." *Then check on Elria*. He wanted to say the words, but he couldn't bring himself. He knew she was dead as much as he didn't want her to be. His heart constricted at the thought. "Just go!" he said a little too harshly. The on-edge feeling he'd sensed from Caerwyn seemed to be catching.

Volf nodded and ran off.

Jais healed Barami. It didn't take long. Resetting the shoulder was a lot easier while the man was unconscious, as it would have been quite painful. Once he was done, he let Barami rest.

He stood and glanced around and couldn't help but look toward Elria.

Moving slowly, his feet traced a path he desperately needed to take yet just as desperately didn't want to.

He knelt next to her and put a hand on her cold, far-too-pale cheek.

She was dead. There was no healing her from this.

He nodded to himself as he swallowed a heavy lump in his throat, which didn't seem to go away. Tears formed around his eyes, but he gritted his teeth and wouldn't let them fall. Yet he couldn't stop himself from gazing upon her, his eyes drawn to hers, which stared up into nothingness. They were perfect, those brilliant green eyes. That green, with the growing pallor of her skin, was set in stark contrast to the bloom of dark blood at her throat.

He tried. He had to.

He pushed a little healing energy into her only to feel it dissipate, wasted upon a corpse.

"I'm sorry," he whispered. "I should have been here to protect you." He leaned down and kissed her cold forehead.

Then the tears came.

With them came a flood of emotions he'd been restraining: regret, anger, loathing, hatred, love, and so many others.

"Why did you have to go on?" he asked her. "You could have waited for us to catch up." But she'd been brave. He wasn't sure he'd ever given her full credit for her strength and bravery since it was hidden behind her kindness and compassion for people. Yet it was clear now. She'd come here, knowing there was danger. She'd come, and she'd died.

"I don't think I ever really knew you," he whispered, still leaning over her, his tears wetting her face and hair. "I so wanted to, but..." Then he couldn't speak anymore.

A voice nearby drew Jais out of his mourning. "I'm sorry I couldn't get you here in time to save her." It was Volf.

Jais nodded, sniffling. "You did everything you could."

He rose then.

He'd been kneeling close enough long enough that there were two imprints of his knees in the darkening pool of blood around her.

He drew in a long breath and his voice turned hard. "I will kill that man."

Volf nodded, then his gaze flicked away to something else.

The cave was dark, lit only by a few flickering torches, but in the distance Jais could see the pile of what looked like ash, that had once been a dragon. "I guess we'll never get our answers now," he said softly.

Volf cleared his throat. "Actually, Caerwyn and I, we did get some before the wizard showed up."

Jais turned to him, trying not to appear envious or heartbroken. "You did?" Perhaps they might be able to help shed some light on his own abilities, tell him more about who and what he was.

Volf nodded. "I'm sorry you didn't get the chance. It was a... changing experience."

"What did you find out?"

Volf grimaced. "I know all of what I can do now, and it's amazing. I was given my bloodline, back to the dragon that spawned my ancestors."

"So, we did actually come from dragons?"

Volf nodded. "The dragons had decided their time was ending and sacrificed their eggs to give birth to our kind to help and protect humanity."

"But you wouldn't know anything about my bloodline or my abilities." It wasn't a question.

Volf sighed heavily. "I am sorry you didn't get to speak to the dragon."

Jais was certain he would always remember this day as one of missed timing and disappointment. Jais looked down at Elria's dead form and something hardened in side of him. "I'll never let this happen again." His gaze drifted upward to no specific point. "And when I find that Holn-damned wizard I swear by Suur I'll kill him."

He turned away at that and went back to Barami. He easily lifted the still unconscious man and brought him over to the area that had been set up as a sort-of camp.

Hildr looked worn and tired.

He set Barami down and asked her, "What are your customs for the dead? The ones back at your village were burned, is that the usual way?

Hildr nodded. "But not without the cleansing ceremony first."

Jais sighed. "What does that involve?" They wouldn't be able to get Elria's body back to the village, which meant dealing with it here most likely.

"They are washed and tended. Then wrapped in white cloth and a prayer is said for them."

"We have no white cloth. Do you know the prayer?"

Hildr shook her head.

"So, what do we do with Elria?"

Hildr looked like she didn't want to be making this decision now, but Jais didn't want to wait. He couldn't think of her lying in that pool of blood. He needed to do something now.

"If we leave her—" Hildr began.

"And let scavengers tear at her? No."

"There is little here to use as a pyre." Hildr shook her

head. "And no scavengers will get at her here. This place is protected."

Jais closed his eyes and pressed his lips together. He didn't like the thought of just leaving Elria like that. He wanted to yell at the world, but yelling at Hildr now would do nothing. "Is there anything we can do for her?"

"Pray for her."

"I've already said my prayer," he said, stoic and stern. His had been to Suur and it been concerning vengeance. He rose and stalked away to Caerwyn. He couldn't think of the dead anymore. He had to... he didn't know what.

The stone that was his soul cracked a little to see Caerwyn so broken. She remained kneeling next to the wall, leaning against it, her posture and position one of defeat and fragility. She no longer wept, but her breathing was erratic like one still sobbing.

He knelt next to her.

Words died on his lips. He didn't know what to say to her, whether to be compassionate or to try jarring her from this state with harsh words.

"You're alive," he said and found his voice was still hard, unyielding. He tried to moderate his tone but found it did little. He remained stoic. "That's more than some people here. Use it. Be strong. Fight back." He felt an odd mix of pity and revulsion rise within him, and it came out in his words. "This isn't you."

He waited for a reply, something, but she didn't even acknowledge his presence. After a long moment of waiting, and with nothing else he could think to say, he shook his head and stood, turning away.

"I killed her." The voice was a mouse's whisper behind him, hoarse and choked with sorrow.

He froze.

Killed... there was only one dead 'her' in the room. But that wasn't right. The wizard had killed Elria. He'd seen it happen.

"He asked me to choose."

Those words froze Jais' soul.

"Choose?"

"The wizard. He had Barami and was hurting him. He asked me to choose who would die between Hildr and Elria." A wet snuffling and a single sob preceded her next words. "I'm sorry, Jais! I killed Elria."

She'd chosen...

Of course she had. She would never have let Barami die. And Barami seemed to have something for the other woman, Hildr. She wouldn't hurt her longtime friend by choosing a woman he liked. But Jais' feelings for Elria, they didn't mean anything to her, they hadn't been considered. That was clear. It all played out in his head with a sickening logic.

He shook his head, feeling something cold sink into his soul.

"Then you can die too for all I care. Just make sure it's fighting that shadow-spawned wizard."

He stalked away.

JAIS' WORDS SANK LIKE A SPEAR INTO CAERWYN'S HEART.

You can die too for all I care.

She hoped desperately, that perhaps he'd understand somehow. She had expected him to be upset, but maybe he'd understand what an impossible situation she'd been in and...

But no, his reaction was just.

She deserved to die. She'd been a coward. She'd never forgive herself for that. She'd just hoped for some solace. But there would be none. She saw that now.

Just as there had been no one to comfort her after her birth parents had died. She'd been alone in a vast forest, scared and cold and crying herself to sleep every night for months, curled up into a tiny ball.

In this moment she felt like nothing so much as that childhood version of herself. She fell to her side and curled up, hugging her knees close. Tears leaked from her eyes, but she felt like she'd cried herself out. Her tempestuous emotions had died down and in their place was nothing, just a void where her courage and strength had been. She was empty and cold.

Jais was right. She would go and face the wizard and sacrifice herself. That was all that was left to her now. It was little comfort, but it was a direction at least.

"Caerwyn?" It was Volf. His voice was soft, tentative. There was an equally as hesitant touch on her calf. "What do you need?" After a moment he whispered, "I'm sorry I left you so suddenly. I didn't know what to do. I fled. I'm a coward. I always have been. I'm sorry."

Was this a kindred soul?

"We all save ourselves in the end," she said, her voice uneven and hoarse.

"You can't believe that."

She hadn't before today, but a few hours could change a person. She was not the same woman who had entered this cave.

"You did. I did. We all do."

"But I came back."

"Too late." Too late to save her from the horrible choices she had to make. Too late to change anything.

"I know. I'm sorry."

"So am I. You'll need to find someone else..." She wasn't quite sure what she meant by that. He'd seemed interested in her, but she knew now she'd never be with him or anyone else. Her dream of a child was gone. Who was she to want such a thing when she'd never be able to take care of it, protect it? No, she would have no child. She'd die soon enough. And there would be no one to teach Volf weapons. Perhaps Jais or Barami could, but she wouldn't be around to do so. Whatever he needed from her, he'd need to find someone else to provide it. She was worthless.

She heard him sigh, and his hand left her leg.

"I still believe in you. Even if you don't."

She didn't have the strength to tell him it was a fruitless belief.

She heard him walk away.

Good.

She deserved to be alone.

Barami woke famished. Jais must have healed him, as he felt much better than he had. Yet still he groaned as he opened his eyes. Far too much had happened, far too much evil. He looked around, tentatively at first. He needed to know if that wizard was still close by and a threat. What he saw was not good.

The wizard was gone. There was no body, which he assumed meant the man had vanished once again. The big man who'd been holding him was dead, that was a blessing, but his friends did not seem all that celebratory of this small victory.

Hildr and Volf, both seemingly lost in dark thoughts, sat around a small oil lantern. The glow wasn't much, but in the gloom of the cavern after the dragon's death, it was enough to illuminate a small area around them in dim light. Caerwyn was huddled into a ball farther off. That didn't look good at all. Jais was nowhere to be seen.

He rose, tested his shoulder, which felt fine, and walked over to Volf and Hildr.

"What happened?"

It was Hildr who responded. "Volf wounded the big man enough for the other man there to kill him." She pointed at the other body. Barami hadn't recognized it. Someone else had joined with them? "Jais has said little, but that other man, I think he was one of the attackers on our village.

Apparently, he changed sides and turned on his companions."

That was interesting.

Hildr sighed heavily. "Caerwyn tried to kill the wizard but the man disappeared again. She be not well. I know not what to say to her."

Volf spoke up. "She blames herself for all of this. I tried to tell her it wasn't her fault, but..."

No, it was Barami's fault. He should have never let down his guard enough to be taken by that brute. He should have sacrificed himself.

Yet even one look at Hildr told him he couldn't have. He was so very grateful to be alive.

But that had taken a toll on another, on Caerwyn. He grunted and moved over to her.

"Go away." It was a soft hiss from a trembling voice as he approached Caerwyn. It didn't sound like her at all. "Barami please, just leave me be." Her voice was hoarse. She sounded like she'd been crying, but he'd never known her to weep.

"I am sorry," was all he could think to say. If he'd been more willing to risk his own life and happiness, Caerwyn wouldn't have had to go through what she had.

"Aren't we all," was the terse response.

What could he say?

He stood there for a while trying to think of something, but this wasn't his strong suit. He wasn't one to comfort others. Eventually he just sighed and repeated himself. "I'm sorry." Then he left.

"What do we do now?" Barami said returning to the others.

"Return to the village," Hildr said. "They must know of the dragon's death."

Of course. Returning to the village was really their only

possible course from here, or at least the necessary first step to anywhere else.

"We should rest first. We're all tired," he said. No one objected.

Yet he felt strong enough for the moment and didn't feel like resting. Somehow, resting felt like giving up.

Hildr rose. "Would you like to walk?"

He'd love to. He nodded to her. Hildr joined him and they moved away from the others. She took one of the few remaining torches and they began a trek along the wall of the massive cavern.

"Give them time," she said once they were out of earshot of the others. "They have been through... too much." She sighed.

"I know. But they're all just so still. I feel like I need to move, to get out there and find the bastard that did this to us!"

"And what if it be me instead of Elria. Would you be so quick to act, or would you need time to mourn?"

"I..." He closed his mouth. He had only just started to get to know her, yet somehow her hand was holding his as they walked. When he was near her, next to her, the feelings within him were unlike any he'd ever known. If she'd been the one to die...

"I'd want revenge."

"Jais seems to want the same thing, but he watched the one he cared for die. He may need more time to recover." She sighed heavily. "A cousin I lost today. I still mourn her. I know we need to be moving, but I too feel the loss deeply and would like to have more time to deal with it."

"And Caerwyn..." He couldn't understand her reaction most of all. Yes, she'd been forced to make a horrible choice, but she was still alive and could still fight. Yet it seemed like all the spirit had gone out of her.

"You cannot see?"

"See what?"

Hildr gave another heavy sigh and punched him in the shoulder. It stung for a long moment. She hadn't pulled that punch too much. "Men be quite blind sometimes." She hesitated. "Well perhaps it be not men. Perhaps we all can be blind sometimes."

"Blind to what?"

"When in that man's grip you were, how did you feel?"

"Useless."

"And how, think you, she felt? Able to fight yet not. She could fight, could win, but could not risk your life. What must that feel like?"

"Probably fairly useless too?" He understood that. What was Hildr getting at?

"Yes. Useless you felt, because you could do nothing. She could do something but had to choose not to. Do you see the difference?"

He did, but he still didn't understand what she was getting at. "What are you saying?"

Hildr stopped walking, releasing his hand, and turned to him. "You could not act so you didn't. It be horrible, but there be no choice for you. She could do much, but at the same time, she could not. She had to choose not to act." She stared at him for along moment. "In making that choice, she gave up a part of her. She lost her strength, her resolve. She chose to be useless. How do you think that would feel after? You bluster and push onward, but she has to deal with being powerless. That be not an easy thing."

"But she's just as powerful as she was before." Barami understood what Hildr was getting at now, the greater depths of Caerwyn's defeat. Yet he still didn't understand why it was taking her so long to recover.

"In body, perhaps, but in mind, in spirit, I think not. Part of her was torn away and taken by that wizard. It may still be within her to regain those lost parts, but such a restoration be much harder than what you had to do. Do you see?"

He did.

"So, what do we do?"

"Let her not fall too deep into despair. Keep telling her she be strong until she believes it. But I have seen the spirit go out of men before and, sometimes it never fully returns. I hope, for your friend, that be not the case.

They continued walking and slowly made a circuit of the giant cave. A little while later, a thought came to Barami. "When the dragon touched you, what did he give you?" So much had happened he'd almost forgotten.

Hildr nodded. "It be something which involves you, I believe."

"Me?"

"Aye. The dragon sensed my desire for many children, a large family. So many of my kin have died recently. Thinking I had been, of a large brood of children to help us regain some strength. So, the dragon gave me the boon of fertility and ease of birth." She looked over at him. Her hand sought his and when they met, she squeezed his. "We shall have many children."

"Oh."

Children.

It hadn't been something Barami had ever thought of. He'd never imagined himself as a father.

"Oh," he said again, realizing he sounded a little odd.

She raised a brow. "Do you want children? You never answered me when I asked before."

No, he'd fallen into the stream... and they hadn't continued the conversation after that.

"I'd never thought of it." So, he did now. Taking a moment to consider. Certainly, he felt strongly for the woman with him and would love to help her provide a strong new generation for her people. "I think perhaps I do."

She smiled and gave his hand another squeeze.

They continued in silence for a time after that.

As they began their return trip around the massive circle of stone, Barami saw a great bloom of fire back where their camp was. He took a few hasty steps forward to see what had happened.

Hildr joined him in moving more hastily back to their camp, but Volf met them soon enough.

"What was that?" Barami asked.

Volf glanced back for a moment, then back to them. "Jais wanted to be alone. He took what materials he could find, nearly all of our torches, most of the oil for the lamps, and anything else that would burn. He made a pyre for Elria."

"Oh," Barami said softly. So, that was Elria's cremation.

Hildr sighed heavily. Her voice was soft, yet perhaps sympathetic, when she whispered. "It be not our way."

Volf meandered off back the way Barami and Hildr had already come.

When Barami and Hildr finished their circuit of the cave. Jais still stood over the smoldering form. The fire had not incinerated the woman, it had burned hot, but not for long. What remained was only a charred corpse, no longer identifiable as Elria.

Hildr's look at Jais was harsh, but only for a moment, then she simply shook her head and knelt to have some silent words with the spirit of her lost cousin.

Barami returned to the camp and found Caerwyn sleeping.

They should all get some sleep, to be ready to leave tomorrow.

"Good night," he said softly to his friend. Then he found and lay down on his bedroll. That was where Hildr found him. Without a word, she laid herself down next to him.

She turned to him and pulled him close to her, kissing him with great force and passion. It lasted much longer than he expected and when they finally drew back, he asked her, "Where did that come from?"

"Life is short. I should take what I can, when I can." Her gaze into his eyes was intense. "I want you to know how I feel."

He nodded. "In that case." He drew her into a long and heated embrace as well. When finished, he was a little breathless. "I hope that tells you how I feel as well."

She nodded. "When we return to the village I will announce our betrothal."

Barami was only a little shocked, but it wore off quickly. At first, he'd balked at the idea of being betrothed, but then he realized that's what they had just proclaimed to each other with their actions. They each wanted to be with the other.

He smiled. "I can't wait to see your father's reaction."

She nodded. "It shall be... interesting."

They put their bedrolls together that night, sleeping in each other's arms.

But Barami was roused rudely by shouting.

"Wake up! Everyone you have to see this! Come on. Wake up!"

Barami and Hildr extricated themselves from each other and sat up. Volf was agitated and pointing back in the direction of the dragon's ashes.

Barami didn't know how long had passed, only that he didn't feel that well rested.

"You have to see this!" Volf said animated. Once everyone was paying attention he added, "I found something in the dragon's ashes. I found an egg!"

33

VOLF'S HEART WAS RACING AS HE LED THE OTHERS BACK TO HIS discovery.

He'd felt the need to wander, and had walked the caves for a while, unable and unwilling to sit and rest and sleep.

He'd explored many of the little nooks and larger caves off this one. It only occurred to him after he'd been doing this for some time that he didn't have a torch. His night-vision was truly exceptional. It seemed he could see well enough in near perfect darkness. When he'd discovered that, he'd tested his other senses.

That was when he'd heard—or perhaps even felt—the egg. It was moving slightly, shifting and in doing so was dislodging some of the great pile of ash that covered it. He'd heard the ever so slight tumble and fall of that ash and he'd thought he'd even felt the barest of tremors through the floor of the cave itself. Between those two things, he'd been able to find the egg quickly enough. He'd waded into the ash, which was the remains of the dragon, feeling a little uneasy about doing so, but his curiosity was too great to be dissuaded.

He had reached the spot only after nearly swimming

through the ash. He'd had to move great swaths of it out of his way since the pile was taller than he was at its center. He'd become quite filthy, covered in great black smears of ash. But then he'd reached it.

Clearing away the ash around it was a nearly heroic task —there was so much—so he'd only cleared away a path to it and uncovered it partially. It was taller than he was, perhaps ten feet from bottom to top and half-again as long in its ovoid shape. Its surface was rough, like coarse stone, and it gave off a faint light, like the dragon had, only at a much lower level. He leaned in close and felt it shiver again. It was warm, and it felt like something was moving about within.

That was when he'd decided to go and get the others.

They followed him, some seemingly more energetic than others. Caerwyn was still sluggish and seemed little inter-ested. Jais just seemed distracted and the other two were tired, that was easy enough to see.

But he hadn't wanted to wait.

This seemed like something good after a day of so much pain and sorrow.

"It be glowing!" Hildr said as they drew near. To her eyes perhaps the contrast against the darkness must have been much greater than to his, so attuned was he to the dim light.

"Gods, it's huge!" Jais said.

"So was the dragon," Barami said.

"Forgive me, I only saw it for a moment before it died."

"There is a lot of this ash." Caerwyn said, her voice sounding rather dejected. "I don't think I can go in there. It seems... disrespectful." She shuddered and stayed back. Volf wanted to go to her, to tell her it was fine and to come close to feel the egg, but he didn't have the words. She seemed too lost and he wasn't going to force her to do anything in such a state.

The others followed him into the ever-shifting pile though.

Even as they approached, the egg gave a rather violent shake and great heaps of ash fell off from above it, sending a wave of dust in their direction. They all covered their faces, but still ended up coughing.

They were all filthy now, except for Caerwyn.

But that last shake had cleared away much of the ashen remains from around the egg. The others followed him, wading through chest-deep ash to get to it.

"Oh! It be warm!" Hildr said laying a hand on it.

Jais and Barami had their turns touching and gawking at it before they all just stood there for a long moment looking at it.

"What does this mean?" Volf asked Hildr. Though he realized only after he asked her, he probably knew more about the life cycle of dragons than she did. Part of what he'd received from the dragon was the knowledge of how they reproduced, creating offspring with a genetic memory of all their ancestors.

She shrugged. "I know not. The dragon never spoke of such things. I know not if this be a natural part of its death... or something else."

Volf was about to tell her what he remembered when Jais spoke.

"It means there will be another dragon for you and your clan to care for," Jais said softly. "It means Elria... didn't die for nothing." His voice was becoming heavy with emotion by that last bit.

Volf had little to add to that and remained silent for now.

"Indeed," Hildr said laying a hand on his shoulder. Both hand and shoulder were equally black with ash.

"Caerwyn you need to see this. Feel this!" Barami called out.

"I won't go in there," was the shouted reply, though it sounded like she hardly had any energy to call out at all.

Barami huffed. "What's it going to take to fix her?" he breathed quietly.

"Time," Hildr said and Volf hoped she was wrong. There was still a wizard out there—now possessing the power of a dragon—that had to be dealt with.

He laid a hand on the egg for a moment and got the impression there might still be much time before the new dragon hatched. But he drew strength from the miracle that was the egg before he stalked out of the ash.

"Can we talk," he asked Caerwyn.

She shrugged.

That would have to do.

He left the others behind and drew her away. "Don't you care that the dragon's death—even Elria's death—wasn't in vain? Doesn't that mean something to you?"

"Perhaps," was the only leeway she'd give him. "It still doesn't change what I did."

"And what did you do?"

She gave a heartless half-laugh. "More what I didn't do: fight."

"And if you had fought and died and Barami had died and Hildr had died would that have changed anything that happened? Those men were too powerful for you three alone. If anything, I should be the one wallowing in sorrow since I left you three with him. Don't get me wrong. I feel bad about that, but I still have hope that now, together, we can defeat him. He doesn't have his henchman anymore—"

"No, just the power of a dragon's soul. I'm sure that's nothing," her tone was derisive and harsh, but he didn't let that deter him.

"So?"

"So, he's too powerful. We don't stand a chance. You yourself just said that we couldn't fight him before, so what chance do we have now?"

Damn, he had said that. He hadn't meant it that way though. "There is always a chance. Before, when that maniac had Barami prisoner, there may have been a chance then, but it was too slim to take, and you knew it. That's why you didn't act. But now, with all of us against just the one man, even with his new powers, I think our chances are much greater. Especially if we hit him sooner rather than later. You know how we felt after we were touched by the dragon. I still haven't had the time I need to fully comprehend it. Perhaps he still hasn't had time to figure out his new power either."

She looked at him sidelong. "You don't really believe that."

"I do."

She shook her head and looked away. "I..."

He waited, but she didn't go on. "What?"

"I... can't."

"Can't what? Fight? I've seen you. I know you can."

"I'm... scared." Her voice had diminished to a mere whisper.

"Is that all?"

She turned back to him then, a questioning look in her tear-filled eyes.

"We're all scared."

She sniffled a little. "You don't understand." She shuddered, her head falling forward, chin to chest.

"Let me guess," he said softly, putting a finger under her chin and lifting her face until she met his gaze again. "You freeze up when you think of fighting that man? You can't move? Your gut turns to jelly?"

"Yes." The barest of whispers.

"You mean to tell me, with all the things you've faced in your life, you've never felt like that before?" He was a little stunned.

She shook her head.

He laughed, but it was short lived given the hurt look on her face. She looked confused.

"Caerwyn." He put an arm around her. She seemed shrunken, not her usual tall, proud self. He drew her a few steps farther away from the others, his voice low, just for her. "I'm laughing because that's how I feel *all* the time. That's probably how most of us feel. We go into every fight, into every challenge, scared stiff. We don't want to be there, we want to run, but we go in anyway. Recently we've gone in because we've had people like you leading us. When you are so scared your legs won't move, but the woman you admire most in your life gets up and rushes in, well, you follow her."

She sniffled. "You've run from every fight we've been in."

That stung, but it was true. He nodded. "You're right. I did, but I also came back to every fight, for you, to help you. Now it's your turn. So you ran from the last fight, well now you can come back as well. Do it for me, or Jais, or Barami, I don't care. Do it because of those who died, or for revenge, it doesn't matter to me, just do it. Come back to us and help us fight."

She looked away. It was her turn to let out a harsh laugh, clipped as it was. "You do always come back, don't you?"

"I do."

"You're insane."

"Perhaps." He pulled her closer, putting his other arm around her. She melted into him and for a moment, he enjoyed the sensation of her in his arms before he remembered it was only because she was so vulnerable and weak at the moment. This wasn't her. "You can join me in my insanity. Let's go do something crazy and fight this wizard. You don't have to do it because you want to or because it's right. You don't have to do it because anyone tells you to. Do it for me, the man who always comes back because he's a little crazy... crazy for you."

She drew herself up a little and pulled out from his embrace. She nodded.

With another sniffle, she gave a sad smile. "Here's to insanity."

34

"GIVE ME A MOMENT, WILL YOU?" CAERWYN ASKED VOLF. SHE moved away as he nodded. She needed a moment alone to sort through everything.

"Take whatever time you need," Volf said from behind her. "Just be ready to go soon."

She smiled. He had a way of saying things, of finding the silly or bright side of nearly anything. He wasn't that practical, nor adventurous, nor strong. He wasn't a fighter at all really, but she found herself liking him more and more. She'd always thought that if she met a mate, it would be a man like her, practical and strong, a warrior. That's why she'd been drawn to Jais. He was everything she'd thought she wanted in a man. He was just young and uncertain. She didn't blame him for that; in fact, she understood that more now than she had before.

Jais had been through a lot, losing his family and the dear friend and lover he'd known most of his life, all within the span of a few days. That hadn't crushed his spirit, but he'd been tentative, careful around anyone, even her. After what had happened to her these last few days, she understood that now. Her own soul had been crushed. She could see that now. It wasn't easy to look at, but Volf had given her enough perspective to see she'd gone through her own ordeal with the wizard. Now she felt she understood Jais a little better. True, she too had lost her family, twice, but she hadn't seen them die. But having been here, having stood by and watched as Elria had died and she'd done nothing, she felt like she understood a little of what that might be like.

She drew in a long shuddering breath.

Jais...

He'd lost so much. First his family and his first love, now another lover... or so she assumed Elria had been. And in such a short period of time. Perhaps she didn't really understand what he had lost.

Perhaps they were just going through their own separate trials.

And she'd pushed him away when he'd tried to comfort her. That stuck like a burr in her soul.

These two men, both so giving, wanting to help her, and here she was still unable to look at either of them as a match for her.

Perhaps it was for the best. She assumed that going against the wizard was a death sentence. She'd not have her child. So, what did it matter what she felt for these men?

All she had left to her was to fight.

And she would fight. She knew that now.

She could see the gaping crack in her spirit. She could feel the terror at the mere thought of going up against that man, but Volf had convinced her. It was necessary. They had to try, or he'd continue to wreak havoc on so many others.

Something else Volf had said stuck with her.

You don't have to do it because you want to or because it's right.

He'd been telling her to fight because he was fighting, and he was just as scared, but she wouldn't fight for him. She'd fight because it was right. That's what she'd always done. She'd always protected others and she'd continue to do so, even if she was afraid of her foe and was nearly certain she'd die.

She clung to that and used it to propel her forward.

Even if it was toward her own doom.

JAIS FELT AN ODD CONFLICT GROW WITHIN HIM. HE WAS SO angry and sorrowful at Elria's death and not having had the chance to speak to the dragon, and yet a hope was springing up within him as he laid his hands on this egg. The not-yet-living dragon held so much potential, not only for him, but for the world.

Everyone thought the dragons were long dead, but perhaps, like this one had been, they were simply in hiding. Perhaps they had kept on, perhaps they had lived and had many other eggs like this one. It gave a certain light to the darkness he'd felt closing in around him.

He waded out of the ash, the remains of the old dragon, and sat heavily on the stone floor.

What did this all mean?

He drew out his father's sword, laid it across his knees, and put a hand to the wide blade.

Father?

Yes son, I'm here.

I'm feeling...

I know, I can feel it too. I'm sorry for your loss.

But... I still don't know so much about who I am!

The soul within the blade laughed a little. *Yet you are*

talking to your long dead father. To many this would be more than enough. I am sorry I cannot tell you more of our heritage, even I don't know much about where we came from. But I can tell you about your mother and me. I don't have all my memories. Being in this place is not natural, and part of me was lost in the transition to the blade. But I do have flashes and there are many things I can recall. I cannot give you your heritage, but I can give you at least a little of your family.

But would that tell him who he was? Would he know all of what he could do? His father's spirit within the sword had already told him he didn't know that information. As much as the soul may have felt his feelings or know what he'd been through, it didn't know him, only what it had experienced with him.

Yes, I am sorry for that. I wish I could tell you more. There was a pause and what felt like a heavy sigh. *I wish I could have known you, my son. I am so sorry we had to leave you behind with your aunt and uncle.*

Why did you? Aunt Sarelle never told me. She only ever said it was to protect me. Why was I safer with her than with you?

There was another hesitation from the spirit within the blade. *Your mother and I were a bit more militant in our beliefs than your aunt. Sarelle saw the world turning against the drahk-sani and thought to hide, to become just another human. We could not do that. We weren't looking for a fight, but we tried for a long time to change how people saw us. It worked, for a while.* Jais got the impression of a shaking head. *But in the end, your aunt's approach was better. By being so open about what we were and trying to help others, eventually even those we were trying to help turned against us. Sarelle had the right idea. Be a human, act like one of them and only use your power when you need to, to help them.*

It didn't work out in the end for Aunt Sarelle either, Jais reminded his father. *The village that she'd helped and healed for years turned on her in an instant.*

We are just out of place in this world, now, his father said wearily. *You need to be constantly careful.*

Yes, thank you. Jais put the sword away and rose.

That hadn't helped him much. He felt more discouraged now than before.

It also didn't help that he was still so very tired. He'd rested a little before Volf woke them to see the egg, but it hadn't been enough. His body still ached, and his mind was hazy. He was bone-weary and needed a good long rest to even begin to feel normal.

He didn't think he was going to get it.

Caerwyn approached him.

Her voice was low when she spoke. "Jais, I'm sorry I... I'm sorry for everything. Elria..."

"That wasn't your fault, and I'm sorry for what I said. I didn't mean it."

The words rang in his own head: *you can die too for all I care.* He shuddered.

"But I chose her."

Jais stepped forward and reached out, holding her shoulders, but keeping at arm's length for a moment. "You made an impossible choice." He still didn't understand it, but then he hadn't been here. That's what niggled and burned within his soul. Maybe if he'd been here Elria wouldn't have died, maybe Caer wouldn't have had to make that choice. Maybe...

"We all have things we need to deal with. I can't say I'm not all torn up inside about..." He still couldn't quite say the words. He swallowed a lump in his throat and went on. "But I don't blame you. I blame that wizard. And I'm sorry you had to go through that."

She nodded. "Thank you. Volf wants to go after the

wizard." There was something odd in her voice when she said this. He couldn't quite place it. "How do you feel about that?"

He gave a mirthless single breath of a laugh. "I'm tired as all the souls in Holn, but *that* I have enough strength for."

Another nod from her.

She broke from his grip and stepped in closer, wrapping her arms around him. He returned the gesture a little unsure where this was coming from but sensed her fragility in that moment and wanted to comfort her.

Her voice was a breath of a whisper over his right shoulder. "Then we'll d—" Her breath caught, and he felt her shiver. "We'll do this together. I'm sorry."

Then she was gone, breaking away and moving stiffly off.

He thought he heard a faint sniffle.

Something was still very wrong with her.

He took a step to go after her when a voice broke through the silence and darkness.

"I'm going after that Shadow-blasted wizard. Who's with me?" It was Volf.

"I am!" He heard Barami's voice from somewhere behind him calling out.

"Agreed!" Hildr called out as well.

Jais sighed heavily. "Count me in." He'd have to figure out what was up with Caerwyn later.

"Then let's get this man before he becomes even more powerful. My spirit link tells me he hasn't gone too far, perhaps back to the area around Hildr's village. Caerwyn and I both are still recovering from our interaction with the dragon. We're hoping to catch him before he's had time to assimilate whatever powers he acquired. But that means we must go now. I can help us move faster than normal, but it will still take us some time to get there and we don't want to give him any more time than necessary." He took a breath. "Are we all ready to go?"

Jais moved toward Volf. "Let's do this."

Caerwyn arrived at the wiry man about the same time as Jais did. He noticed an odd look she gave him and Volf as she nodded her acquiescence.

He hoped he'd have time to talk to her before they had to fight the wizard, but something told him that wasn't to be.

35

OTHER THAN CLIMBING DOWN THE MOUNTAIN SIDE AND MOVING back across the wall-walk over the river—which had luckily dropped its level far enough that it was no threat to any of them—they had traveled the entire distance back to Hildr's village using Volf's shadow-walk.

Barami found it highly disconcerting, the world flashing by as he took but a single slow step.

Dawn had come as they'd descended out of the mountains. Now, standing at the base of the hill on which Hildr's village sat, long shadows still covered them, but the sky was a clear blue above them, the sun risen over the mountain peaks to the east.

"Holn!" Caerwyn swore.

"What?" Jais asked.

But Caerwyn turned to Volf. "You feel that too?"

Volf nodded turning to the rest of them. "It seems the wizard didn't retreat to somewhere near the village, but to the village itself. He's somewhere up at the top of this hill."

Now Barami understood Caerwyn's cursing.

"Let me see what's going on up there." Volf stepped away from them and sat on the ground, his eyes glazing over.

"What's he doing?" Hildr asked. Barami was curious as well.

Caerwyn shrugged. "I don't know. I'm guessing it's one of his new abilities. It sounds like he's able to see what's happening in another place?"

Jais stiffened a little at the mention of 'new abilities.' Barami felt sorry for the boy. He'd been the one who'd so desperately wanted to know more about who he was, and he'd been the only one not to speak to the dragon.

They all waited for Volf to finish whatever it was he was doing. Time slipped by. The shadows grew shorter and the sun peered down on them as it cleared the hill next to which they stood.

Volf drew in a long, shuddering breath, and his eyes snapped open.

Barami caught the flicker of the other man's gaze toward Hildr as his expression went from neutral to horrified.

"I'm sorry," he said to the Dronnegir woman. "You're people..."

"Are they dead?" she asked and Barami was surprised at how composed she sounded. He looked to her. She didn't look composed. Her eyes were haunted, her lips pressed together, nearly bone white with the pressure.

Volf shook his head. "No. Though whether this fate is better or worse I don't know. The wizard has them all in some trance. They are guarding him. Their eyes are vacant, lost. We'll have to go through them to get to him."

Hildr nodded, though Barami could see she didn't much like this news. "Then saved they can be, still."

"Where is the wizard?" Jais asked.

"In that same long-hall where the leaders lived."

Barami felt a surge of hope. "That's not far from the secret entrance. If we use that to go back up..."

"Secret entrance?" Jais looked confused.

Hildr answered. "There is a secret way in and out of the village. We are right next to the lower exit actually, through those bushes." She pointed. Jais looked skeptical.

"Into the side of the hill?"

Hildr nodded.

"I don't know how much good that will do," Volf said rising and stretching. "As much as we'd be getting past many of the villagers, there are still a fair amount within that long hall. We need a plan. I can hide some or all of us if needs be."

Barami nodded. That wasn't a bad idea. Though the tall, skinny man did look much drained from having gotten them here so quickly. He wondered how much the rogue still had in him.

"I agree. I do not wish for any of my village to be killed in fighting this madman. We must spare them." Hildr was adamant.

"That may not be possible," Caerwyn said. Barami knew she was being practical, but he also had a good idea how Hildr was going to respond to that.

"Make it possible! I will have no more of my kin die today!"

That was the response he'd expected.

Barami decided he needed to step in. Everyone here was tired and disheartened, some more than others. There needed to be a reasonable voice to guide them, and it was going to be his.

"If we can come up with a good enough plan then nobody has to die."

"Bara—" Caerwyn began, but he cut her off.

"No! I will not be told what can or cannot happen, not

today." He looked Caerwyn in the eyes. He'd once thought her to be perfect—the epitome of strength and courage—but now he easily won the battle of wills between them. She looked away. "Yes, Caerwyn, we will need to fight. But—" He turned to Hildr quickly. "That doesn't mean anyone has to die."

Already a plan was forming in his head. He threw a question out to the group. "I know little of wizards and such. Do we think that if we slew this man his hold on these people would end?"

Caerwyn nodded. "Yes. I learned a little about other drahksani abilities from the dragon, and that would be in keeping with what the dragon knew. Most if not all magic is dispelled when the originator dies."

"Good. Then I have an idea. Although..." A flaw in his plan occurred to him. He turned to Volf. "You can go unseen, but is there any way to mask your... drahksanness from another such as yourself? Otherwise, even if hidden that man will know you're coming."

Volf nodded. "Yes." He smiled slightly. "It's something I didn't know I could do before the dragon, but when I'm in my shadow-form I cannot be detected by other drahksan."

Barami nodded. "Good. Then here's the plan. We'll all go up that tunnel into the village. Hopefully, the wizard knows nothing of its existence and won't have it guarded. Even if he does, we'll fight our way out—making sure not to kill anyone in the process, just defend ourselves. That will be Jais, Hildr and myself. We'll be the distraction."

"All-the-shadows-in-Holn! I will be no distraction!" Jais shouted. "I'm going to kill that man!"

Barami stared down the husky youth. Jais looked incredibly tired: large bags under his eyes, his gait was sluggish, his shoulders slumped. "Which would you rather have? Killing that man at the expense of the lives of Hildr's kin? Or simply having him dead, in a way which saves as many lives as possible?"

Jais fumed. Barami could see the young man knew the right answer but didn't like it. He'd like what was to come even less. "Caerwyn and Volf will be hidden from sight and the senses of that madman. They will sneak out of the tunnel and get themselves to a position behind the wizard and take him down with little fuss, hopefully." He hadn't taken his eyes off Jais. The young man didn't look upset. It must have been a testament to how tired he was. Barami was sure he'd be complaining about why Caerwyn was going instead of him. Barami would deal with that now, just so it wouldn't become an issue. "Caerwyn goes instead of you, Jais, because she's the veteran warrior and she has just as much desire and reason to want that man dead as you. Trust me."

Jais opened his mouth but said nothing. His eyes darted over the Caerwyn and he nodded slowly. "I'd ask you to make it painful, but I fear quick will be best for all of us," Jais said. His words were dead calm and all the scarier for it.

Barami looked them all over slowly. "The hope is to distract the man and defend ourselves, drawing as many villagers as we can to us, while you two kill him and make sure he never threatens anyone again. Understood?"

There were nods and grunts of agreement all around.

"Then let's go."

Hildr pushed aside the bushes to reveal the hidden portal behind them and then stepped closer to open the heavy door.

Hildr let them all through. Barami went last. He wasn't fond of this place, but to help Hildr free her people and to get vengeance on that wizard, he'd endure it once again.

Volf had a torch lit by the time Hildr was closing the door behind them. Volf led the way down the straight tunnel, and

Caerwyn and Jais followed him. Barami stayed back a bit with Hildr as she lit another torch.

"Do you think my plan will work? I am sorry we'll have to fight any of your people at all, but I fear it is the only way."

She nodded in the flickering light of the newly lit torch. "I agree. It be not ideal, but it be the best way. I can think of no better plan." She looked him in the eye. "Thank you." She stepped forward and with her free hand touched his face. Drawing closer still she guided his lips to hers. The kiss was sure and strong and deep. He felt the heat of her body next to his and held her close. She kept the torch away from them and finished her ministrations.

"If this works," she said softly. "Then I shall make sure you thoroughly enjoy the celebrations afterward."

"Oh?"

"I shall bed you and ensure you be well satisfied."

He had to smile at her blunt recitation of such things. "Then I'll make sure this works." He pulled away and they began to walk swiftly to catch up to the others. After a moment, he turned to her with a half grin, thinking of his reward. "I'll make sure you are well satisfied as well."

"I have no doubt."

Good.

But first they had to kill a wizard who'd taken an entire village under his control, *and* somehow not hurt anyone too badly while doing it.

36

AFTER THE LONG STRAIGHT TUNNEL UNDER THE HILL, THEY HAD ascended the tight spiral stairs, carved from stone, to the landing below the secret entrance through one of the fire pits in a longhouse used mostly for storage.

Volf watched as Hildr moved quietly up the ladder to the metal grating covering the secret entrance. They had doused their torches, as there was enough dim light filtering down from the fake fire pit above for them to see. Hildr peered about cautiously, through the sides of the fire pit.

"It be clear," she whispered down to them before carefully and quietly lifting the grating aside and exiting.

Barami and Jais quickly followed her out.

Volf was tired, incredibly so. His lack of sleep the night before was quickly catching up to him, especially after having used his powers all day. He knew now his shadow-walk wasn't meant to be used over such long distances. In addition to that, he'd been using a lesser version of his shadow-form—which still allowed them to be seen by Barami and Hildr—to hide the drahksani nature of himself, Caerwyn, and Jais for the past trek through the tunnels and continued to do so. He could feel the limits of his power drawing nigh. He just hoped he'd be able to last long enough.

"You ready?" Volf said to Caerwyn behind him.

In the dim light she nodded.

He proceeded up the ladder and out, with her close behind him. The longhouse was empty save for his friends. It seemed they hadn't been sensed and the wizard knew nothing of this entrance.

Good.

"Jais, when I hide myself and Caerwyn, I will have to release my limited shadow-form on you," Volf said. Jais raised a brow. Volf got the feeling the other man didn't know what he was talking about. He simplified. "In a moment the wizard will be able to sense you. He'll know you're coming."

Jais gave a feral grin. "I don't care."

Barami added. "That will work well for our plan. We want the wizard looking our way, not yours."

Volf nodded.

He turned to Caerwyn. "Take my hand." He held it out. Taking a great breath, she took it. He didn't know what was going through her mind, but he feared she might not be up to the task ahead. He certainly wasn't.

He wrapped them both in his shadow-form. The three others had fanned out, weapons ready. The blazing sun was allowed in through the doors at either end of the longhouse as well as several smoke holes in the roof, though the overall effect in the longhouse was still a dim, diffused light.

Hildr was leading the other two toward the passageway at the center of the longhouse, which would connect it to the next one over. "We are only two houses over from the main house. This will get us there fastest. Hopefully the wizard has not thought to guard these." The other three moved down into the darkness as Volf led Caerwyn to the far end of the longhouse, the side facing the outer wall. He knew where he needed to go now: two houses over.

He stopped before they stepped out into the sun.

"You ready for this?"

Caerwyn was close, her hand still in his. It made it easier for him to keep his shadow-form extended for so long if he didn't have to hide a great area. He felt a tremor run through her. She was near enough that, stopped as they were, she was partly leaning against him.

"You keep asking me that." Yet her tone wasn't perturbed, more afraid.

"I'm worried for... for us. I'm no fighter. We both know that, and I'm the only one you'll have with you when you go up against that man. We should be able to surprise him, but if he doesn't go down with one hit..." He shrugged. "You've been through a lot recently."

"I don't need reminding. Let's just get this done." Her tone was clipped, tight.

He nodded, then pulled her along as he slipped through the doorway.

He nearly ran into a guard who'd been stationed close to the door outside but moved carefully around the man.

"His eyes," Caerwyn hissed.

Volf looked to see the man's eyes were glowing with a faint orange light as he looked around slowly. It must be some effect of the magic controlling him. Volf didn't want to think about that too much.

As he moved on, he instantly saw a problem with their plan. There were guards galore around the longhouse which they were heading for. If he hadn't known where to go, the guards would have been a good indication. Not only were there several on the peaks of the houses using that vantage point to keep an eye out, but there was a group of about twenty men and women crowded around the entrance Volf and Caerwyn needed to go through.

They approached slowly.

"How will we get past them?" Caerwyn whispered, her breath warm on his ear she was so close.

He had a way, but he didn't know if it would work on her. He'd never tried it on another person before.

He could manipulate his own form making himself smaller, flatter, if needed to get through tight spaces. He couldn't become too tiny or paper thin, but if he slid along the wall, he could make himself slender enough not to brush by those near the doorway. He'd be able to slip in that way.

But could Caerwyn?

There was only one way to know for certain.

He stopped, and she bumped into him lightly.

"What?" she asked, her voice hushed. Even though no one outside of his shadow-form should hear them they were getting close enough to that large group that he understood her hesitancy to speak any louder.

"I'm going to try something. Come this way." He directed her to the outer wall of the longhouse and stood with his back against it.

Before he could explain, she said, "They're too close to the wall, we won't be able to slip past them."

"We might," he whispered. "I have an ability which lets me flatten or shrink myself when needed. But I don't know if it will work on you. I'm going to—"

Shouts and sounds of fighting erupted from some distance away, somewhere within the longhouse. Before either of them could react, several of those in the group standing outside moved as one and turned, heading in through the wide door to the longhouse.

Of the score of men and women who had been guarding this entrance, half were gone now.

It also meant those who'd been close to the wall weren't there anymore.

"Apparently we won't need to worry about my ability." Volf shrugged. "But we should hurry. If the others have started to fight we don't have much time." He drew in a long breath. "Let's get in there and get this over with."

Caerwyn nodded and they slipped along the wall and through the doorway.

Volf's eyes adjusted almost instantly to the dimmer interior and he stopped, squeezing Caerwyn's hand to give her a bit of warning.

Her eyes must have taken a moment longer to adjust.

"Oh," she said seeing the problem.

As much as some of the guards from outside had come in, and made it easier for them to enter, there were even more men and women within the house between them and the wizard.

Volf could see the tall drahksan man. He was about thirty feet away standing in the center aisle of the longhouse. He was cackling with laughter, looking in the other direction, toward the sounds of fighting.

Between him and them were a couple clusters of guards all looking right at them. Luckily, it looked like his shadow-form was still keeping them from view, but so many pairs of eyes pointed in his direction still made Volf uneasy.

There was also the problem of how to get through the clumps of men and women who stood not only in the wide center aisle, but also on the platforms to either side. There were two sort-of rows of them each a few men thick. It wouldn't be easy to get past them.

"We might need that trick of yours after all," Caerwyn

said. Her voice was barely more than the warm breath which tickled his ear.

He nodded. "Let's see if it works on you." He moved them to one side and up onto the platform, then he concentrated on making them smaller, shorter. Thin wasn't what was needed now. The sloping top of the house would make it hard for them to move at speed past these men. They'd have to crouch or crawl, and that wouldn't work anyway. The hanging furs and cloths which separated different areas along the platform would keep them from moving along too far toward the sides. Mostly they just needed to be a bit smaller to keep hurrying as they moved around all the barriers, guards and otherwise.

He felt himself shrink, an odd sensation as the world grew and enlarged around him. He was a tall man, but most of the Dronnegir were taller and bigger in general. Now they just looked huge. He looked back at Caerwyn hoping she'd shrunken as well.

She had, and looked a little stunned.

He felt her shiver through the hand he was holding. "This is odd. Let's not stay like this any longer than we have to."

He agreed. He knew just how to move to avoid people. He'd been doing it his entire life. He led her in a winding course through and around people avoiding the hanging walls as well.

Soon enough they were within striking distance of the wizard, and the man seemed to have no idea they were there. His attention was still focused in the other direction.

Volf turned to Caerwyn and found her right next to him, his face so close their noses touched. "Once you go in to attack, you won't be hidden anymore. Those men and woman behind us will know you're there."

"Then I'll just have to end this quickly." She tried to give a confident grin, but the tremor in her voice and the uncertainty plain on her face belied her words. She seemed to realize it too. She closed her eyes and drew in a breath. "I can do this."

"I know you can."

She opened her eyes and kissed him quickly. It happened so fast he didn't quite register it. "For luck."

He nodded still stunned.

Then she released his hand. With a muttered word, a spear appeared in her hand.

She'd be visible now, but no one was looking in this direction. She'd have one good attack.

She threw.

But fate was not on their side.

The spear bounced off some field around the man which shimmered when struck. It was a rough ovoid shape, covering him like an invisible egg-shell.

The spear returned to Caerwyn's hand quick enough, but their surprise was gone.

The man spun and stared at her, then laughed.

With that, Volf lost all hope.

JAIS WAS DRENCHED IN SWEAT. HE'D BEEN EXHAUSTED EVEN before starting this fight, and his body throbbed with one united ache. He worked harder and harder just to keep away the Dronnegir, who were trying to kill him, without hurting them.

But there were too many.

He spun like a top, his two blades whirling so fast they were barely visible. He was defending only, as the others were, but this was taking too long, even though this fight had barely begun.

He'd have to stop soon.

Far too soon.

There was only one thing to do.

"I'm going through them!" he called out to Hildr and Barami. If they registered any shock at this, it was lost in their own intense concentration as they battled to keep weapons away from them.

"You can't!" Barami shouted.

But Jais didn't have a choice.

He was not a tall man and couldn't see past the hordes of

people in front of him. He didn't know if Volf had managed to get Caerwyn in, or if they were still sneaking around somewhere. It didn't matter. He couldn't wait.

The trick would be to do this without harming anyone.

It was going to hurt, but he hoped his healing ability would save him in the end. It was a desperate gamble, but he had to do something now.

He let out a scream, more to invigorate himself then intimidate the mindless people in front of him. Then he ran headlong into that wall of flesh and armor.

He was right.

It did hurt a lot.

But he was strong, stronger than any normal human by some degree. He pushed people aside and bull-rushed through them. Blades cut lines of fire through his flesh. Fists hammered him. Shields bashed at him. His head rang, and his body's ache became a living breathing entity of pain.

But then he was free, out the other side of the horde of people. Some were turning to grab at him, but he ran. His legs were exhausted, but he forced them to propel him forward in a stumbling shamble of a jog.

There was yet another group before him with weapons ready, but beyond that, he could see the wizard and Caerwyn.

He had a brief moment before he reached the next group as he watched what happened beyond. Volf was nowhere to be seen, probably still hiding. The wizard unleashed a great gout of fire at Caerwyn, and Jais screamed as it engulfed her.

Charging forward, he continued his anguished cry, crashing against the next wave of Dronnegir before him.

The mind-controlled barbarians closed in around him, clustering close and cutting off his view of what happened beyond. He tried to push through them as he had with the last group, but these seemed more prepared for such an attack.

He was moving forward, but it was slow, step by agonizing step, and the force against him was immense. He'd forgotten how strong these people were. They didn't use weapons against him this time. That would have been futile as bunched together as they were. They would have been cutting themselves as much as him. But their fists were weapons, and they used them with abandon, smashing down on him as he tried to get past them.

He wasn't going to succeed. For every step he took, trying to push forward, he found his feet sliding backward in the dirt of the floor.

More hammering fists rained down on him. His strength waned. His Body began to give way as his mind grew hazy. If he survived this, everything above his waist would be one great bruise of lumpy flesh.

He surged his healing ability to give himself what strength he could, but precious little happen. He was too far gone into fatigue.

One of his hands found the hilt of his sword and he gripped it. He wouldn't draw it fully. He'd made a promise to Hildr and he'd keep it even if it meant his life. No, he drew it out only enough to lay a finger on the blade.

Father... I need...

His father's spirit read his thoughts quickly enough and did as he'd hoped.

Energy flashed into him.

He funneled everything he could into healing and rejuvenating himself. He could feel it working, his flesh mending, his muscles strengthening, but even as the sword push the last of what it could into him, he feared it wouldn't be enough.

He cried out again, in a great wail of pain, fear, and frustration.

Even as he did, the force of the people around him pushed him to his knees despite all his newfound energy.

From his knees, he was pushed lower still, to all fours.

People must have been piling on above him as the great weight on him increased.

Tears leaked from his eyes, his lids clenched shut.

He let out one last bellow...

CAERWYN HAD SUMMONED HER IMMUNITY TO MAGIC JUST IN time to avoid the fire spewed at her from the wizard. She'd had it lowered so Volf could keep her hidden. But when the wizard had turned to her with that hideous laugh, she'd remembered it and raised it just in time.

The fire washed around her, warm and harmless.

When it died, the wizard's eyes went wide.

She grinned. She still wasn't feeling particularly hopeful, but the look of shock in the other man's eyes was pleasing.

She didn't know if the ability would affect her weapon, whether that might allow it to penetrate through his magical shield. It was worth a try.

She threw Davlas with all the pent-up fury and rage she felt at her own impotence. It bounced off the wizard's barrier once again. Though there was a moment of terror in the man's eyes. Perhaps he'd doubted his own magic.

Apparently, her ability to negate the magic of others was only on things actively affecting her, not passive defenses.

She summoned the spear back to her hand and reassessed her situation, but in that moment, the wizard figured out how he could fight someone immune to his magic. He did after all have an entire village of slaves at his disposal.

A group charged at her.

Now she had a problem. If she wanted to keep Hildr happy, she couldn't fight them with her weapons. She'd kill someone if she went all out. She could defend herself and had just enough time to take her shield from her back and slide it onto her arm before the people arrived. She kept Davlas nearby but didn't wield him physically. She could control the spear with her mind and did so, drawing her sword to deflect any attacks at her.

It quickly became apparent that though she was pulling her attacks so as not to seriously harm anyone, the villagers were not.

She had to retreat from the onslaught of so many infuriated and skilled warriors. Her calf, just below the knee, bumped into something as she stepped back. She nearly toppled over, but only just managed to keep her balance.

She didn't have time to look behind her but hoped what she'd encountered was what she thought it was.

She leapt up and back and thankfully found she was now atop the platform which dominated the side of the longhouse.

She had something now, if not much and not for long. She was a good foot and a half above her attackers. She had some high ground. Her mind whirled through the years of tactical training. She didn't have much to work with, only a little height advantage, but she be damned to the darkest shadows of Holn if she didn't use that to its fullest extent. She hammered down on several attackers with her shield. They'd hurt, but it wouldn't be anything fatal, she hoped.

Two men tried to step onto the platform on her right. She

sent Davlas back behind their legs, then pulled it forward, toppling them backwards into others.

She had a moment, a few heartbeats at most, to pause.

She couldn't get past these people, which meant she couldn't fight the wizard.

There was nothing she could do. It would take all her ability and tactical knowledge to just keep these people at bay. Moving past them without harming them would be near to impossible.

She could do nothing to affect the wizard now.

It was all up to Volf.

And that's when the earth shuddered and heaved beneath her.

38

Volf felt the tremor. It shook him so violently he let his shadow-form drop. He was exceptionally agile, but still went to one knee at the violence of the quake. Dust and debris from the rafters was shaken loose and fell on everything around him. For a moment, all was obscured by the haze.

Before the sudden and inexplicable tremor, the wizard had been focused on Caerwyn, one hand outstretched and eyes near-to-closed as if it took some great concentration to control those attacking her.

Volf had stood so near, but terrified to act.

What did he know of fighting, of killing? He didn't even have a sword on him. He'd left the one Caerwyn had been using to teach him back with his pack. He hadn't thought of it at all, he wasn't a fighter. Stealth and secrecy were his weapons. All he had on him was a single long knife and that was in his hand. But what to do with it?

A few times he'd taken a tentative step toward the wizard but had backed off every time. If Caerwyn's spear hadn't broken through the man's shield what made him think his knife would do any better?

Even now, as the dust settled and he tried to regain his feet after that odd tremor, he realized he'd dropped the weapon.

He knelt again and rummaged around in the dirt, but he still could not see well through the settling dust. His hand brushed something, cutting a finger. He plucked up the weapon by the blade, slicing his palm, but at least he had a weapon now.

He switched the knife to his other, unwounded hand as he rose.

It was only then—as the dust settled—that he saw what he guessed had caused the earth to shake as it had.

Jais was on his hands and knees at the center of a small crater. There had been a group of Dronnegir there before. They had all been thrown away, flung to all sides, creating a small cleared area around Jais.

The wizard was also down.

Jais tried to rise, but it took him several attempts and when he did, he swayed on his feet as he staggered forward toward the wizard.

The wizard was quicker to his feet and faced Jais.

"I do not think you will be resistant to my fire," the wizard said, hissing out his words with a ragged vehemence. He raised a hand, but then a form—shrieking and flying through the still dusty air—knocked him to the side. The wizard's gout of flame missed Jais, but only by a few inches and Jais raised an arm, ducking to one side to shield his face from the heat.

Volf could now see it had been Caerwyn who had hit the wizard, and she was following up her flying attack by physically battering on his magical shield. The wizard was still standing as Caerwyn bashed with her shield and slammed her fist against his defenses again and again. Her sword had been knocked from her hand when she'd hit the wizard and lay on the floor a few feet away.

Volf rushed over to the weapon, thinking to toss it back to Caerwyn, but once it was in his hand…

He was behind the wizard.

Jais had closed distance. He and Caerwyn were pounding on the wizard's shield and the man seemed to be hard pressed to keep them at bay. He wasn't throwing any magic at them and for a moment, Volf wondered what the man was doing.

But then in his periphery he caught the villagers closing in slowly and carefully behind his allies. The two were so focused on trying to bash down the wizard's shield they weren't seeing the attackers gathering behind them, weapons ready.

Volf felt his mouth go dry and his stomach heave and clench. His palms were slick and his breathing quick. He had to do something.

But what?

He'd just be battering the wizard's shield as well.

His mind flashed through everything the dragon had given him about his own abilities and as it did, it snagged on something. It was some bit of knowledge, some ability he hadn't had time to think on or test since he'd gained his newfound awareness of his skills.

It was a variation on his shadow-walk. That ability allowed him to move quickly over-land despite a leisurely pace, but there was a deviation from that which would allow him to step through barriers. He didn't fully understand it. The insight came in a flash, and he knew what to do without truly knowing how he was doing it.

He held out the sword in his one hand and concentrated just on it and his arm. It faded a little, becoming transparent. It seemed to shake with a great intensity, such that he could feel the rapid tremors through the rest of his body as well.

He didn't think.

Thrusting forward with the sword, it encountered no shield.

The blade plunged into flesh.

The feel of a blade jarring through a man's body was too much for him, and he stumbled back, releasing the sword, horrified. His stomach churned, and he felt himself growing faint.

Both Jais and Caerwyn stumbled forward a step as their attacks hit nothing.

They shared a revelatory glance then both pounced on the wizard.

Even as they did, the men and women who had been gathering behind them swayed and staggered. The faint glow of their eyes was gone. They'd been freed of the control on them.

Volf let out a giddy laugh of shock and joy... and fainted.

CAERWYN'S FISTS CONNECTED WITH THE WIZARD'S JAW. HER knuckles were already torn and bloody from pounding on the magical shield, but she didn't care. It felt good to feel his skin and bone give way with the blows.

She was on the man now. He lay prone and she was half atop him and half kneeling. She surged her strength and endurance with a wild cry and hammered down on his face with the wild fury of a cornered bear. She'd lost her shield and was simply pummeling the man with both fists. Her scream did not let up until her voice could cry out no more, and her arms did not stop descending on the wizard with rapid blows until someone grabbed her.

"He's dead, Caer," Jais said.

She couldn't see him—nor the wizard—through the glazing of tears in her eyes. She blinked, but the tears did not go.

She wiped her eyes as she staggered to stand. Yet that did little. Her hands were covered in blood. Still, she could barely see.

Her throat was raw and her face wet. She'd been sobbing through her screams, she knew that now.

Jais' voice was close. "Gods, you're a mess. Here let me..." She felt his tender hands wiping her face. When she could see again, she looked around, still dazed.

Jais stood next to her. He was holding her, supporting her, or perhaps she was supporting him. He looked completely drained, barely able to stand.

But despite his fatigue, he wore a weary grin. "We did it." He turned his head slightly and nodded.

She looked and smiled grimly. The wizard was no longer recognizable. His face was well caved in, near to crushed. A sword tip poked through his belly as he lay at an awkward angle, propped up slightly by the hilt of the sword behind him.

"I..." But she had no words. Her fury was spent, and her emotions surged within her.

She fell to her knees and Jais went with her. It seemed they had been supporting each other after all.

"I know," he said softly as her tears returned and she doubled over weeping. His hand rubbed her back. "I know."

BARAMI—CLOSELY FOLLOWED BY HILDR—CAME UPON A strange sight. They'd known something had happened when the villagers they were defending against had suddenly stopped. The villagers' eyes had returned to normal, and they'd stood, confused, blinking and recovering from their possession. He and Hildr had pushed their way through several groups of villagers to see what had transpired. They'd come across a group of villagers recovering and groaning, tossed about like twigs from some strange attack that had scattered them so. Then they'd reached where the final battle had been fought.

Caerwyn was lying on her side, curled into a ball, weeping. Jais was nearby, kneeling, face down in the dirt... snoring. Volf was a little ways off, splayed like a ragdoll and similarly out of it. The wizard was dead, quite so.

With no one to tell them what had happened, Barami could only imagine the various and odd scenarios which had led to this scene.

"It's over," he said softly.

Hildr put an arm around him. "Thanks to you and your friends."

39

"SKOLL!" BARAMI CHEERED, CLASHING HIS METAL FLAGON WITH many others. He didn't know what the word meant. The Dronnegir used it as some sort of toast to health. Also, he didn't much care as he was getting well drunk from their strong and sweet honey-mead.

A great celebration was being held, a festival and a funeral. Several days had passed and life was ever so slowly moving on in the village. Several clan members, Elria's father among them, had gone up to the dragon-cave and brought back her body for the proper rights. Her remains lay on an unlit pyre to one side of the large village center. The pyre would be lit at dusk, or when Jais had awoken to give his final respects, whichever came later.

Jais had been asleep for days, unable to be woken by any outside force. He'd risen for brief periods to eat great quantities of food, but then had succumbed to his fatigue once again.

Caerwyn had been abed for much of that same time as well, though Barami could tell her weariness was not of body, but of soul. He'd been meaning to talk to her but hadn't had the heart, not yet.

Volf had woken not long after the fight, only to be sick. He too had rested for quite some time. Now he stayed near Caerwyn tending to her.

That had left Barami on his own. He'd rested for some time as well. He wasn't as young as any of the others and had no special powers of endurance. But he had something to get up for.

Hildr had seemed to sleep little. She was much younger than he and still well in her prime. He had no doubt she'd slept, but not for near as long as he. The woman was a blessing, a wonder, a miracle. Just seeing her made him feel ten years younger.

She came for him now, pulling him away from the celebration with the group of Dronnegir.

"Be you ready?"

He grinned. "Ready as I'll ever be."

"You be drunk. Do you think that wise?" Her tone was scolding.

He could only grin wider at that, and he chuckled a little to himself. So many times in his life he'd seen men chided by their women in similar ways. He'd seen it with his own father and with friends who'd been bonded. He'd laughed at those men and the trouble they'd caused, thinking he'd never be in such a position. And now that he was, he found he thoroughly enjoyed it. One could not be scolded by a loving woman, unless one had a loving woman, and he did.

"I can handle my liquor. And I think I need just a little fortification to face your father again."

She laughed a little. "Perhaps. Even I wish I were drunk when dealing with him at times."

"You could have a drink."

"No, not for this."

Barami nodded. He couldn't help but have his silly grin grow wider as he looked her over. She was washed and, for once, not wearing her armor—which seemed ever-present on her. Instead, she wore a dress of white, made of some thick material—probably wise given the climate here. It covered her entirely, from a modest neck-line to wrists and ankles. Her fiery hair was braided in a single thick knot, falling to her mid-back, pulled back tightly. Her skin was pale and, as always, her eyes that brilliant green.

"I'm the luckiest man alive," he whispered and leaned in for a quick kiss. His lips only just brushed hers as she moved back a bit and blushed.

"Not yet. Not here."

He quirked a brow. "What's changed?" Was she having second thoughts?

She was blushing as she leaned close and whispered, "There be a ritual to this. The woman wears a dress of white and must not be seen to be... intimate with the man. Not until this is done."

"Oh." He nodded. For a moment, he'd been a little concerned. It was the first time she'd ever been so reserved in her actions or words. "Then let's get this done."

She nodded and, taking his hand, turned to her father's hall.

"Holding hands is not too much?" he asked. He was teasing a little, but also actually curious. If a chaste kiss had been too much, perhaps...

"Holding hands be well, yes."

They passed by many on their way to and through the long hall. Everyone who saw them began to follow along behind.

"We're gathering a crowd," he said quietly.

She gave a light laugh. "They know what be happening and wish to watch."

"This isn't a private thing then?"

She shook her head still smiling. "No."

"Ah."

Finally, they came before her father.

Barami guessed that the man had had some warning. Either that or he was dressed in his own finery for the feast and funeral tonight. He wore a thick cloak lined with white fur, but the exterior was a pristine light blue, like a winter river. He was also washed and done-up. His long red-and-gray beard was braided, and his fiery hair was loose and laid out evenly over his shoulders. He looked every inch a king, even if it his kingdom was rather tiny.

"Father," Hildr said with a bit of a bow. She dipped, bending a knee, but did not kneel, that would only mar her dress in the dirt. She looked at Barami then.

"Great Egir," Barami said and did the same, bowing with a bended knee and rising. That had been what she'd told him to say. Now came the hard part, his own words.

He met the chief's eyes. It was the first time he met the man's unyielding, intimidating gaze and felt no fear or worry. He felt at peace, and he even smiled.

Hildr had told him to use his own words, just don't insult her father... too much.

"I am a simple man, so I shall keep this simple. I wish to be bonded to your daughter. I love her."

The Egir waited, perhaps to see if there was more. His face betrayed no emotion. After a long moment, he drew a deep breath and turned to Hildr.

"Do you wish to be bonded to this... simple man?" the large man rumbled.

"I do." She nodded.

Another long pause as the Egir turned that green-eyed gaze of steel back to Barami.

From what Barami understood, the Dronnegir were unlike most cultures he'd heard of. Permission was not needed to be bonded. The two in question needed only to profess their devotion to each other before at least five others. What he and Hildr were doing now was a bit more formal. Also, this wasn't the bonding. This was just addressing the Egir for his blessing, which, though not mandatory, was customary. The fact that the Egir was her father made things more interesting.

The Egir spoke. "You are a strong and wise man, Barami of the Afgenni. I do not think you 'simple' in any way. You have my blessing to be bonded with this woman, and she has my blessing to be bonded to you."

The crowd around them cheered, and Hildr leaned over to him. Her voice was only just loud enough for his ears over the noise of the others. "You can kiss me now if you like."

He did, and it wasn't all that chaste, but then, she was participating in it as much as he.

Out of the corner of his eye, he caught the Egir's expression.

The man was actually smiling.

BARAMI BEGGED SOME TIME AWAY FROM HIS NOW OFFICIALLY betrothed.

Seeking out Caerwyn, he found her easily. She was where she had been for most of the last few days, at her bunk, laying down, eyes staring off into nothing.

Volf was nearby, of course, and Barami asked if he could

have a word with Caer alone. Volf passed a concerned gaze over the woman and nodded, leaving.

Caerwyn rose to a sitting position. She'd heard him.

"Barami? What do you need?"

He came to sit on the edge of the platform, close to where she'd spread out her bunk. She slid over, so she was a little closer.

It was heartbreaking to look at her, especially when he felt so light and happy. Some of his elation melted away. She no longer seemed like the woman he'd known. The toll of the recent events still wore on her deeply. There were bags under her eyes where there had been none before and her posture was different, not as rigid or firm, but slumped slightly. Mostly it was minor things that might not seem of any great concern, but to one who knew her, these were telling signs of a spirit that was—if not broken, then—altered.

"I have good news. Though perhaps you may not see it as such."

"Oh?" She did not seem upset, but curious and a little worried.

"Caer," he began and reached out to her. She put her hand in his and he smiled. "I need to ask a favor of you, a large one."

"Go on."

"I need you to discharge my life-debt."

Her brow furrowed. "Not that you haven't repaid it a dozen times over, but why?"

He gave a halfhearted laugh. "I may have repaid it that many times, but you've saved my life even more still." He looked away for a moment and drew in a long breath. "Caerwyn, I've found something here." He pressed his lips together for a moment before going on. "I am sure you know how I felt about you. I will always admire you. But I have found... someone, and I need to pledge my life to them now."

"Hildr."

He nodded.

It was her turn to look away. "You're staying." It wasn't a question. After a moment, she nodded and repeated—in a more final and grave way— "You're staying."

"I am."

She just kept nodding to herself.

"But," he hastened to add. "I will always be here if you need me. As much as this place is as far from my home as I have ever known, I will be making a new home here. If you need anything, you have but to return and ask it. I'll give you whatever you need." He shrugged, and the next words sort of slipped out, though he wasn't sure he meant to say them. "You could make a home here too."

She shook her head. "No." The gaze she turned back to his was hard even if her tone wasn't. After a moment, she said the word again, but softer still and squeezed his hand. "No. I'm happy for you, Barami. I'm glad you've found someone and..." She drew in a long breath. "I am sorry I could not give you what you wanted. You have always been—" Tears were coming to her eyes now, another sign of her changed spirit. She would not have wept before. "You've been such a good friend, the best friend a person could have. Thank you... for everything."

She withdrew her hand from his and that was the end of it.

The end...

He rose and nodded. "As have you, Caerwyn. Thank you."

She was smiling as he turned away, but it was a sad smile and her eyes were still tearing.

He left a little bit of his heart with her in that moment. If she had been her old self he was sure he could have made a clean break, but now... she was so vulnerable. He hated himself for leaving her, even if she'd be the one leaving this place not him.

He swallowed a lump in his throat and exited through the far end of the long-hall. He didn't have the heart to rejoin the celebrations.

Not now.

Not yet.

40

JAIS WOKE JUST BEFORE DUSK.

He was ravenous and, as had been the case in the—however many—days since the wizard's death, food had been left on the edge of the platform for him. He scurried over and ate it all, despite it being well cooled. He cared little.

He cared little.

That phrase stuck like a burr in his thoughts. It seemed to sum up the entirety of his being at this moment. So much had happened. He should have felt excited or victorious. They had defeated the wizard, and he'd discovered a new ability. He didn't know where it had come from, but under that pile of men and woman trying to crush him he'd done something. The earth had shaken, and he'd thrown everyone off him. It had been amazing and eye-opening and allowed him to get to the wizard to help Caerwyn. But that felt like it had been so long ago. Now, he felt... nothing.

Hollow.

Nearby, someone cleared their throat.

He paused in shoving food into his mouth and looked up to see a young man standing not far away. He was Dronnegir, that was clear enough by the tall lean build and red-blond hair.

"I be told to tell you, if you woke before dusk, that that be when we will perform the rites for Elria." The young man motioned to a large wooden basin filled with water and some fresh clothes, all in white. "If you wished to bathe and change we shall wait for you." He nodded and left without waiting for any response.

"What if I didn't want to come," Jais mumbled to himself, but he knew it was meaningless. He'd go.

Finishing his meal, he stripped and stepped into the tub. The water wasn't frigid, but it was far from warm. He cared little and sunk in, scrubbing himself.

He wasn't sure where the others were.

When he'd fallen asleep after the battle, they had all had their bunks spread out somewhere nearby on this platform, but all their things were gone now. Had they left without him, heading south already? He didn't think that likely, but he grew more concerned.

How long had he been asleep?

He knew only that he felt well rested now.

Finally.

It felt like it had been ages since he'd felt this way.

And what would he do if the others had left him?

Would he follow after them? He was a good enough tracker to find them if he wanted to. But, what did he want?

He felt so... empty.

He scrubbed hard to remove the layers of caked on grime, then dunked himself a few times. There was a cloth for drying himself, then he dressed. The clothes were not his, so they were ill fitting, there were few people in this world with his build. The Dronnegir were tall and muscular, he was even more muscular than most but stocky and short. Anything which fit him across the shoulders was usually too long for him.

He made some adjustments to the clothes with his knife, caring little for the garments he might have ruined or the loose threads he left hanging from every hem. He put on his boots and walked out into the growing dimness of a gathering dusk.

He'd been wrong. His friends had not left. They were all still here... but then why had they moved their bunks away from his? He shrugged and moved forward to join the large group which surrounded a pyre.

Elria's pyre.

"We are all gathered," a great baritone voice boomed into the dimness. Jais looked around to see Elria's father standing with a torch, the only torch. "Who wishes to speak of my daughter before she be sent to Vala?"

Jais froze, a tear in his eye and a lump he couldn't quite swallow in his throat. He wasn't ready for this.

"I will." Hildr stepped forward. All eyes turned to the chieftain's daughter. "My cousin, though she trained with us in weapons, was always a kind soul. As a healer, she loved to help others. Yet she had no fear when it came to battle. Her heart be Dronnegir!" That got a bit of a cheer from the crowd. "Never doubt that she died fighting. Her spirit resisted until the end. She was the best of any of us... of all of us. I know not any woman like her and can only hope she will inspire us to be better."

A few people gave restrained cheers or affirming comments as Hildr stepped back.

Jais had to move now.

But he couldn't.

Tears were on his cheeks, and he feared he'd have no voice to speak with. That and his legs refused to move.

Yet again, another stepped forward before he did.

It was Caerwyn.

"I cannot apologize enough." The words were clear, her voice raised. But Jais could sense something from her, a bitterness underlying what she said, a self-loathing. It seemed to taint all her words, making them just a little too harsh, too abrasive. "It is my fault that this woman died."

Oh gods. No, don't do this to yourself Caerwyn. Don't tell them. They don't need to know the details. Please just stop.

"If I had not sought her out in Cold River to heal my friends. If she hadn't known we were coming north, she may have stayed in that town. But she knew her duty..." Caerwyn faltered and her voice broke. It took her a moment and several breaths to recover. "She was strong and came north with us to warn you of our arrival." Caerwyn shook her head a sour look on her face. "I should have heeded her warning, your warning. If I had, none of this would have happened. I am so, so sorry," She wiped away tears and tried to speak again a few times, but in the end simply said, "I'm sorry." She returned to her place tears running down her cheeks.

Jais moved.

His legs unstuck. He stepped forward. He didn't know what he'd say, but he was committed now, moved by Caerwyn's speech.

He came to stand before the pyre, uncertain, in front of the gathered mass of Dronnegir. For a long time, he simply stood there trying to find words as tears traced his cheeks.

He had to say something.

"I—" His voice cracked with that one word. He couldn't help himself. The noise he'd made had been so pathetic and his emotions so tense and taut that he had to laugh. He laughed in a jerking, sobbing sort of way for a long moment before it became sobs and the words fell out of him like the tears from his eyes. He wasn't speaking loudly or perhaps even clearly, but he didn't care.

"I loved her. The gods only know how I loved her. She was unlike anyone I'd ever met. She was pure and loving and wonderful, and I wish to all the heavens that I could be there in her place and she here with you. I too am sorry that I and my friends dragged you and her into this mess. I can't ever make up for your loss. If you feel her loss half as deeply as I do, then I know it will mark your soul just as it has marked mine. She was... she was... everything Hildr said she was: strong and brave and kind and wonderful and so helpful and, and, I'm so sorry. I... my heart... she..." He was stammering, and he knew it.

Strong arms enfolded him and pulled him close to a large barrel chest.

"I understand."

It took Jais a moment to figure out who was holding him. He looked up into the tear-streaked face of Elria's father.

"It be clear now, your feelings for her. I be sorry if I doubted you. I hold no ill will against you. She died a warrior, defending the dragon. That is all we can ask."

Jais nodded, and the man released him. Jais moved back to the crowd, feeling drained and with a new weariness coming over him. Though he felt just a little lighter for having released those words from his soul.

Elria's father spoke.

Jais didn't really hear the words, he was still a little lost in his own mourning. He only was drawn back as the man lit the pyre.

"...and so we send her soul to Vala to be with her ancestors and the gods."

The flame caught quickly and spread, licking like a hungry wolf through the timber. Soon the white-wrapped bundle atop the pyre was no longer visible through the flames. Yet Jais stayed to watch the fire. He had to. He felt like there was nothing else for him in the world at the moment. He stayed, as did her father, late into the night until the pile was only embers. Then he returned to his bunk and returned to sleep. This time it was not the slumber of a fatigued body, but a weary soul.

41

CAERWYN STOOD ON THE ROOF OF THE HALL SHE SHARED WITH her two companions: Jais and Volf. Barami was living with Hildr now. She was happy for him.

If indeed she could be truly happy about anything.

She stared out over the hills beyond the wall of the village, but the amazing vista did little to inspire much of any emotion within her.

She shivered despite the warmth of the late summer morning. The cold wasn't without, but within. Where before within her there had been certainty and daring, now there was just a gaping hole, frosty and hollow.

She'd had time enough to think about what had happened to her; to assess the events in the cave and afterward. Logically, she knew she wasn't a different person, but she felt like some part of her had been ripped out. The wound was healing, but in its place was only scarring. And as with all new scars it didn't feel right, less sensitive and rough. She'd come to terms with what had happened, but they weren't great terms.

She was questioning things she'd never questioned

before, which was odd. She knew more about herself and her power now than she had, but that was only part of who she was. That was what had been given to her through generations, but her heart and soul were her own and until now she'd never questioned her wants and desires.

Now she questioned everything.

Her keen ears picked up the footfalls of someone approaching. It was a testament to those superior senses that she even knew who it was. Jais and Volf had very different gaits and strides. This was soft and long, not sturdy and sure.

Volf.

He stopped about ten feet behind her. She'd let him announce himself.

"Caer?"

He'd taken to using the short form, and in truth she didn't care that much. Jais used it too. Yet she wasn't sure she felt that close to either of them anymore. How close could a person get to another person without a heart? Hers was cold.

"Yes."

"I'd been meaning to ask you... can you feel the others?"

She sighed.

She could. She'd been wondering how long it would take before Volf asked about them. Apparently, that time was now.

"Yes."

"To the south?"

She let out a bitter laugh. "Everything is south of here."

He laughed a little as well. "Yes, I suppose..."

She finally turned to look at the man. "You want to go find them?"

"Isn't that what you and Jais were doing? Finding other drahksani? Isn't that why... how you found me?"

Yes, that had been what they were doing, but she didn't really know what she was doing anymore. She nodded to his questions and let out a long breath. "We should seek them out."

His face darkened, all frown and furrows. "Is that what you want?"

I don't know what I want. Yet instead of saying that, she tried to sound more positive when she said, "Yes. I'm just..." She smiled and hoped it looked genuine. "I need a little time to get back to being me." That's what she'd been telling people. They seemed to accept it, but in truth, she didn't think she'd ever be back to her old self.

He smiled. "Good. When shall we leave?"

She picked a date. "Tomorrow, first thing?"

He nodded, his smile widening.

She could imagine his thoughts, *look how decisive she's being, perhaps she's recovering!* He was a bit of an optimist. But it wasn't really decisiveness, more a need to give him what he wanted so he'd leave her alone again.

He nodded a goodbye. "I'll go tell Jais."

He left, deftly and lightly moving down the side of the sloped, grass-covered roof.

She turned back to the mountain vista.

She knew that Volf was interested in her. She also suspected that Jais would turn his attentions back to her now that Elria was gone. She didn't much care.

Her desire to have a child was gone. It had been a part of the old her. This new incarnation didn't want to have to take care of anyone. That would require her to care.

And right now... she didn't.

———

VOLF WAS SMILING AS HE ENTERED THEIR LONG-HALL AND found Jais.

"We're leaving first thing tomorrow."

"Oh?" Jais looked up, seemingly distracted. He shook his head and looked at Volf. "Why?"

"Caer and I have been sensing other drahksani to the south. We figure it's about time we moved on and found more of our kind." He shrugged. "Perhaps they can help you figure out who you are?"

"Perhaps." Jais seemed to fall into another stupor, but a moment later shook his head again. He'd been doing that a lot. "I'll be ready first thing tomorrow."

"Good," Volf said. He turned and left, something about being around the man brought him down. He didn't blame the man for feeling lousy after the loss of a loved one, but that didn't mean Volf had to be nearby and feel bad as well.

He walked back out into the sun of the day and took a deep breath. They'd be on the move again soon and that thought cheered him up. Even speaking with Caerwyn a moment ago, she'd seemed a bit more certain and happy than she had in the past few days. Perhaps she was getting over the horrors they'd all faced.

That brought a flash to Volf's mind, the sensation of stabbing the wizard. He shuddered as the thought fled, but it had shattered his happy mood.

He forced a grin.

He'd have to get used to fighting. He was out in the world now and there were dangers all around him. He'd need to be prepared for the next one. He'd need to know how to fight.

He told himself he could handle it. That the next time it wouldn't be so bad.

Mostly he told himself that anything was worth it to be near Caerwyn. She was still the most wondrous and fascinating woman he'd ever met. She was so strong. Well she had been, and would be again, he was sure.

He had faith.

JAIS HAD FEW BELONGINGS, BUT HE STUFFED WHAT HE HAD INTO his pack and closed it.

It was morning. The sun just up over the mountains.

A week had passed since the funeral, and they were leaving... without Barami. That had come as a surprise, which it shouldn't have. In truth, Jais had to wonder: if Elria had lived, would he be leaving?

He stopped what he was doing. It was a question which had plagued him for several days, even if it was entirely hypothetical. He honestly didn't know. At the funeral, he'd professed his love for the Dronnegir woman, but there was still so much he didn't know about... so many things. Chief among those things was who he really was.

Caerwyn and Volf had talked to the dragon and uncovered their abilities. He had his father's sword and the spirit within it, but...

The earth shaking he'd done to throw those Dronnegir off him during the fight with the wizard, that had come out of the blue, a complete surprise to him. He wasn't even sure if he could repeat it. He didn't even know what had happened, really.

So much he didn't know.

Elria's father had said that when he'd gone to get her body he'd seen and touched the egg. The villagers would be sending people up to the cave regularly to check on it. There was hope here now. They still had a dragon to protect. They had been doing it for so long, they wouldn't know who they were without a dragon nearby to keep safe.

Jais considered staying until the dragon hatched, but he

didn't know how long it might be until then, or even if the new dragon would be able to help him.

Jais shook off his ruminations and finished tying his bedroll to his pack.

He'd found out why no one had been around when he'd woken, why their stuff was somewhere else. Barami was staying with Hildr now, and Caerwyn had wanted to be alone, off by herself, so she'd claimed a section of the hall much farther down. Volf had moved his things closer to hers, while still giving her room to be 'alone.'

Jais sat on the edge of the platform, his pack over one shoulder.

So much had happened recently.

Too much.

They'd met Volf only a couple of weeks ago. Then there was Gosse, the conflicted dragon-hunter-turned-drahksan. In the end, he had been a good man, had sacrificed himself to help those he'd once hunted.

Was that all that mattered? Who they were in the end?

Elria had faced her death fighting as much as she could, and Gosse had died freeing drahksani. Perhaps that *was* all that mattered?

So, who did Jais want to be in the end?

He still didn't know.

Would it make any difference if he knew who he was and what he could do?

He shook his head. He wasn't going to figure out anything today sitting here. He took a look around this strange hall that had been his home for a short period.

He had no true home now, so everywhere he went he had to make his home while he was there. This would have been just as good as any.

He sighed and left the hall.

Volf and Caerwyn were waiting for him by the gates to the village. Barami and Hildr were there too, as well as a few others, Elria's father among them.

Jais had been spending time with the large man, learning about the woman he'd loved. Everything he learned told him he would have been happy with her. He'd be leaving a part of his heart here.

Yes, this would have been a good home, but for now, he was left to seek for more in his life.

He said his goodbyes.

Elria's father bound him up in a great bear hug and told him he was welcome any time.

Barami shook his hand and they shared a knowing look.

"I'll look after her," Jais said softly to the dark-skinned warrior.

Barami nodded. "Thank you. She is still…"

"I know."

Jais knew how the man had felt about Caerwyn and what it must have been like to leave her now after knowing her most of his life. Yet he wished the man well. Barami had found something precious and was holding it tightly.

"You take care of yourself. Have some kids. Relax," Jais said trying to find some lightness in his heart. He could not find much, and in the end, hoped he hid his envy for the other man.

Barami grinned. "Hildr wants a large family, many children."

"Well, hopefully you'll be a father of a few by the time we return."

"I wouldn't know what to do with children!" Barami looked more afraid at the concept of being a father than he had facing any monster or man. "And for you. I hope you find what you are looking for."

Jais nodded. "Thanks, me too."

The others had said their farewells, and the day was young.

They began their trek down the hill, away from the Dronnegir village, southward to find more of their kind.

To learn more about R. Michael's books and to sign up for his newsletter to receive exclusive announcements and new release notifications visit: www.rmichaelcard.com

OTHER BOOKS BY R. MICHAEL CARD

BLOOD OF DRAGONS

Book 1: Soul Seeking

Book 2: Shadow Soul

The King's Outlaw

GUARDIANS OF LIGHT

Book 1: The Last Scion

Book 2: Scion Rising

Book 3: Scion's Sacrifice

TALES OF THE SEVEN KINGDOMS

The Goblin King

The Swordmaster's Apprentice

ABOUT R. MICHAEL CARD

R. Michael Card has loved fantasy since he read his first Dragon Lance book so many years ago. He has been writing for twenty years but has only recently decided to start sharing his work with the world. He has always enjoyed the lighter side of epic fantasy, the grand adventure, and has infused that love into his works.

He lives near Toronto, Ontario with his beloved wife and their cat. He has had a plethora of careers, working in software, insurance, trades, and education, with jobs ranging from washing cars to career counseling.

www.ingramcontent.com/pod-product-compliance
Lightning Source LLC
Chambersburg PA
CBHW031159020726
47499CB00002B/422